Barefoot with a BAD BOY

Barefoot Bay Undercover #3

roxanne st. claire

Barefoot Bay Undercover

Barefoot With a Bad Boy

COVER ART: The Killion Group, Inc.
INTERIOR FORMATTING: Author E.M.S.
Seashell graphic used with permission under Creative Commons CC0 public domain.

ISBN-13: 978-0-9908607-7-8

Published in the United States of America.

Critical Reviews of Roxanne St. Claire Novels

"St. Claire, as always, brings a scorching tear-up-the-sheets romance combined with a great story: dealing with real issues starring memorable characters in vivid scenes."

— *Romantic Times Magazine*

"Non-stop action, sweet and sexy romance, lively characters, and a celebration of family and forgiveness."

— *Publishers Weekly*

"Plenty of heat, humor, and heart!"

— *USA Today's Happy Ever After blog*

"It's safe to say I will try any novel with St. Claire's name on it."

— *www.smartbitchestrashybooks.com*

"The writing was perfectly on point as always and the pace of the story was flawless. But be forewarned that you will laugh, cry, and sigh with happiness. I sure did."

— *www.harlequinjunkies.com*

"The Barefoot Bay series is an all-around knockout, soul-satisfying read. Roxanne St. Claire writes with warmth and heart and the community she's built at Barefoot Bay is one I want to visit again and again."

— *Mariah Stewart, New York Times bestselling author*

"This book stayed with me long after I put it down."

— *All About Romance*

Dear Reader,

Welcome to Barefoot Bay Undercover...where love is in the air and suspense will heat up the sand. Like every book set in Barefoot Bay, this novel stands entirely alone, but why stop at just one? Barefoot Bay is a whole world of romance, friends and family, and unforgettable stories, divided into bite-size trilogies so you can dive in to the water anytime and stay as long as you like!

The Barefoot Bay Billionaires

Secrets on the Sand

Scandal on the Sand

Seduction on the Sand

The Barefoot Bay Brides

Barefoot in White

Barefoot in Lace

Barefoot in Pearls

Barefoot Bay Undercover

Barefoot Bound (prequel)

Barefoot With a Bodyguard

Barefoot With a Stranger

Barefoot With a Bad Boy

Want to know the day the next Barefoot Bay book is released? Sign up for the newsletter! You'll get brief monthly e-mails about new releases and book sales.

http://www.roxannestclaire.com/newsletter.html

Acknowledgments

Many thanks to some dear individuals who help me along the way. Tatiana Lammers helped with the Russian, Rossella Re assisted on the Italian, and Mia Frisiello chimed in with some very cool linguistic information that helped to write about a translator. Writer friends Leigh Duncan, Kristen Painter, and Fiona Roarke not only helped untie plot knots, they were never far when I needed tissues, wine, and chocolate salted caramel.

As always, there's a team of professionals who make my job easy and joyous. Most especially, huge love to Kristi Yanta, the Picky Editor who has an eye for the big picture and a heart for a good story. In addition, many thanks to keen-eyed copyeditor Joyce Lamb, super-sharp proofreader Marlene Engel, brilliant cover artist Kim Killion, and über-patient formatter Amy Atwell. Behind the scenes, amazing assistant Maria Connor leads the charge, backed up by our fantastic street team. (Join the Roxanne St. Claire Street Team, AKA the Rocki Roadies, on Facebook if you enjoy my books! We have a blast and they get secret scenes and book info!)

On the home front, there is love, understanding, great food, and tremendous patience from my dear and precious family. This time, my wonderful husband created a "Revision Week Menu" that reminded me why he's mine until death do part us. I like to think he's Gabe, but he's really Nino.

Barefoot with a **BAD BOY**

Barefoot Bay Undercover #3

roxanne st. claire

Dedication

Barefoot With a Bad Boy is dedicated with love and gratitude to the thousands of readers who've reached out and asked me to write Gabe's book. Thank you for plucking this secondary character from the pages of older books and falling in love with his dirty mouth (you've been warned: he swears a lot!) and his clever wit. I hope that his love story meets and exceeds your fantasies.

Prologue

"Gabe?"

"Mmmh."

"Are you awake, sweetie?"

"No."

"Please wake up." A finger trailed over his bicep. Soft. Enticing. Inviting. Like the woman who owned it.

He eased around, sucking air when his morning boner jabbed a luscious hip. "Okay." He grunted the word. "I might be awake." He slid a hand around Isadora's waist and turned her so they were facing each other. "Awake…enough."

She hesitated for a second, then melted into him. "It's impossible to resist you."

"Why would you want to?" He used his knee to spread her legs, heat and blood surging as his dick found its way home.

"Because I have tell you something that might be…hard."

He opened one eye just to see if she could possibly be serious. "That joke is too easy for me, even at this hour."

"No joke is too easy for you, at any hour. But I do want to talk."

There was an edge in her voice. The predawn light

slipping in through the cheap metal blinds revealed bright green eyes that had definitely been alert for longer than he had. A hint of shadows under them made him suspect she might have been awake for hours. Even so, Isadora Winter was beautiful, and when she was the very first thing he saw when he woke up, Gabe Rossi was a happy, happy man.

Happy and hard.

"Talk later." He gave a little thrust, nesting in her warm, wet center. She let out something that fell between a sigh and a moan, which he took as permission to proceed without caution, slowly building the rhythm and the heat between them.

"We're perfect together," he mused, fading sleep and growing need making him feel expansive and honest.

No, it was Isa who made him feel that way. Isa with her jade eyes and wavy chocolate and caramel hair. Isa with her quick wit and tender heart and sweet, sweet soul. Isa who got him like no woman he'd ever met and had him like no woman ever would.

"Isadora..." He nudged his way inside her, earning a quiet gasp of pleasure. "I adore ya."

"And poetry at dawn." She laughed under her breath, turning onto her back with another sigh, this one pure resignation.

"It's working, isn't it?" He moved over her but kept his face nestled in the smooth skin of her neck. There, he could flick his tongue under her earlobe because he knew it was step one to making her lose it.

Shuddering under him, she bowed her back, letting him deeper into her. Which would be step two. He slammed into her, not bothering to hold back or use any finesse.

They'd finessed the holy hell out of each other last night. Every night. But right now, all achy morning wood, he just wanted to start the day right, buried inside the woman he loved. He inhaled the lingering fragrance of Chanel No. 5 mixed with the remnant aroma of a hibiscus flower she tucked behind her ear when they went out on hot Cuban nights.

All those sexy, spicy scents that his brain would forever associate with this woman. *His* woman.

She dug her nails into his shoulders, and her whimpers grew more desperate as the sound of her imminent orgasm dragged him to the edge. His balls clutched in agony and ecstasy while his lower half seized up with blinding, crazy pleasure. Everything faded until the world was gone.

Only Isadora and Gabe, one unit, one thing, one…*one*.

"Oh, Gabe. Gabe. I can't…"

"Yeah, you can." He ground into her slick skin, holding her so tight he felt every muscle tense. "Just…like…this." Opening his eyes, he lifted his head to see her face. He loved to watch her come. It did him in.

Pleasure punched its way through, wicked and wild and…*wait*. Were those tears in her eyes?

Of course they were. Because…this was it. This was the real fucking deal, and he was all in. *All in.*

Literally and emotionally. *All…the…way…in.*

He squeezed his eyes closed, a warning to slow down flittering through his brain, but it was instantly wiped out by the need for her. Need and heat and exquisite, sweet torture collided into one long, achingly perfect release of everything he had into her.

Oh, hell *yeah*.

He collapsed onto her, vaguely aware that she hadn't come.

Digging for strength, he pushed up again. "We're not done, baby," he promised her.

"Yeah." Her voice was soft and uncharacteristically

uncertain. "Yeah, we are…for the time being."

He managed a dry laugh, slipping his hand between them, working his finger over her. "I don't think you've actually met Gabe Rossi, orgasm deliverer." He rubbed the spot where they joined. "I should have introduced myself that way when we met at headquarters. Right"—he made a tiny circle, guaranteed to make her melt—"on the damn CIA insignia. Remember the spot?" He underscored that by rubbing *her* spot.

But she didn't move, didn't arch into his hand and let him pleasure her the way he'd done a hundred times since the day he spied a beauty of a recruit and teased her right into his bed that very week. And every time he needed a translator on a job, he requested Isadora, and they always fell a little bit harder into each other's arms.

And then they hit Cuba. Guantanamo Bay. Of all the craptacular places to fall in love. For these six months, it wasn't just hot sex and good times. This was *it*. Forever.

They both knew it.

"I really need to talk to you," she said, still not giving him full access to the tender skin between her legs.

Is that what she wanted to tell him? How serious this was? Because he was totally down for that conversation. As soon as he delivered what he'd promised.

"Not until you are weak and under my spell."

Her eyes, still misty, narrowed at him. "I am not weak." The statement sounded like a well-practiced mantra…or a protest. "Nor am I under your spell."

His finger stilled, more from the tone than the words. Her tone from the minute he woke up, come to think of it. Isa laughed during sex. She never gave up without full satisfaction. She delighted in everything they did in the sack and out of it.

But not today. She wasn't delighted at all.

Very slowly, he removed his hand and, worse, himself. Pulling out, eyeing her with a mix of trepidation and curiosity, he let his weight fall on his side of the bed.

On his back, he took a slow, deep breath. Without a word, she inched closer and placed her head on his shoulder. A shoulder that he swore God made for the sole purpose of letting Isa rest on him.

"What is it?" he finally asked.

"I've been reassigned. Long term. Possibly years. Undercover. And I'm leaving Cuba in about an hour."

He closed his eyes as the knife ripped right through him. "*Fuuuuuuuuck.*"

Isadora slipped out of bed before he could finish his favorite exclamation, or change her mind. Which she'd like to think she was too strong and determined to let happen, but it *was* Gabe. And, despite her protests, she *was* completely under his spell.

But some things trumped love. Like…duty. And lives—precious, innocent, important lives—that needed to be saved.

"Where are you going?" he demanded.

"The bathroom."

"Isa." All humor was gone. Eyes the color of a perfect summer sky turned to stormy slits. "Where the hell are you going?"

"You know I can't tell you." Especially because she wasn't entirely sure herself, just that it was far and deep under.

"*What*? You're serious?" Gabe gave a disgusted choke,

running a hand through his thick, dark hair as if he wanted to tear out the truth that was finally processing. "They can't reassign you. Who else could translate *shut up you needle-nose dick* in Punjabi *and* Urdu? I need you here."

"Well, *they* need me somewhere else. Last time I checked, I didn't work for you, I worked for the Central Intelligence Agency, and I go where they tell me to go." Or, in this case, where she asked to go.

She headed across the tiny studio apartment to the bathroom, closing the door without slamming or locking it, the very act of being so in control giving her the adrenaline shot she needed.

"Isa." He was right outside the door now. "We have to talk about this."

Oh, *now* he wanted to talk.

But he was right. They did have to talk. If she couldn't convince Gabe that she was strong, driven, and doing the right thing, then how could she infiltrate a covert operation and stop deadly attacks? This was just the first of many obstacles she was about to face.

But if she opened the door, there would be gloriously naked Gabe, ripped, built, and hung like no man she'd ever met, leaning against the doorjamb with just enough of a crooked smile to let her know he had this fight in the bag.

Think of Mom and Dad, Isa. You could save someone the pain you've been through.

She called on Dexter Crain's words to give her the strength she needed, slipping on a cotton robe before she opened the door.

He was glorious all right, and naked. And built to make a woman weep with want. But there wasn't even the shadow of a smile on his face.

"How long will you be gone?"

How could he even ask that question? "How long have you been a consultant for the CIA?"

"Coming on eleven fucktastic years."

"And have you ever, in that entire time, known the length of an assignment?"

"I might have had an idea. And your stuff, the translation stuff, they know how long they need you."

Translation stuff. There it was, that subtle dismissal because the *stuff* that Isadora Winter did for the CIA wasn't exactly the *stuff* that Gabriel Rossi did. He was a badass contract agent who kept the company at arm's length, and she was a low-level translator and employee who jumped as high as they demanded. Higher.

And this assignment? Over the top, which was why it appealed to her.

"This is different," she said vaguely. "And…important."

"It's *all* important, Isadora." He found his voice now, and his brain was fully engaged as he pinned her with his eyes and barely hid a low-grade bubble of anger.

"This is antiterrorism, Gabe, and you, of all people, know how important that is to me."

"What the hell do you think we're doing here? Why do you think we've spent the last six months in this particular corner of hell trying to convince asswipe terrorist detainees to go home to some fuckistani country and spy for the US? That's antiterrorism."

Indirectly. And her translating job was pretty mundane. This new one would be anything but. "I want this assignment," she said.

He pushed by her, grabbing his toothbrush and twisting the faucet hard enough to pull the rusty thing out of the wall of her dilapidated Cuban apartment.

Of course the Italian temper would flare. Because he heard "I want this assignment *more than I want you.*" Which wasn't what she'd said, but maybe it was implied.

She *did* want this assignment, she thought as she pulled a suitcase out of the tiny closet. Not only were her linguistic and translation skills critical, she knew the targets and their weaknesses. So did Gabe, of course, and a few others who'd been at Gitmo these past few months, but none of them spoke a dozen languages. None of them could slide under the radar, unnoticed and unrecognized.

"Why didn't you tell me about it sooner?" He stood in the doorway, a mouthful of toothpaste, the brush frozen in midair.

She shrugged. "I thought you were going to take that assignment in Miami and we'd go our separate ways. Again."

"I never wanted that job in Miami, Isa." He turned and spit noisily into the sink. "I was planning to tell them this week to shove Miami and their Cuban Mafia up their asses because I didn't want to leave you. *Again.*"

She refused to let that sway her. "Well, I didn't tell you because I wasn't absolutely sure I'd get it. I've been waiting for word from Washington, and that just came through overnight."

"Washington and not Langley?" He yanked a towel from the rack and swiped it over his mouth.

"Both."

"So Sexy Dexy's given you a plum job in Europe with stupid benefits and easy hours."

"Not in Europe," she said, plucking some jewelry on the dresser into her hand. There were no benefits, and the hours would be 24/7.

He came out of the bathroom and got right in front of her, his eyes cobalt blue with anger now. "But it is a Senator

tropical Christmas was. And last, she'd have to carefully and believably reveal things that only Isadora could know.

The crowd was already well lit, and she didn't mean the faux Christmas stars on the two trees that flanked the party, complete with seashell ornaments and mermaids on top. Three open bars were set up around the open-air dining, and drinks were flowing, along with animated conversation punctuated by bursts of laughter.

For the thousandth time since she'd learned he was here, Lila wondered what in God's name had brought Gabe to Barefoot Bay. To this posh resort famous for destination weddings and dreamy honeymoons located on a small island off the coast of Florida.

No, it had to be because of the proximity to another island near Florida...Cuba. And there would only be one reason Gabe would be interested in the goings-on in Cuba. A reason he now believed to be dead.

He'd used his considerable spying skills to learn that Isadora had been killed in a car accident in Cuba. Then, because Gabe was wanted by the Cuban Mafia and not safe in that country he'd sent his sister and close friend to search for a child who was most likely his.

But there, they were told that child died as a baby in Cuba.

But tonight, Gabe would know the truth.

The real question was, would he believe any of it?

"Are you in line?"

Lila looked up and dug for every ounce of her training not to react at the sight of Malcolm Harris, a former agent who'd worked in Cuba with Isadora and Gabe, and the very friend who'd gone there to find Gabe's son.

"For the bar?" he added at her silence, which probably lasted a millisecond too long. "I don't want to cut you off."

"That's fine," she said, recovering as she realized she was standing near one of the bars, not actually in line. "I'm not in a rush."

"England?" he asked. "I hear the accent."

"London, yes, originally. But I've been living in the States for years."

"And you're here on holiday?"

She nodded, appreciating his use of the European term for vacation. Mal was a great guy, a tough but truly endearing man. And he looked as handsome as ever and far more at peace than when he'd been working undercover as a guard at Gitmo. "Yes, I am on holiday."

"Mal, there you are." A dark-haired young woman approached, and it took Lila only a split second to figure out she was looking at Francesca Rossi, the younger sister Gabe protected so fiercely. Behind chic horn-rims, her eyes were the precise color of crystal blue trimmed with navy, and there was something just so...*Rossi* about her. Attitude, confidence, warmth, and that spicy Italian passion simmering just under the surface.

"This is my fiancée, Chessie, and I'm Mal." Mal made the introduction as he wrapped his arm around Chessie's shoulders.

Fiancée. She hadn't heard they'd gotten engaged after their mission. That explained the peace in his expression.

"Lila Wickham." She reached her hand out and shook Chessie's, then Mal's. "A guest at the resort. Are you here to check the place out for a potential destination wedding locale? I understand they have an expert team here."

"They do," Chessie said. "But we're getting married in Boston," she said. *Bahston*. Lila could easily hear the distinct, if subtle, accent of a native of that city. "We've been staying down here near my brother, who...oh, there he is."

Chessie's gaze shifted over Lila's shoulder, and suddenly, Lila froze. Everything in her went ice cold, then fiery hot, a thrumming at the base of her neck like a warning siren. She ached to turn and see him, to look him right in the eyes and dare him not to know the truth.

But she couldn't. She absolutely *couldn't.*

"'Scuze me," she said quickly. "I see the resort owner, and I want to thank her for the invitation."

Without waiting for a response, Lila slipped around them, purely incapable of enduring this moment yet. She wasn't ready for this particular pain.

With that emotional hurricane on the horizon, she absolutely couldn't "meet" him in front of all these people, she realized. She couldn't have her first words to him be in an English accent, a casual introduction, a fake how-do-you-do, when everything inside her would be imploding.

She'd seen him before, of course, the last time she'd been at the resort. And even that had had a debilitating impact on her.

She neared the group of people that included Lacey Walker, the resort owner, but purposely steered around the table so she wouldn't have to talk to them.

Instead, she found a pocket of privacy and slowly turned, bracing herself for the blow of seeing Gabe.

And still she wasn't prepared.

Gabriel Rossi was more breathtaking than ever. His dark hair was longer than when he was a contract agent for the CIA, thick and curled around his collar. His face was still hollow-cheek handsome in the most surprising and arresting way, strong and deliciously shaped. And his eyes, deep blue, intense, sparking with dry wit, and fringed with sinfully long lashes.

But those eyes were flat tonight, like a light had gone out behind them.

And she knew why. How could she tell him that she was the woman who could erase that? Well, it wasn't something you walked up to someone out of the blue and announced.

So, she'd wait for her opening. She surreptitiously watched him examine his sister's left hand, making a comment that elicited a laugh. She could only imagine the Gabe-ism that would mix humor, profanity, and charm. *Shot your fucking wad on the ring, huh?* Then he hugged Chessie and gave Mal a brotherly embrace and—

Caught her staring at him.

Mother of God, she nearly fell over. Blue eyes, vaguely interested, mostly cool, shockingly unemotional, met hers and still pierced her heart.

Okay, it's okay, Lila. Just stare him right down like any woman with a pulse and a working hormonal system would do.

The eye contact lasted at least five beats of her thumping heart.

Gabe tore his gaze away and slammed his drink on the table, splashing the liquid, an f-bomb easily heard at twenty feet. "I'm not in the mood for Christmas Eve," he said gruffly. "Give my regards to Nino."

She, along with others, watched him power through the tables and onto the open sand.

"Gabe," Mal called, following him.

Lila casually inched a few steps closer to use her well-honed eavesdropping and lipreading skills.

Gabe gave his friend a dark look over his shoulder. "I don't want to—"

"I have something from Isadora."

Isadora? Lila sucked in a silent breath, her whole being tensing up.

Gabe turned slowly around to stare at Mal, who held out a blue slip of paper. Good God. The letter.

"I found it in the Country Club when I nabbed that gun," Mal said. "I haven't read it, but I'm sure it's from Isadora to you."

She didn't know if she should be relieved or terrified. The note, which she knew verbatim, would certainly support what she was about to tell him. But it also might make him refuse to believe her.

Mal stepped closer to Gabe. "I didn't know if I should give it to you, or—"

"It's mine." Gabe ripped the paper from his friend's hand.

"I didn't want to make things worse," Mal said.

Gabe nodded, his attention already riveted on the note. "Leave me alone. Just…leave me alone." He started to walk away, already opening the paper and reading the first words, which were simple but strong.

Gabriel, my angel.

Suddenly, he stopped and whipped around. Lila bit her lip, fearing he'd tear it up or shove it back in Mal's hands like something delivered from the devil.

"Hey, man, thanks," he said to Mal, sliding into that heartbreaker of a smile that made men want to work with him and women want to strip for him. "Thanks for what you did in Cuba. And thanks for loving my sister. And thanks for…knowing how important this is. Merry Christmas," he added, walking off.

And now she had her chance to talk to him alone.

She waited, observing his every step, though she made it look like she was admiring the party decorations on the beach. She got a good long look at his broad shoulders and narrow waist as he strode away from the party, music, and lights, toward a deserted part of the beach.

She saw him sit on the sand in the shadows and open the letter. Her brain recited the words he was reading, like a memorized prayer.

You will be told that I'm dead. I am not.

Even from here, she could see him stab his fingers into his hair and pull back hard.

You will be told our son died when he was less than two years old. He did not. I am under deep cover and so is he. I promise you will understand when I explain it to you.

But *would* he understand? It was time to find out. Lila set out in the same direction, slipping her hand into her shoulder bag as an idea took hold.

Committed, she kept walking as he read, and she imagined each word hitting his heart like fire-tipped darts.

Gabriel, wait for me. Promise me you will wait for me. It might be years, but the very moment I am free, I will find you, I will come to you, and I will tell you everything. But I give you my word, on our love, that I am not *dead. And neither is Rafe, who is a carbon copy of you in every way.*

She could practically taste his torment. He put the letter down, looked out to the bay, picked up the paper again, hunched his shoulders in pain.

No matter what, my darling angel Gabriel, wait for me. I will come to you as soon as I can. When that day comes, you may not question me. You may not doubt me. And you may not recognize me.

No, he would not, that much was certain.

She cleared her throat to warn him of her approach, and he looked up, not even attempting to hide his disgust at being interrupted during his private moment. Too bad. She lifted her chin, squared her shoulders, and defied him to send her away.

She imagined the string of mental profanity singing

through his head. But, to his credit, he didn't say a word.

She stopped right next to him. She had to make it completely clear who she was. Completely. It was her only shot.

"Gabriel," she said.

His eyes shuttered in unadulterated disinterest. "Look, lady, I—"

"Like the angel."

That shut him up, especially spoken not in the Queen's accent but in Isadora's unrounded, flat-voweled non-accent.

He drew back a little, narrowing his eyes to slide his gaze over her. "Do I know you?"

There were so many answers to that. So, so many. Her smile was slight and tight.

He started to push up, but she held out her hand as if to stop him, opening her fingers to let her villa card key tumble into his lap. And without another word, she stepped away and headed into the shadows.

He'd follow her. He had to.

You may not question me. He would.

You may not doubt me. Oh, he definitely would.

And you may not recognize me. He would not…until she proved to him who she was and convinced him this was real.

Chapter Two

There were two possibilities. The blonde was a sex-starved lonely heart stuck in paradise and looking for a roll on the sand…or she was an operative sent to contact him and deliver information about Isadora.

Gabriel…like the angel.

Those were the first words Isadora had spoken to him. Right in the middle of headquarters, standing on the iconic CIA insignia, that easy laugh and volley of banter, that gorgeous cleavage over a precious heart. Damn, he might have fallen in love with her that very moment.

Gabriel…like the angel.

He'd been in the business long enough to know a code word when it landed in his lap. Along with a room key. His money was on operative.

Except, her voice…it was identical to Isadora's.

Gabe inhaled deeply, trying to clear his head of ridiculous thoughts, but the Florida air held more than sickeningly sweet honeysuckle and magnolia tonight. The path to Rockrose was sliced with the spice of Chanel No. 5, a scent that twisted his gut and made him want to howl at the moon.

But he kept walking toward the villa at the northern

border of the Casa Blanca property, still checking off possibilities.

Horny tourist with good taste in perfume? Or an agent about to mess with his head? He glanced down at the paper he still held.

You will be told that I'm dead. I am not.

Well, there was one other possibility. One other out-there, patently ridiculous possibility.

"I knew you'd come."

He didn't react, even though the voice in the dark—British now—totally took him by surprise. Which didn't happen often, if at all.

So, a spy. Anyone who could sit on a patio in the moonlight ten feet from him and be so still he didn't know she was there? Trained. Well trained.

He approached the walk that led up to the deck that wrapped around the villa, the whole house and patio raised off the sand by stilts. He let his eyes adjust to the sight of her leaning into the corner, her arms crossed protectively, her shimmery white clothes catching the moonlight, ghost-like.

Was *that* what was going down here?

"Of course I came," he finally replied, pausing at the bottom of the stairs that led up to the deck. The position gave her a considerable advantage of height and power, but he let her have it for the moment. "I find that room keys handed to me by a beautiful woman can open up the most interesting doors."

She laughed, soft and throaty and...familiar. Like a favorite old song he hadn't heard for years. Like a taste of something he used to love but hadn't enjoyed for a long time. Like...Isadora.

He put his hand on the wood-carved newel, hoping it

wasn't obvious he needed to brace himself thanks to stupid thoughts.

"What's so funny?" he asked.

"That you would call me beautiful."

Using just the moonlight, he took the closest examination of her he'd had to date. He'd definitely seen her on the beach while Mal and Chessie were in Cuba on Mission Miserable. He'd noticed her then and, of course, tonight. The timing of the visits could be coincidence…or not.

She was interesting to look at, not classically, traditionally, by-the-book beautiful. Not like Isa. He shook his head again. Had to get rid of that thought.

"So you agree I'm not beautiful," she said.

"I didn't say anything."

She inched out of the corner, shimmering again, a long, lean woman who was no stranger to the gym but managed to keep it all very feminine. Under the thin silk top, trimmed with rhinestones that flashed and twinkled, he spied small breasts, perky enough to skip the bra, and chilly enough to pop with sweet little gumdrops.

A narrow waist, tiny even. Decent hips, but nothing like…

Damn it, stop comparing, Gabe.

"You don't have to say anything," she said. "I'm fluent in body language."

He stumbled on the first step as a memory flashed in his head. A bar in Beijing. Smoky. Loud. Some karaoke dickwad annihilating a Black Eyed Peas song. And Isa across from him, her emerald eyes full of concern. He could still hear her voice.

I can tell something's wrong, Gabe. I'm fluent in body language, too.

He regained his cool so quickly, it was possible she

hadn't noticed the slip. Yeah, and maybe Santa flew down from the North Pole and pissed in the middle of the party he'd just left.

"So read me, blondie." He took the next two steps as one, just to prove how steady he was. "Tell me what my body is saying."

She came to the top of the stairs, still more than a foot above him, maintaining control of the situation, which he'd have to change. "Let's start with hello."

She reached her hand out for a standard shake, but he grabbed her wrist and tugged her down, forcing her off balance. In a flash, he was up two steps and she was down two, and that left them face to face, eye to eye, and mouth to mouth. And she didn't even ask why he'd done that, so she must not have been too surprised. Come to think of it, she barely lost a moment's control.

A spy. Definitely a spy.

She held his gaze, her eyes so dark it was impossible to tell where iris ended and pupil began. Smoky, seductive eyes that…looked unusual on a woman with such blond hair.

Was she CIA? Or something deeper and darker?

He tipped his head, feigning casual interest. "This is a pretty elaborate come-to-Mama ploy," he said. "What gives?"

Her eyes flickered, and she drew back but didn't retreat completely. If anything, she subtly squared her shoulders and lifted her jaw. "I wanted to talk to you."

"Talk?" He dropped his gaze, noticing how her chest rose and fell with tight breaths and a little vein in her neck pulsed.

A vein that…

Damn it. *Every fucking woman has that vein, stupid.*

He brushed by her and bounded up the last two steps, landing on the deck with enough force to announce that he'd officially taken charge. "Great. Let's talk inside. Got any booze?"

She turned slowly, forced to look up at him, while he loomed over her, openly checking her out. Face to tits to hips and down to the cute red toes that he'd seen on the beach.

While he was reading a letter from a dead woman.

She stayed where she was for a split second, then nodded. "Fine. We'll do this your way." She came up the steps and walked across the deck, tipping the power scales again, but he snagged her arm before she got to the door.

"Do what?" he demanded. "Am I going in there to unwrap a Christmas present, or are you planning to slam a bullet in my brain?"

Her eyes widened, the response seemingly genuine. "I'm not going to shoot you. But I might..." She slipped out of his grip and used her free hand to casually graze his jaw, the touch so light it could have been air. Hot, electric air. "Rock your world a little."

She went inside, and he stayed right where he was. Okay then. World rocking sounded...promising.

A few seconds later, he entered a dark living room, hearing ice clinking in a glass in the galley kitchen, dimly lit by soft, under-the-counter halogens. He followed the sound—and the perfume—to find her pouring amber liquid into two rocks glasses.

Not just any amber liquid. Johnnie Walker Blue. His brand of Scotch.

She set the bottle on the counter and looked right at him. "Single malt Scotch is for try-hards who like craft beer."

His words—spoken in private more than five years ago—burned like lousy Scotch going down.

"I've heard that." Only, if his memory served him right,

he'd said something more like, *Single malt Scotch is for snot-flicking hipster try-hards who like craft beer.*

She handed him the glass. "And Johnnie Walker is highly underrated."

What the *fuck*? Was she just going to toss back random shit he'd said to Isadora all night? And how the hell did she know these quotes? Were the rooms bugged when he'd been with Isadora?

He didn't reach for the glass, but only because he wasn't entirely sure his hand would be steady.

She inhaled as if gathering her thoughts, then lifted his drink to her lips, staring at him over the rim. "If it makes you feel any better, I'm more nervous about this than you are." She punctuated that with a healthy gulp, and no girlie cringe as it went down.

She handed him the same glass, the intimacy of sharing not lost on him. He drank some, swallowed, and set the glass on the counter. "Okay, you've proven you're not poisoning me. Those formfitting clothes aren't hiding a pistol. What in the name of ever-lovin' fuck is your deal, woman?"

She flinched. Hard.

"Fair warning. If dirty words turn you off, you picked the wrong guy to lure into your holiday honey trap."

"No words turn me off," she said, just pointedly enough to make him pause. Was she trying to remind him of Isadora, who'd loved words?

Because nothing about her reminded him of Isadora. She didn't have wavy hair or playful freckles or a light in her eyes. She didn't have a turned-up nose or a delicate chin or luscious D's and a handful of hips. But she had words and memories and stuff no one but Isadora could have.

Why? Because she knew something about his dead lover? Worked for someone who'd paid her so he'd end up the same way? Or maybe she just wanted to barter information.

Whatever the spy game, he could play. And he would win.

"Then let's get this party started." He took the glass and pivoted, heading to the hall that led to the bedroom on his left or the living room on his right. "Sofa or sack? Pick your pleasure, Mata Hari."

"Living room."

He headed there and plopped onto an overstuffed sofa, leaving enough space to lure her closer and let her think he was all in for her booty call.

She brought her drink and the bottle in there, and sat in a club chair on the other side of the coffee table. There was just enough light to see her blond locks and sparkly party clothes and pools of dark, dark eyes.

"You read the letter, I noticed."

A chill hit his veins, but he covered by taking a mighty swig of Scotch. And another. Then he finished the drink and slammed the empty glass on the table so hard he almost cracked the crystal.

"How do you know about the letter?" he asked, easing his head back to the armrest and propping his feet on the sofa, as unfazed as humanly possible for Miss I Can Read Body Language.

She didn't answer right away but crossed her long legs and took a sip, faking plenty of cool on her own.

"Because I wrote it."

Fuck being cool. Fuck body language. Fuck everyone and everything. He shot straight up and sliced her to pieces with a look.

"What the hell do you mean *you wrote it*?" He hadn't had time to process what he'd read, since he was instantly summoned to her lair. Of course, it was possible, probable even, that someone other than Isa had written that letter. But why? Who was left in the world who wanted him that bad?

"Exactly what I said. I wrote every word, and every word is true. I left it in the interrogation room at Gitmo, the Country Club."

The air and life just seeped out of him, leaving behind nothing but confusion, anger, and a black ball of hate. He leaned forward, squinting at her.

"Who are you?" Rage rocked him, pushing him up to a dominating stand. "Tell me right now. *Who. Are. You.* And every blasted word better be the truth, or I *will* get it out of you."

She stared at him. "You really don't know." It was a statement, and one that made zero sense.

He slowly walked around the table to get in front of her, staring down, placing his hands on the armrests of her chair to trap her. "Who the fuck are you, woman?"

"It's me, Gabe. Isadora. It's me."

Chapter Three

He'd never been any good at hiding his emotions. Not around her, at least. And tonight, Gabriel Angelo Rossi was wearing his anger, hurt, and deep distrust of mankind in general all over his gorgeous face. Sapphire eyes deepened and tapered, and under a shadow of whiskers, his jaw locked and throbbed. His neck corded with tension. His chest heaved with indignation and confusion and raw, raw fury.

Lila waited for a blistering barrage of creative curses, but he stayed silent, staring down at her with a glare that was somehow far more frightening than a profanity-laced tirade.

"I told you the assignment was...different," she said, hating that her voice sounded weak. Lila Wickham was not weak. She was a lot of things Gabe didn't know and might not like, but she was not *weak*.

"Sit down and I'll tell you everything," she said.

"You'll tell me everything whether I stand on my head or jump up and down. You'll talk fast, clear, and if you lie, you die." He leaned even deeper into her space, his hips at the same level as her eyes, so she either had to look down in deference, look up in need, or stare at his crotch. She'd seen him use the technique on plenty of detainees in Gitmo.

"Got it?" he demanded.

She shoved her chair backward, and it scraped over the hard wood, giving her enough space to stand up. He had her by a good five inches, but her move added a tiny bit of power to her side.

"Who are you?" And that low, slow growl of a barely restrained fury shifted all the power back to him.

"I am Isadora Winter."

He suddenly turned and reached to the end table to turn on the lamp. The golden glow warmed the room, but he marched to the other lamp and turned it on, too. Then he hit the switch for two sconces in the dining area and tapped on the kitchen light.

"There's a flashlight in the drawer," she said. "And I bet I can find a magnifying glass if you'd like to look closer."

Still near the kitchen, he stared at her. "I might. Don't move," he ordered. "Except your mouth. You can move that anytime. And for the love of sweet baby Jesus, please know that I was associated with the CIA for more than a decade, and there is not a trick of that trade I don't know."

"Then you know about the use of facial-reconstruction surgery to create an undercover disguise."

Still staring at her, he took a few steps closer. "Facial-reconstruction surgery, yes. Not body, height, hair, voice and...soul."

She let out a sigh. That was it, of course. She didn't just look different; she *was* different. "You know there's more. Body reshaping, chemical changes of hair color and texture, surgical alteration of fingerprints, permanent eye dye. And, of course, training on how to stand, walk, speak, and behave differently. A person can be remade, Gabe. I was."

He approached her, openly looking her up and down and up again, and then he began to circle, very, very slowly, examining her with his arms folded, eyes intent, an appraiser looking to see if the art was real or a forgery.

He reached out and lifted her chin, turning her face one way, then the other, looking for scars she knew were artfully hidden but could be seen if he looked carefully enough.

He rounded her back, grabbed a handful of hair, and then slid his hand down the length of it, probably unable to feel the artificial straightening that gave her well-colored hair a glassy sheen.

He stroked a shoulder, one finger grazing her bicep, which she flexed, as she did regularly in weight training after having her once-feminine curves taken away, along with her curls and green eyes.

Finally, he was facing her again, that finger sliding to her throat, her collarbone, her breastbone, and over the rise of one barely there breast, a mere shadow of its once-formidable glory.

Of course, he lingered there longer, circling the nipple that jutted against the silky top, his gaze down as he watched his finger torture her. His touch still raised chills on her skin and shot fire through her whole body.

That much had not changed.

She breathed slow and steady, waiting out his assessment. She knew Gabe's tastes, and they didn't include lean, structured women. He was a big-tits and soft-ass kind of man. He liked laughter and lushness, a woman who'd rest on his shoulder, not on her laurels.

This new model of an old favorite had to disappoint him.

"I don't believe you," he said.

"Because you don't *want* to believe me. Which, as you know, is the most effective element of any disguise."

His eyes flared like she'd turned up the heat on a gas flame. "If you think I don't *want* Isadora to be alive, then you haven't done all your homework, spy girl." He spat the words, shaking his head. "You can try to convince me you're Isadora, for whatever effed-up mission you're on for whatever coal-black op you work for. But I know every trick in the CIA handbook because I either invented them, used them, or rendered them useless. Which I'm about to do with this little game."

"I know things only Isadora could know."

"You could have interviewed the sweet shit out of her, read her journals, cracked her e-mail, stolen her computer, or dragged conversations from her brain using some Dr. Evil memory-retrieval software."

She leveled her gaze at him, knowing her ebony eyes could land a very effective glare, and she decided to make her point by using her natural American accent again. "I *am* Isadora Winter, your former lover and an undercover agent for the United States government."

His jaw and fists flexed as he scrutinized her, his razor-sharp brain obviously in high gear. "What I want to know is why," he mused, ignoring her statement. "Not that I'm expecting a word of truth from you." He turned his back on her, then grabbed her barely touched drink on the table and knocked it down his throat. "So I'll have to figure out a very clever way to get you to tell me the truth. Torture. Coercion. Or maybe I can fuck it out of you. That's why you brought me here, right?"

"Why don't you just sit down and hear me out, like a smart, experienced intelligence agent who knows this is entirely possible?" She put her hand on his shoulder and tried to turn him around, feeling the ice in her words which, for the past five years, felt normal. With Gabe? That cold tone felt wrong.

"Please listen to me," she said, softening her voice,

letting the tiniest glimmer of Isa come through. "Even if you don't want what I tell you to be true."

He let her turn him, but she almost wished she hadn't. The fire had dimmed, drenched by the Scotch or her words. Either way, pain was back, and she knew why.

If she was lying, it hurt.

If she wasn't lying, it hurt even more.

"Gabe, I know you don't want *this* woman"—she made a sweeping gesture over herself—"to be Isa. But I am."

"You're wrong," he said, reaching into his pocket. "When I read this tonight..." He pulled out the thin blue paper. "I felt alive for the first time since I found out she'd died. Just the chance that she is not dead, that I..."

The words, or maybe how he couldn't finish the sentence, almost cost her balance and control, making her close her eyes for a second. He cared. He still cared.

"Don't do that," she said softly. "Don't go there."

"Go where?"

"I didn't come here to fall back in love with you, Gabe Rossi." That would ruin everything; that would put Rafe at bigger risk. "I need help. And only you can give it to me. And Rafe."

"Rafe? That would be a child I thought was buried under a gravestone that said his name was Gabriel Rafael?" He got right in her face. "He's alive?"

She put her hand on his forearm, squeezing the taut muscle. "I can't tell you until I am one hundred percent certain you believe me."

He wrenched out of her touch, pushing away. "I am one hundred percent certain that you are a fucking liar. Also, one hundred percent certain that this charade has ended. Come and find me when you're ready to tell me who you are, what you want, and why you went to this much trouble." He brushed by her, practically knocking her over with his shoulder. "I'm out."

"I get that you're angry but—"

He whipped around and vaulted right back into her face. "Angry? You haven't seen anger, babycakes. If I find out you had anything to do with her death…" He inched closer, heat rolling off every cell in his body. "If you, or anyone you know or have ever met, touched one hair on her head or that of my child, you'll have plenty of scars to show the world. Plenty."

She closed her eyes at the threat and kept them closed at the sound of his retreating footsteps and the slamming of the door.

Letting out a sigh, she lifted the Scotch and took a swig straight from the bottle. Not because he didn't believe her. Not because he threatened her. And not because this would be a hellacious uphill battle.

But because she still loved him. And if she wanted to stay alive and make sure her son was safe, she could not love Gabe Rossi, not ever again.

Chapter Four

Gabe opened his eyes and stared at the position of the moon, trying to guess how many hours he'd been lying on the sand. Long enough for that holiday party from hell to be over.

Long enough to careen through every emotion a man really ought to be able to avoid.

Long enough to figure out what that lying sack of sorry woman was really up to.

But he hadn't. All he'd done for the past hour, or four, was make side trips into memories best forgotten. Not the ones with Isadora, oddly enough. He'd think that after standing in front of someone who claimed to be the only woman he'd ever loved, he'd be focused only on memories of her.

And for a while, he had been.

But the deeper he dug himself into the cold sand just by lying there, the deeper he let his soul drift even further back. Two years before he had the good fortune to bump into Isadora Winter at headquarters, he'd made the mistake of believing who a woman claimed to be.

He could still feel the blood on his hands and see the shock in Darya Andropov's eyes as she realized she'd been caught and shot.

Some spies, the most cynical and darkest, say that the first time you fire a bullet into a traitor, there's a rush of satisfaction. Even pride. All it had done to Gabe was make him want to throw up, and swear he would never, ever trust anyone again.

Even on a sleepy beach in a remote location.

Especially on a sleepy beach in a remote location.

The fact was, there lived on this planet at least a few people who would like to see Gabe Rossi destroyed one way or another. Sending a woman who claimed to be his former lover miraculously changed by the powers of medicine and counterintelligence, and who knew things she shouldn't and couldn't know?

That could be the most brilliant ploy in the history of spying.

He didn't glance over his shoulder in the general direction of Rockrose, but he sure didn't want to go to the little bungalow he and Nino called home. So he brushed off the sand and meandered back toward the resort, relieved to see the Casa Blanca staff was cleaning up.

Except he'd sell his left nut for something left to eat. What had he been thinking missing Nino's signature holiday dinner to listen to some liar who claimed—

"Mr. Gabriel!" Poppy's voice yanked him from his reverie, and he looked up to find the housekeeper grinning at him, carrying a tray of dirty dishes. "You jus' about broke your grandfather's heart tonight."

"And he's drowning his sorrows in post-Christmas Eve limoncello."

"How did you know?"

"A lifetime of living with him. Please tell me there's some calamari left. Or a crespelle."

Her big brown eyes rolled to the sky. "Those crepes were

divinely inspired, it pains me to admit. I saved you a plate up in the restaurant, where some folks moved to the bar. And I covered for you leaving like that, like the good spy I am learning to be."

"You certainly have the makings," he admitted, taking the heavy tray from her.

Ever since he'd first arrived in Barefoot Bay to start his own privatized witness protection business here, he'd depended on this talkative Jamaican housekeeper's uncanny ability to know what was going on around the resort. She was observant, obviously, but also had a knack for drawing information out of people. Even him, he had to admit.

"But I didn't need a cover for disappearing," he said, lifting the tray toward the main building of the resort. "To the kitchen?"

She nodded and put a hand on his back, leading him there. "Mr. Gabriel, I don't think they all should know where you were. I mean, it's Christmas Eve, and…" She let out a big sigh. "I know God forgives all your sins. Every time you make one."

"Must be a full-time job keeping track of me. But this time, my sin was sleep."

She shot up a doubtful eyebrow.

"On the beach," he added.

Both brows lifted.

"Alone."

She tsked noisily.

"Don't give me the head shake of judgment." He elbowed her. "I'm not lying." Unlike *other* people he'd met tonight.

"I saw you, Mr. Gabriel. I saw you talk to the blond lady named Lila."

Lila. He snorted at the name. Emphasis on *lie.*

"She left, and I saw you stroll like a peacock up to

Rockrose and disappear for a long time. Now you are covered in sand and looking a little"—she inched back to rake him with a gaze—"disassembled."

"I'm assembled just fine." He nudged her along with his elbow. "But props to you for observation powers, Pop-Tart. Damn impressive."

Instead of looking grateful for the compliment, she scowled at him. "That'll be three dollars for the D-word."

"Oh, sh…shoot me now for hiring you."

She put a hand on one of her ample hips. "It's been lucrative. The swear jar overflows thanks to your filthy mouth."

"Why don't you empty it? I thought you were using those ill-gotten gains to get those nephews of yours to the States."

She didn't answer, but some of the joy left her expression. "Not yet, but working for you, it accumulates. Tell me about Miss Lila. The clean version."

"I hate to break it to you, but there was no *ahem* with the fake"—*Isadora*—"blonde."

"I don't think that color's fake. And I've looked closely, ever since she asked about you last time she was here."

Damn, his game was off. Of course his budding spook resort housekeeper knew shit about Lila Wickham, because she'd mentioned her the last time Lila was here. And why hadn't Lila jumped all over him then and tried to bury him in her ugly lies?

He had to clear his head and get intelligence.

"So, did you notice anything funny about her, then or now?" he asked.

"Funny?"

"Just off. That's what a spy looks for, Poppy. Something that doesn't quite jive with appearances. Something interesting or weird about her. Unusual conversations or habits?"

As they reached the back entrance to the resort kitchen, Poppy slowed her step, furrowing her bushy brows to think. “Well, I can tell you that she’s a good mother and puts her son before everything else. It’s so obvious.”

Gabe stopped, icing up inside and out at the word *son*. “He’s here? You’ve met him? She really has a son?”

She gave him a slow smile. “So you talked to her instead of *aheming*? My prayers were answered.”

“Answer *me*,” he fired back. “Have you met this kid? Is he here, on the island?”

“I’ve only heard her talking to him on the phone. And by talking, I mean reprimanding. That child must be bone-bad, considering the number of times I’ve heard her tell him he shouldn’t do something or try to set him straight. And then tonight, she told me he gives her headaches. What kind of mother says that?”

A lying bitch of a fake mother. But still, if there was a kid, he had to know if it was his kid. Sure, there was a gravestone in Cuba that covered the remains of a not-yet-two-year-old boy with the first name Gabriel and Rossi as one of three last names. Still…

“Where is this kid, Poppy? Has she told you?”

“I don’t know. Maybe still up in Washington, DC, where she’s from.” Poppy searched his face and broke into a smile. “You know, Mr. Gabriel, it wouldn’t be so important if you didn’t like her some.”

It took everything in him not to throw the dirty dishes on the ground and tear ass back to Rockrose and squeeze the fucking truth out of that woman like she was a human tube of toothpaste. Was the kid really alive? Because that would change *everything*.

And could that mean…Isadora was, too?

Hope practically strangled him.

He couldn't go demanding answers from her, though. He'd never get them. He'd get more lies and half-truths and tricks. No, he had to be as smart as she was. Smarter.

"Mr. Gabriel, you are practically vibrating, child." Poppy put a steadying hand on his shoulder.

"Have you seen this kid?" he asked. "Even a picture?"

"Last time she was here, I saw a picture of a little boy on her dresser, but then when I was on my way back to clean her room, I noticed she slipped it into a drawer."

"And you didn't think that was strange?"

"Strange enough to report to you? No. Lots of people go private when maids come in the room. But I did tell you that she was asking about you and had a picture of you on her camera, remember?"

He did, and the report had been odd enough for him to go to the villa where the woman had been staying at the time, finding it empty. Except for the lingering scent of Chanel No. 5.

"I know my job for you, Mr. Gabriel," Poppy said. "And what I don't know, I'm willing to learn."

"I know you are, and you have boatloads of spy potential, Poppy. In fact…"

She reached to open the door into the kitchen, but he stopped her. "How would you like a new assignment tonight?" he asked.

"Before or after I finish cleaning up the party?"

"Now."

"Whatever you need, Mr. Gabriel." No hesitation in her answer, or a split second of doubt.

"Get that kid's picture and bring it to me."

She stared at him, a million questions in her big, dark eyes.

"We can come up with a reason for you to get in the room," he added. "You can say that—"

She held a thick finger to his lips. "Shh. I know what to do. You just gotta trust me."

Never easy for him, but he nodded. "Okay."

"Now take those into the back for bussing," she ordered. "And you'll find your plate in the warmer, with extra crespelles."

Without another word, she turned and headed toward the sand, her big ol' hips swaying as she marched off to her mission. God, he loved that woman.

Past midnight, Lila was still on the chaise lounge on the long deck outside her bedroom, a mother of a migraine in full swing. She squeezed her throbbing temples, looked up at the stars and nearly full moon, and then down at the picture on her lap.

She angled the frame to catch the moonlight, running her finger over the picture of Rafe but seeing his father. The smile was a little higher on the right than the left, a hint of dimple, an overdose of attitude.

And the eyes. Beautiful, bright, blue eyes the color of the morning sky over Barefoot Bay. She loved him so hard it hurt worse than the headache.

"This is all for you, buddy," she whispered. Yes, Gabe had left, but he'd be back. It was just a matter of time.

A soft hum of an electric engine made her sit up, reach for her weapon, immediately on alert. She recognized the sound as one of Casa Blanca's golf carts the staff used to get around the expansive resort property. A slow tingle of anticipation mixed with trepidation slipped up her spine as she thought of that last text from Dex.

You're never really safe, Lila. There are spies among us.

Maybe her friend and mentor was being overly cautious by using the phrase she'd heard him say a thousand times as a subtle warning to keep her mouth shut and her eyes open.

Or maybe he knew something he wasn't telling her.

Either way, the sooner she got this plan underway, the better. Even though it meant—

The golf cart slowed in front of her villa. Was that Gabe back for more information? She let the hope curl around her heart, despite the fact that he'd call a golf cart a walker on wheels.

And now that vehicle stopped and shut down completely.

She had a visitor, that was certain. Rockrose was the northernmost villa on the property. She'd chosen it purposely because it backed up to the large gardens and had a lovely wraparound porch built on stilts, giving it the utmost privacy, a wall of shrubbery, and no neighbors.

So who was up this far on the resort property, and why?

Her chaise was tucked into the corner of the side deck, impossible to spot from the front entrance. But that also meant she couldn't see who was coming to the front door.

Still holding Rafe's picture, she stood without making a noise and took two silent steps to get close to the railing so she could see the stairs that led up to the deck. She'd stripped out of her white outfit, changing to a simple black cover-up. With her hair pulled back, she could easily hide in the shadows to see who was here.

She peered at the heavyset woman carrying an armload of towels and one of the Casa Blanca terry-cloth robes draped over the top. Lumbering up the steps to the deck, the maid hummed softly, as if it were perfectly normal for a maid to drop off towels and a robe after midnight.

It wasn't.

There are spies among us.

Before Poppy spotted her, Lila moved across the side deck, soundlessly, hiding around the corner just outside the French doors that led to her bedroom.

"Miz Lila?" the housekeeper called out with a tap on the front door, her voice easily carrying around the side of the villa. "Delivering the towels you called for. And an extra bathrobe, case you get chilly."

She hadn't called for towels, and despite the December date, chilly wasn't common in the tropics. Poppy wanted in for some reason. Lila's instinct said this wasn't a hired assassin, but instinct could be wrong.

Why else would the woman make up a reason to come here at midnight, this woman who was always trying to hook Lila up with…

Of course. She worked for Gabe. There *were* spies among us—him.

He always had an asset or three on the ground and believed firmly in slipping cash to local eyes and ears to help out an operation. She knew Gabe was running a business that was equivalent to a for-profit wit-sec program, which was one of the reasons she was here, so of course he'd enlist a snooping housekeeper for help.

He'd sent the woman to dig around for information. *All right, Poppy, have at it.*

Lila slipped through the French doors and tiptoed down the hallway to the front door, arriving just as Poppy knocked and called again, repeating the whole speech.

Soundlessly, Lila lifted and opened the security lock, then

lightly darted back to her hiding place on the side deck.

After the third attempt at knocking, Poppy used her passkey and, without the security lock on, opened the door. Heavy footsteps hit the hardwood floor, loud enough for Lila to hear through the open bedroom doors.

"Anyone here? Miz Lila Wickham? It's Poppy from housekeeping. Don't want to scare you." She continued to use a loud voice, but Lila knew this was not Casa Blanca Resort & Spa protocol. A housekeeper would never walk into an occupied villa after midnight, even if a guest had called for towels. They'd leave them outside the front door and call on the house phone.

This was a Gabe Rossi B&E if she ever saw one. Lila stayed quiet, tucked into the corner so she could see through the sheer curtains but not be seen.

"Miz Lila?" Poppy tried one more time, moving noisily into the bedroom, giving Lila a direct view through the sheers over closed doors. Poppy looked side to side and then slipped into the bathroom, presumably to deliver her armload, and a minute later—longer than it took to place towels on a shelf—she stepped into the bedroom and looked around. Then she hustled right to the dresser, opening the top drawer as silently as a professional thief.

But she wasn't a thief. She was under the Rossi Spell, a powerful and heady thing.

Poppy felt around the top drawer, then abandoned it, moving on to the next. She searched that one, then repeated the move on the next two drawers, her shoulders lifting and dropping with frustration. What was she was looking for? A passport? Files?

She turned and looked around the room again, stepping to the nightstand to try that drawer, and then Lila remembered Poppy walking in just as she had slipped Rafe's picture into the top drawer. Of course that's what he wanted. He wanted to see his child.

Lila looked down at the framed five-by-seven in her hands.

Poppy gave up her search and left the villa through the same door she'd entered, moving with a little less speed and purpose. Probably sad to have to report a failed mission to her boss.

As she started up the electric motor and started to drive off, Lila scooted around the corner to the front of the villa. "Poppy, wait!"

The woman gasped loudly and slammed on the brakes. "Miz Lila!" she exclaimed. "I…I just…just delivered your towels…that you called for."

"I fell asleep on the chaise outside the bedroom." Lila walked down the stairs. "I appreciate you running out here so late at night for me. And on Christmas Eve."

In the dim moonlight, she could see the look of abject confusion on the other woman's face. "Um…yes, ma'am. We aim to please."

"One more thing," Lila said as she reached the side of the golf cart. "Would you mind doing me a favor?"

"Yes, yes, I'm happy to do whatever you like." Her Jamaican accent thickened, probably as a result of getting caught red-handed in all kinds of lies and subterfuge. But she held it together, and Lila had to admire Gabe's instinct and judgment. "What can I do for you?"

"Give this to Mr. Gabriel Rossi." She held out the picture frame. "Tell him I said Merry Christmas."

Chapter Five

As the sun rose on Christmas morning, Gabe sat on the edge of his bed staring at the picture he'd held most of the night. Out of the frame now, carefully examined for clues, changes, or photographic trickery that he happened to know quite well, he stared at the freakishly familiar face.

Oh, hell, *yeah.*

Far, far more familiar than the face of the woman who'd ordered the picture to be delivered to him.

Now he had a plan. A purpose. A reason. And raw, real emotion surging through him again.

He still mourned Isadora, because no matter what that blonde ice queen claimed, he knew in his deepest soul that the woman he loved was dead.

But not their son. All he had to do was look at this kid and he knew what gene pool this boy splashed around in.

He put the photo down and headed straight to the bungalow's back patio, restless with newfound energy.

Everything had changed. In fact, last night was the best sleep he'd gotten since he'd seen those words on the computer screen after his sister Chessie had done her masterful hacking…

Isadora Winter...deceased

But moments later, Chessie discovered that his ex-lover left behind a child named Gabriel. Yeah, sleep started eluding him that night. His appetite caved, too. Along with his overall mood as the world seemed to deliberately piss him off at every turn.

Then, because he was so not welcome in the country of Cuba, Chessie and his friend and fellow spy, Malcolm Harris, had gone there to track the kid down. Shit really sailed south then. Gabriel Rafael Rossi Winter, they'd discovered, had been adopted by a woman he and Mal knew from their days at Gitmo, and the child had supposedly died of a mysterious illness before his second birthday.

But last night, with a picture of a healthy, living, breathing, cocky-as-shit four-year-old who could be Gabe's clone, sleep was deep and dreamless. He didn't know who that human icicle was or what she wanted from him, but Lila Wickham had what he wanted most, so he was ready to play ball.

He popped down to the wooden deck and dove right into his routine, hitting sixty-two one-armed push-ups when the door opened and his octogenarian grandfather came lumbering out.

"*Buon Natale*," Nino said. The rare use of his native tongue, even to say Merry Christmas, made Gabe stop midway, balancing his entire weight on one arm.

"Same to you, old man. Why the Italian?"

Nino harrumphed with the ease of a man who harrumphed a lot, dropping onto a plastic Adirondack chair that had been at this place, sometimes used for staff housing, when they rented it from the resort. The two of them hadn't done a lot of decorating in the few months they'd been in Barefoot Bay. Hid a few people, set up a couple of new identities and lives, and made some good cash while Gabe used the proximity to Cuba to dig for news about Isadora. But no decorating.

Nino lifted a cup of coffee to his lips and nodded to Gabe. “All that reminiscing last night and I got cobwebs in my head.”

“All that limoncello last night gave you the cobwebs. The strolls down the Amalfi Coast circa 1950? Priceless.” He counted in his head while talking, long used to this with Nino.

“You left the bar so suddenly when Poppy came in,” Nino said. “Why?”

Because life changed in a heartbeat.

For one crazy second, he considered confiding in Nino. He told the old man everything he could, on every subject, more than he told anyone else in the world. He trusted him completely and had moved heaven and earth—and exposed the truth about a pesky old lady who tried to set Nino up for disaster—to get his grandfather to come to Bareass Bay with him.

Bringing Nino along might have ticked off the family they left behind in Boston, but Gabe hadn’t done it just so he could eat well.

Nino was his best friend, and if anyone could be trusted to know about what transpired last night, it would be him. But Nino was no spy; he wouldn’t understand. And, like Gabe, he’d been by what Chessie and Mal had discovered in Cuba, deeply affected by the loss of a great-grandchild. Yes, he had a few, with more on the way.

But Gabe’s child would be different, because Gabe was Nino’s favorite. His siblings and cousins might think they were, but Gabe knew the truth.

“I left ’cause I was tired,” he finally replied in answer to the pointed question.

"You're lying."

Gabe stilled on push-up number ninety-nine, looking up through squinted eyes at the old man.

"Something's up with you." Nino sipped. "Think I don't notice when your mood changes?"

Okay, there was a price for being the favorite. The old bastard knew him better than anyone. Gabe abandoned the push-ups and rolled onto the hard deck, flat on his back, staring at the marbled clouds in the morning sky.

He couldn't tell him everything, but he could tell him something. "I met a chick," he said.

"Mmm." Nino's reaction was masked by another noisy sip. "So that's why you took off without so much as a bite of scungilli salad."

"The blonde in the sparkly white trumped your tasty snails. Sorry."

"Actually, scungilli is conch."

Gabe rolled his eyes. "So did you see her?" he asked.

"No."

"She's staying up in Rockrose. I think I'll go visit her in a little bit." Gabe turned his head to get Nino's reaction, who just looked at him over his cup.

Then Nino sighed heavily and shook his head.

"What?" Gabe asked. "You've been on my case about my general dick-like behavior lately, so I thought I'd..." His voice trailed off at the look on Nino's face. "What is wrong, Nino?"

"Gabriel, you haven't been through all the stages of grief yet."

"I'm not grieving." Not since he saw that picture. "And, for the love of *Christmas*, stop reading those damn pop psychology books."

"There are five stages of grief, you know." He put the

cup on a table next to him and leaned forward. "I remember every one like it was yesterday after my Monica died."

My Monica. Sometimes Gabe's grandmother's name was like one word in Nino's mouth. *MyMonica.* And Gabe knew better than to even consider a sideways comment about her.

"Well, I plowed through every stage real fast," Gabe said. "So don't give me blowback if I want to spend time with the blonde." A lot of time. Enough time to get his son back, no matter what it took.

"You've been through denial and anger, God knows." It was like Gabe hadn't even spoken. "Next, you're going to try to make deals."

He was going to make a deal. *With the lying spy bitch who has my kid and probably had something to do with Isa's death.* "How about this deal? We shut up about this, and I get to work out in peace? Is that a deal?"

"They call it bargaining."

Gabe wiped his eyes, pressing the heels of his hands hard against them because he so fucking did *not* want to have this conversation. He wanted to shower and get over to Rockrose to start the charm offensive. If Lila wanted him to believe she was Isadora, he'd let her win that war. He'd do anything to get that kid, and calling her on her lies wouldn't help the process.

"You have a long way to go before you let go of this woman, this Isadora you told me about."

Why the hell did he get hammered and tell Nino so much that night Chessie had called him from Cuba with the news that his son was dead?

"And this little boy," Nino added. "You have two crosses to burn."

"Bear, not burn." He corrected Nino's butchered English phrase without thinking, but he couldn't correct Nino's mistake about who was dead and who wasn't. Even though he knew if he showed the picture to Nino, his grandfather would say, *Oh, Gabriel, you took that from your mother's wall of Rossi fame.*

That's how much the little boy looked like his father.

But he wasn't going to show it to Nino. The real thing would be better. "Thanks for the sage wisdom, as always, Gramps, but I got a ton to do today." He walked by, unable to avoid Nino's scowl or the giant gnarled hand that reached out to stop him.

"I know a little bit about grieving, young man. The hole my Monica left in my heart has never been filled in, and you know how I tried. Don't get taken in by this woman," he warned. "You know better than anyone that women can smell vulnerability."

Gabe lifted his arm and sniffed. "Then I better shower mine off before I go tap the new neighbor, huh?"

Nino didn't even smile. "I thought you learned that lesson."

"What lesson was that?"

Nino's bushy brow went up. "It's very easy to imagine a woman is who you want her to be because she happens to be who you need her to be."

Gabe stopped cold. He might have gotten boozy and chatty a few times in the last couple of months, but he was not stupid. He'd never told Nino any other story about being duped by a woman, ever. God knows that couldn't be tortured out of him. "What are you referring to, old man?"

"Remember what happened to me in Boston?" Nino asked. "Thinking that woman was free and interested in an old fart like me?"

Of course Nino didn't know about Moscow. He had his

own checkered past with wily women. "Yeah. Good thing I'm never too far away to save your sorry old ass."

Nino gave a yellowed, loving grin. "Which is why I'm willing to get out of this comfortable chair and cook for you. You want breakfast, Gabriel?"

"No, I want"—answers—"the neighbor. See you later."

"Suit yourself, but remember. You're tender and vulnerable."

"My ass is tender and vulnerable." He headed into the house with one single thought: He hated when Nino was bang on. And he was. Every stinkin' time.

By the time Lila returned to her villa, her head felt like a cement truck had been grinding her brain into mush for the last two hours.

At the time, it seemed worth every second. After all, it was Christmas Day. Who cared if that caused a headache? But now the sun was high, and the heat pounding down made the pain worse. She'd parked her rental car near the main building of the resort and chosen the beach as her route to walk back to the villa, a stroll on the sand exactly what her conflicted soul needed after a morning of the highest highs…and the deepest lows.

Her jumbled thoughts and fears and plans smoothed out, somehow, as her bare feet touched the sand and a tropical breeze fluttered her linen slacks and loose top. She pulled the elastic free that held her ponytail and rubbed her throbbing temples, letting her hair fall over her shoulders, even though the last thing those shoulders needed was more weight bearing down.

The beach was fairly deserted with most of the yellow umbrellas shading empty sand, which was understandable considering what day it was. But she still checked out every stranger she saw, constantly aware, constantly on guard.

That was another aspect of her life that would change with Gabe's help. A new identity and home would certainly help take her farther away from the guarded, worried existence of an operative. If only that life could include—

"I got your present."

She spun around, instantly braced for a battle, one hand reaching for the pistol hidden under her top.

"Gabe." How had he done that? He'd been right on her heels, and she hadn't even realized it. What was wrong with her? She puffed out a breath of self-disgust.

"Where you been?" he asked.

"Out."

"I've been sniffing around Rockrose for hours."

"I was…out." She didn't want to play any more verbal games with him, but she wasn't about to tell him where she'd been. Not yet. It was still too risky. He had to believe her first.

"I came to thank you." He held up the picture.

An unexpected surge of warmth at the sight of Gabe holding Rafe's picture rolled over her. "You like it?"

One side of his mouth lifted in a perfectly delicious Rossi grin, one that matched the smile in the picture he held up. "This is legit," he announced.

Of course he'd know that. Gabe's ability to spot a doctored picture was one of the reasons she was so certain giving it to him had been a good idea.

"And a quality piece of bait, blondie."

"I'm not trying to bait you. I'm here to convince you I am who I say I am, and that he…" *Needs his father.* "He…"

"Is alive."

She laughed softly, the sound of a little boy's laughter and shrill screams of Christmas morning excitement still in her ears. "Very much so."

Gabe eyed her. "That might be the first time I've heard you laugh."

"Don't get used to it." Lila wasn't the laugher Isadora had been. "Do you believe me now?"

Even in the warm sunlight, she could see some color leave Gabe's face. "I believe he's alive," he said again, a little wonder and a lot of thickness in his voice. "I was so sure he was dead."

Pain stabbed her head. Or was that just plain guilt? Hard to tell; they often felt the same. "He's not," she assured him.

His strong shoulders sagged in ever so slight resignation. "How about we start over?" he suggested.

"Only if you believe what I told you last night."

"That you're Isa—"

She stopped him with a hand to his lips, a gesture that would look playful to anyone watching, but she added pressure and a warning look. "Not out here."

He stared hard at her, his sapphire-blue eyes turning to slits. "Why can't I say your real name?"

She lowered her hand, a little reluctantly. His lips were so warm and smooth. Oh, the things those lips had done to her. She got a little weak just remembering.

"That person is dead for all intents and purposes, Gabe. You can't refer to me by my former name, ever."

He looked hard at her, intent and determined, like he was trying to see into her soul, the scrutiny sending tiny sparks to every nerve ending.

But then he shrugged and backed away. "Fine, whatever. I'll call you whatever you want, buy what you sell, and barrel down memory lane with you if that is what gives you a lady boner. But understand I have one goal and one goal only."

"You want to see your son."

"Of course. You gave me the picture, now I want the real thing." He put both his hands on her shoulders, intense again. "And answers. I want honest, complete answers."

She sighed with resignation. "Okay, I'll tell you inside." She started walking toward the path, imagining the conversation. "But be forewarned, you might not like everything I have to say."

On the path ahead that curved around some bushes, a man appeared, sunglasses hiding his eyes, a white T-shirt not hiding his muscles. His face angled toward Lila, but she couldn't tell if he was looking at her.

He half turned toward Gabe, a few steps behind Lila. Instantly, she stiffened, aware of how close and how big the man was, and how direct his attention seemed. And then she saw the gun on his hip.

He lifted his right hand and stepped closer, and Lila reacted without a second's hesitation. She launched to the left, blocking Gabe, and whipped out her pistol from the back holster, the barrel aimed squarely at the man before he took his next breath.

"Whoa!" He threw his arms in the air as Gabe vaulted closer and put his hand on Lila's arm.

"Don't shoot."

"Normally, I'd have an issue with a greeting like that on resort property, but..." The man took off his sunglasses and gave her an intense look. "Maybe Gabe is about to tell me you're here to interview for a job with me and you're showing off your bodyguard skills."

The adrenaline dumped, and Gabe tightened his hand on

her arm, giving her a surprisingly much-needed bit of support.

"Luke McBain, this is my friend Lila Wickham. And this guy"—he gestured to the other man—"is not a threat, but, in fact, is the head of security and owner of McBain Security, our crackerjack bullet catcher team keeping hordes of rich vacationers safe from harm."

Luke, a rugged man in his mid-thirties, laughed easily at the description. "We're growing and hiring. But you can put that weapon down now."

She lowered her Glock and slipped it back into the tiny holster at her back.

"I assume you have a permit for that," Luke said.

"Of course." She reached for her tiny shoulder bag, but Gabe put a casual arm around her, protective but light.

"No fears. Lila's well-trained, fully licensed, and not threatening the locals."

Luke nodded. "Gabe's blessing is all I need. Nice to meet you, Lila. Have you ever thought about personal security?"

Gabe stepped between them. "Don't you have a couple billionaires to protect, Deputy Dawg?"

Luke smiled, getting the message and saying good-bye. When he was out of earshot, Gabe inched closer and pressed his warm, strong hand a little harder on her back. "What kind of trouble are you in, blondie?"

Of course he'd figure out by her over-the-top reaction to an armed stranger that she was on the run. Because he was Gabe, perceptive and smart, and dear God, he smelled good.

"I'm not in trouble, just cautious."

"And let me guess…you need a place to hide and a new identity." It wasn't a question.

"Among other things."

"It would have been easier to just walk into my office and ask for help."

"But not nearly as much fun."

He slowed his step, looking at her. "That sounded like something Isadora would say."

"That's because I am Isadora," she whispered.

She could feel disbelief roll off him as he stared her down.

"But now Isa is Lila Wickham. You have to believe me."

"I don't have to do jack shit except see my son."

"Not until you believe me. I will not, under any circumstances, let you meet him until I am one hundred percent convinced beyond a shadow of a doubt that you trust me."

"Trust? I thought you claimed to know me."

She conceded with a nod. "Until you believe me, then."

"Okay, fine." He nudged her toward the house. "I believe you."

"You don't," she said on a sigh. "But you will before you see Rafe. You will."

Chapter Six

Gabe sat at the counter bar of the kitchen where they'd had their argument the night before. As Lila poured two tall glasses of iced tea, he studied her hands and prepared to lay on a few of his own lies.

He'd make her think he believed her. A few questions, the right answers, and he'd fake-celebrate her home.

Whatever it took to get information and access to the child she called Rafe.

Her hands looked...familiar as she squeezed a lemon and stirred the drink. Except for the bright red nail polish, which Isadora had hated.

These hands were thinner, bonier like the rest of her, but...they *could* be Isadora's hands.

He let his gaze drift up, taking in the way she held her shoulders, the tilt of her head, the shape of her brows. Was it possible? Yes, there was a vague whisper of a resemblance to the woman in his memory. Did she still favor her right leg ever so slightly when she walked? No one else would notice that but a spy, or someone who happened to notice that she wore the soles of her right shoe down faster than the left.

He muttered a curse and stuffed his fingers through his hair to drag some back.

She looked up at him. "I know it's hard to accept, Gabe."

She spoke in that natural, flat Midwestern voice that sounded just like Isa's. Only behind closed doors, though, he noticed. Outside, even with no one around, she was all British proper.

Accept. Hah. He was curious, confused, and pissed off. But he wasn't even in the same zip code as *accepting*. "I'm waiting for your explanation, which better be rock solid, crystal clear, and include the full address and complete security report for my son."

The impatience and force in his tone made her eyes shutter as she handed him a glass. "Come outside in the sunshine."

"Fuck the sunshine." He slammed the glass on the granite. "Sit your ass down on this stool"—he pointed to the one next to him at the kitchen bar—"and start spilling state secrets, and don't stop until I know everything about you, your problems, why you're here, and my son. In fact, start with him."

"Don't tell me what to do."

"Don't tell me what to believe."

She narrowed her eyes at him. "Still the control freak, I see."

Anger sparked. "If you're going to pull off Isa, you might try to be a little sweeter."

"People change."

He inched back, the hint of a smile pulling at his lips. "Was that supposed to be sarcasm?"

"It was supposed to be the truth, which I promised you." She came around to sit next to him, giving her forehead a rub, but he watched her gait. A little different, but he could make the argument that she walked like Isadora.

Son of a bitch.

"I don't want to fight," she said.

"Just tell me about Rafe."

She sat down, sipped her tea, and gave him a rare smile. "He's an incredible kid."

Of course he was. Gabe swallowed the comment with some tea and waited for her to go on.

"Really smart and inquisitive and, oh my God, he's..." She laughed, shaking her head, pressing her thumb to her temple as if the very thought gave her a headache.

"He's what?"

She bit her lip, her dark eyes glimmering in a way he hadn't seen before. "He's bad."

"What do you mean?"

"I mean, he's *bad*," she repeated with a shrug. "The terror of preschool. He spends so much time in the corner there are tally marks on the walls."

He couldn't help it, the image made him smile. "Some genes die hard."

She gave him a rueful smile, and he tried—really tried—to see Isadora in that expression. How many bars had they sat in, cozy and close to each other, laughing about a shared joke, knowing the night would end with ball-blasting sex that would leave them both beyond satisfied?

But this woman? Very little about Lila was like the woman he'd loved to drink and laugh with. This woman was...attractive, if you liked edgy, controlling blondes draped in secrets and deceit. He didn't.

She lifted her iced tea in a pretend toast. "Rafe is your clone right up to and including his, uh, colorful four-year-old vocabulary. Is that genetic?"

"I don't know." The question called for a smile, but when reminded of the child's age, nothing amused him. "He's turning five in June," he said simply. "Nearly five *years that I've missed*."

She averted her eyes, then closed them altogether, like the liar that she was.

"If you really are Isadora..." *If*. Like there was any doubt that she wasn't. "Then you'd better have a good reason for keeping my son from me all these years. Like, you were abducted by aliens and living on Mars until the day you showed up here."

She slid her hand up and down the crystal, thinking for a long time before answering. "I knew the assignment was undercover. I didn't know...how severe. And I didn't know when I accepted it that I was pregnant."

He inched closer, aching for the answer to a question that had plagued him in the middle of a lot of sleepless nights. "Isadora was on the pill."

She nodded slowly. "Isadora forgot to take it one time and thought she'd be okay." She gave him a dark look. "Which is why I didn't dream I could be pregnant and didn't pay any attention to my schedule or the changes in my body. When they started happening, I was deep in training for a new job, totally preoccupied. I didn't gain much weight or experience sickness. It wasn't until a pre-surgery blood test that I found out I was pretty far along. They were willing to make concessions and wait until I had the baby to do the surgeries."

Plausible, possible even. "So you were pregnant when you left?"

She nodded. "Maybe that was why I was so emotional when I tried to tell you. Well, we were both emotional," she added. "At least, we were after we made love and I told you I was leaving."

His whole body tensed and froze. How could she know something so intimate? Who could have gotten that particular truth out of Isadora? This woman *had* to be guessing. It was a huge part of a great cover, something they were all trained to do. Pick up clues and make assumptions and speak with authority, and you can pass.

But the way he'd delayed the conversation that morning was no assumption. That was a *memory*.

"I don't really remember the details," he said gruffly, and even on this stranger's face, he could see disappointment register at his lie. He remembered the details, every single one, right down to the bone-deep pleasure of his last killer orgasm with Isadora.

"I do." She twisted the barstool so she was facing him directly. "And I remember the argument, and how you walked out without saying good-bye, good luck, or good riddance. Or," she added with a surprisingly soft touch of her fingertips to his arm, "three little words we used to say with such frequency."

Neither one of them had said those words that morning.

More blood drained from his head. Memory-stealing software and a hot chick describing sex. This was *exactly* how dark intelligence worked. He had to remember that.

He looked her straight in the eye. "Go on."

"You want more details? What we said? How we moaned? You came like a freight train and I didn't. Then we had a fight, and you mocked my friend and…and you left in a typical Gabe Rossi temper tantrum."

"Shit." He pushed back hard, nearly toppling his stool, giving up on Plan A to pretend to believe her. "Motherhumping scientists. How did they do this, and where the hell is Isadora?"

She didn't even flinch. "I'm right here, and there were no scientists, just a lot of very talented surgeons."

He stared at her, fighting for each breath, feeling his nostrils flare as another round of fury and frustration rattled him right to the bone. "Even if you were…are…" He shook his head and felt the punch of what was *really* killing him.

This could be true. He knew that much. It was improbable and rare, but not impossible. Just like her pregnancy. "How?" he asked.

"How do you think? Countless surgeries, including facial recon, breast reduction, eye dying and chemical straightening and hair-color changes. Don't forget this lovely beak of a Roman nose."

"That's not a Roman nose."

She rolled her eyes. "They called it 'aquiline,' which is a nice way of saying a little too big for my face."

It was prominent, but so were her cheekbones and jaw. It all fit, somehow. She was elegant and structured, where Isadora had been pretty and soft.

But if he looked really hard…he could see things that may or may not be there.

"Look here." She lifted her hair along her temple, pulling it taut so he could see the fine line of a scar he hadn't seen on his first inspection. "And here." She pushed her ear forward to show another. "And these." She closed her eyes and stretched the lid, where a close examination showed a line so tiny it could have been a premature wrinkle.

"There's a lot more changed than your…her…face." He gestured to her body but really meant her personality.

"Trust me, I have scars on my legs, under my arms, and along the bottoms of my breasts. Liposuction, the bone surgery, a complete change of diet, and a year of personal training, and I have a different body. Some would say better, but…" She lifted a shoulder. "I liked my cushions."

He just stared at her.

"And so did you," she added, jabbing her verbal knife a little deeper.

"And the rest? The way you walk and talk and move is different."

She blinked at him. "Training in a new posture and carriage, eliminating gestures and linguistic tics. None of that is twenty-first century. The CIA's been doing it for decades."

"Isa's linguistic tics were overusing people's names and tending to say 'just' more than necessary." Not that he'd noticed, but she'd told him that once.

"And you love alliteration."

And she'd told him that, too.

"We all have language crutches and, being a linguist, it was very easy to change mine. Even easier to learn a subtle British accent." She smiled. "It's quite the natural way for me to speak now," she added, slightly emphasizing the accent that he'd already grown so used to he barely noticed it when she spoke.

For a minute, Gabe stayed silent, taking it all in, processing, judging, and knowing, deep in his soul, this very well could be the truth.

A truth he hated so much it made him sick. "And there was no one else in the entire CIA who could do this job? It had to be you, made over?"

"Yes," she said simply. Without, he noticed saying a word about what the assignment was. "And you have to believe me before I tell you why."

A low-grade simmer of fury started in his blood. "Isadora is dead." He ground out the words because as much as he hated saying them, he needed to believe it. He couldn't fall for this. He couldn't.

"Isadora's death was faked on a rain-slicked road outside of Caibarién, Cuba, and had a body double placed there while I escaped by helicopter. There was no real investigation since Cuban officials, as you well know, are easily bribed."

The simmer grew to a boil as anger flashed through him. If anyone else were to hear this story, they'd shake their heads and call it the stuff of spy movies. But Gabe had spent a lot of years in this world. He'd met plenty of guys—maybe not a woman, but who knew?—who'd changed the way they looked to use a special skill and infiltrate an operation. Some became sleeper agents and essentially disappeared in their target country. Some just left the agency and kept their new identity. Some killed themselves because this wasn't fucking natural in any way, shape, or form.

But those kinds of life-changing assignments were taken by people who had nothing left to live for, not vibrant, gorgeous, brilliant linguists in happy relationships.

Not Isadora. His precious Isadora. *Damn it.*

"She is not dead," she said quietly. "She is right here."

"She might as well be dead," he finally said, trying to ignore the flinch of pain his words caused her, because, too bad. Her pain couldn't be as bad as his. "'Cause this"—he gestured up and down her body—"this model-slick bottle blonde with fake eyes and skinny hips isn't the woman I loved." He shook his head and got off the barstool, ready to erupt.

"I know I'm different, Gabe, but—"

"Different?" He spat the word back at her. "You're…you're…*not Isadora*." He clung to that belief even as the tendrils of truth started wrapping their soul-sucking claws around his heart. "Isadora had heart and soul," he said, hating that his voice cracked from the anguish those tentacles caused. "She had laughter in her smile and a spark in her eyes." He stepped back with every word, feeling himself trying to get away from her, knowing he was hurting this woman—whoever she was—but right then he didn't care because *she wasn't Isadora.*

Even if she was or had been at one time, this bitch had taken his Isadora away, and he hated her for it.

"Gabe."

"No!" He barked the word. "You're not her! Isa had gentle green eyes and a ridiculously cute overbite and…and…no nail polish the color of a fire truck."

She just looked at him like a prisoner taking the torture, refusing to break.

"She was soft and sweet and…" Goddammit, his eyes were misting over. "Mine," he finished, turning away so he didn't embarrass himself any further. "She was *mine*."

He forgot his son and his mission and his common sense and did the only thing he could possibly do…he bolted. Marched through the room, out the door, and clomped down to the sand to get as far away from this phony, lying, conniving, threatening spy.

He *hated* her. Even if she was Isadora. He hated every fucking cell in her brand new body. He shot forward and started to run, his only need to escape this sickening impostor and mourn the woman he loved all over again.

Chapter Seven

Lila caught up with Gabe before he got twenty feet from the steps, slamming her hand on his back and pushing him so hard, he stumbled. Off balance, she threw them both to the sand and flipped on top of him before he had a chance to breathe.

He wasn't even putting up a fight, or she'd be on her back in a second. Under her, Gabe stared up, shocking her with the redness in his eyes.

"Isadora couldn't fight." He barely breathed the whispered echo of his last words.

"At the risk of stating the obvious again, I've changed." She used her full body weight to pin down his shoulders with her arms.

"It was her least favorite part of training."

"It's not so bad." She pressed harder, straddling his hips. With her arms locked, her loose top sagged and gave him a bird's-eye view of her breasts.

Lila rarely wore a bra and today hadn't even bothered with a camisole.

And, of course, he looked, then straight up at her, yet another disappointment registering in his eyes.

"Breast reduction," she said. "My boobs were

too…memorable."

He groaned a little and closed his eyes. "This is a fucking nightmare."

Of course he'd think that. She sat up a little, releasing her hold on his shoulders but not a hundred percent ready to slide off this particularly wonderful saddle. How many times had she sat on Gabe like this, making love in one of their favorite positions?

Too many to count.

"I want to know the assignment," he said.

"You actually were the first person to tell me about it."

Disbelief flashed. "What?"

"Roger Drummand's special snowflakes, as you called the detainees, set free in the United States of America."

He sat up on his elbows, his eyes narrowing even more. "They canceled that program," he said. "Someone got smart and realized it was one thing to send those nitwits back to their own countries to spy for us, but letting them live and work in the US was sheer madness."

"They did cancel the project, but Roger never brought back the ones he'd already sent out to see if they could find domestically based terrorist cells. He was a little crazy."

"And now he's a little dead, thanks to Mal and my sister."

"Which is how I got my release from the CIA."

He looked hard at her. "Because of what happened in Cuba? Chessie and Mal did that when they brought him down for embezzling half a million bucks and letting Mal take the blame."

She nodded. "Until then, he secretly kept those detainees-turned-US-spies alive and kicking, against all rules. My job was to infiltrate his organization, use what I knew against him, and hunt each of the former detainees down and ferret them out. It had to be someone who knew Drummand and the detainees, someone willing to change their looks." At his look of raw incredulity, she added, "No one else had the language skills, the knowledge of the individuals, the insight into Drummand, the ability to transform myself, and an uncanny knack for flying under the radar. Nobody else could do it."

He puffed out a disgusted breath. "Nobody else wanted that shit job."

She couldn't argue that. "I'll give you that. It was a delicate, dangerous, dark operation that required tremendous sacrifice and took years to accomplish. But I saved lives, Gabe. Lives that would have been snuffed out like my mom and dad's lives were. And that's what mattered to me."

He speared her with a look, pushing himself all the way up now, his wheels turning as he took that information, added it to what he already knew, and looked at her, maybe for the first time since she'd arrived, with a flicker of belief.

Finally.

"How exactly did you do that?"

She shook her head. "You know I can't. Everything was top secret. Highest clearance imaginable."

He leaned closer, inches from her face. "Baby, you better dish up a heaping, stinking pile of classified crap. Right this fucking minute."

She looked down and plucked a tiny white shell from the sand, running a finger over its edges. "Drummand had managed to place six former detainees in the US. He did it rogue, because he couldn't get CIA support, and monitored the program himself, with hopes of becoming the big hero of antiterrorism."

"Now that is a chilling thought."

"Precisely. After a complete physical transformation so

he could never recognize me, I was brought into his department in DC as part of an international joint task force, a new agent from the MI6 who could speak a number of Middle Eastern languages, ostensibly to work on some unimportant, bogus project he supervised. Of course, it didn't take long for him to grow dependent on me, which was the goal, and ask if I could translate some messages. Then I really made progress."

"What kind of progress?"

"Three of the spies, it turned out, hadn't completely flipped to side with the United States and were actively planning terrorist attacks. I was able to track them down and work with the FBI and our agents to stop the attacks."

He considered that, and her, no doubt sizing up her ability to handle a job of that magnitude. "And what about the baby? You did all this as a single mother?"

"While I trained, I stayed in Cuba, where the agency has some secret facilities. It worked well. I stayed at a farm and worked there as a cover and made sure I trusted the people who took care of Rafe. After I…after *Isadora* died, Rafe went to live with Alana Cevallos, who adopted him and gave him a safe home. You remember that she worked at Guantanamo and had, at one time, reported to Drummand."

"She was in on all this?"

She nodded. "That was my stipulation, and she was sworn to secrecy. That way, I had someone I could be in regular contact with and a way to see Rafe without having him be in the States until we were ready. When he was two, I was able to bring him home to live with me in DC."

He sat very still, processing this. A non-CIA person would blow his stack or at least pepper her with a million questions. But Gabe knew the agency all too well.

"He's reported dead," he finally said. "That grave said his

name was Gabriel." His voice grew thick. "Chessie took a picture for me."

She swallowed. "It was the only way to get him safely out of Cuba. His name is Rafe Wickham now."

He closed his eyes like she'd shot a nine-millimeter bullet right through his heart. "How'd you explain that undercover?"

"Easily. The deeper I wormed my way into Drummand's good graces and helped him, the more dependent he became on me. So, when I said I wanted to return to London because I'd left my child to be raised by a nanny, he immediately had me transferred full time into his operation and I moved Rafe to DC with me."

His jaw clenched and unclenched as he listened. "Why didn't someone—you or Crain or *someone*—tell *me* I had a child?" The break in his voice was like a hot poker through her brain.

"They cut me off from everyone and watched me very closely," she said.

"Because they're pricks like that," he said.

"Every single piece of communication I had, made, or did was supervised by the CIA and many by Drummand himself. I tried a few times to send test comm, without saying anything specific, and every one was intercepted. I had to stop trying because what good would it have done? It would totally have blown my cover if my old pal from Gitmo showed up to claim his kid. Don't even pretend you wouldn't have stormed DC demanding him."

"As I should."

"So the last time I was in Cuba, when I got Rafe back, I had Alana plant that letter in the interrogation cell. It was my only hope."

He gave the sand a frustrated flick, silent.

"Gabe, listen to me. I made my decisions and have to live with the consequences. But those decisions resulted in three foiled attacks: one at the Mall of America the day after Thanksgiving, one in the middle of the red carpet before the Oscars, and one on a fully loaded plane leaving Orlando. None of them publicized and not a single word leaked. You know this kind of counterterrorism work is not unusual. Hell, there's more going on every day with ISIS."

"Then why'd you quit?"

"We finished the job, Drummand is dead, and the CIA wants the whole thing to go away. Can you imagine the outcry if the media got hold of the fact that someone planted 'flipped terrorist detainees' on US soil? It's one thing if they sneak in under our noses, but if we planted them there?"

He shook his head. "A shit explosion of the highest order."

"Exactly. It's Dex's worse fear."

"And God forbid Dexter Crain lose the presidential bid."

She ignored the sarcasm, unsurprised by it.

"Did you get them all?" he asked.

She took a slow breath, knowing he meant the terrorists. "We think so."

"You *think* so?"

She rubbed her head. "But since I'm not absolutely sure, I hoped you could help me start over somewhere else with a whole new identity."

He backed up a little, blinking. "That's really why you're here? What about Rafe? You expect me to give him a new identity so you can haul him away from me?"

She swallowed and looked down at the shells and sand. "No. I brought him here to...give to you." This time her voice cracked.

"What?"

"You heard me."

He moved closer to her, close enough to put his hand under her chin and lift her face. "Now I know you're not Isadora."

She stared at him, knowing where he was going with this.

"Because that woman would never give up her child."

"She would to keep him safe."

"He's not safe?" he demanded.

"He is. Right now, he's in a secure home with a trustworthy Secret Service agent acting as his bodyguard. But…" She turned away, shame and guilt making it impossible to look at him.

"But what?"

"I just want you to have your time with him, okay? Do you believe that?"

He smiled. "You *just* want that? What was it you called that, a linguistic tic?"

"And a little more proof that I'm not lying."

"Oh, you're lying," he said. "I don't know why or how much or even what parts of your far-fetched story, but you are lying."

She sure was.

Chapter Eight

Dexter Crain closed his eyes, blocking out the rolling, snow-covered hills of western Pennsylvania and the sounds of laughter and Christmas carols emanating from the family room. He didn't want to be in there when the call came in and have to excuse himself to take it.

He had a feeling it would be bad news.

All he wanted was for the whole operation to be over. For years, he'd lived with the tension that this potential land mine could blow up, and the closer he got to the nomination, the more deadly that explosion could be.

But all of the flipped terrorists were detained or dead now. Drummand had graciously put a bullet through his own head. Even Lila, who'd worked the hardest and sacrificed the most, had been released from the CIA and had assured him she would be disappearing with her son, taking their secrets with her.

He hoped. She was the only real thread still dangling that could turn into a rope to actually strangle him.

But when he received a text ordering him to stay near a safe phone and available all day, his heart had grown heavy. Had the media gotten wind of the project? Was someone writing a tell-all that would bring him down?

This thing had to end.

So he listened to the happy noises from the holiday scene unfolding in his ten-thousand-square-foot McMansion and prayed he didn't lose it all in a scandal that could end his career. His kids, his grandchild, and his dear wife.

Anne would be heartbroken to give up that dream of the White House.

"We're ready for the annual picture." Anne's voice pulled him from his reverie, making him turn from the picture window to see the petite woman with a sleek black bob, not a hair or jewel out of place, warmth and hope in her golden-brown eyes. "It's hardly a family Christmas picture without you."

There was just enough of a note of sadness in her voice that he let guilt squeeze his chest. He'd been so preoccupied and distant. He knew he'd stretched her patience thin, and she was beginning to think that it wasn't a dark operation that fell under his purview that had him spending so much time whispering on the phone or in secret meetings in undisclosed locations.

And he couldn't blame her for assuming the worst, even though she'd be so wrong.

"I'm waiting for a call," he said, holding up the cell phone—the untraceable one, of course. "It's a CIA issue. Classified and urgent."

"I see."

"Anne. Lives are at stake. You know the world we live in and the role I play." Actually, the chairman of the Senate Intelligence Committee shouldn't be playing this role at all, but she knew very little about his work, and he liked it that way.

"When you're done, then?"

Before he answered her, the device in his hand hummed.

"Here's the call," he said, holding up his phone. "Get everyone a drink, and I'll be there in just a few minutes."

"Dex, I—"

"Hello?" A woman's voice came through the speaker he must have accidentally touched.

Anne's eyes widened like she'd been slapped.

Dexter turned around, thumbing the phone to get it off speaker. "This is Senator Crain," he said.

"Can you hold for Director Hollings, Senator?" Of course it was an executive assistant placing the call, but Anne didn't know that. Now her worst suspicions seemed confirmed.

And so were his if the director of the CIA himself was on the line. On Christmas Day. This was not good.

"Yes, of course." He walked down the hall to his study, his mind spinning over the possibilities. A number of CIA higher-ups had been putting pressure on him for some time now to get Lila Wickham out of the picture and out of the country. She knew too much about programs that could blow up in the face of the intelligence committee and cost too many people their jobs…or the jobs they wanted to get.

Was that why the director was calling? He could assure him she was doing just that. As long as a reporter hadn't gotten too much information about this damn operation.

In his office, he closed and locked the door behind him just as the booming voice of Jeffrey Hollings came through.

"I'd like to say Merry Christmas, Senator, but I'm afraid it's not."

"What's the problem?"

"We've received intelligence of a credible threat against Lila Wickham."

Dex drew back, frowning at the phone, the statement not at all what he'd been worried about. "From whom?"

"We don't know, they are encrypted and classified."

In other words, even Dex wasn't getting that information.

"Could it be someone associated with one of the cells she helped take down?" Dex asked.

"It could and we're investigating that possibility."

"Can you protect her?" Dexter asked.

"She's released and out of our care," Hollings replied. "She's left no forwarding information, and her apartment in DC is empty. That's what we agreed on, but obviously we want her to know and take precautions. While we look for her, I assumed you were the best and safest way to reach her. Is she still in the country?"

"I'm not sure." And that was the truth; she'd refused to tell him where she was going or how she was getting assistance. They agreed it was better if he didn't know.

"Are you in touch with her?"

"Occasionally."

"Then tell her to get out of sight and be on constant guard. We think this is a real threat. We also think it could be someone with access."

Dexter frowned. "How much access?"

Hollings let out a low, long sigh. "Someone with access to seriously classified information."

An insider? Someone Lila might trust?

There are spies among us, he thought bitterly. And he always knew it.

"We'll be in touch," Hollings added. "And Merry Christmas."

"Sure." Dex disconnected the call and fell into his chair with a soft moan. He'd dragged her into this, knowing that having an insider in the operation assured that he'd never be out of the loop. He knew from the beginning it meant a complete change of her identity and had made the calculated decision not to tell her.

He had no idea that the woman he hand-picked for the job would be pregnant, but she'd handled it. And quite well. But this cloud over his head had to go away, and if she—

"Dexter?" Anne's voice and a sharp rap on the door startled him.

He got up and opened it, his chest squeezing at the sight of her tears. "Who is she?" she asked on a half sob.

Of course her mind would go there. Anne had no idea the intricacies of the intelligence community.

"She's no one you have to worry about," he assured her.

"That's what you said about the woman at the Brazilian embassy."

Who was no more his lover than Jeffrey Hollings was. He was tired of her constant suspicions, but, deep inside, he understood them. She lived with a level of subterfuge the wife of a senator shouldn't have to endure.

He closed his eyes and puffed out a breath. "I swear to God, Anne, I'm not cheating on you."

"Then what was that phone call about?"

"An undercover CIA agent, actually former CIA, is being threatened, and they need to find her."

"And you know where she is? Why? Are you sleeping with her?" And she jumped to ridiculous conclusions.

"God, no."

She crossed her arms and worked so hard to look furious, but all he could see was the hurt. She sighed and closed her eyes. "I can't take this anymore. The lies and the secrets. I just can't. It wasn't always like this."

"Of course not, but—"

"Ever since Isadora died. Ever since."

He stepped back, surprised by the connection, determined not to let on that even the mention of her name meant anything anymore. "It just seems that way."

She wrung her hands and made her fretful face. "I guess it's the holidays. They make me blue. They make me miss her."

"Don't...be blue." He started walking back to his desk to hide the secure phone.

She took a slow breath and closed her eyes. "I know you were in constant contact with her. You know what really happened to her, don't you? It wasn't an accident in Cuba, was it?"

"Anne." He whipped around. "What do you mean?"

"She died of a brain tumor, didn't she?"

"Why on earth would you even suggest that?"

"Because...because..." She bit her lip. "I know things, too, Dex. Things her mother told me before she died."

"What did Mary Lou tell you?"

"Everything. She was my closest friend." Anne put her hand on her chest, her eyes welling. "I grieve for that whole family every single day."

"What are you talking about, a brain tumor?"

She blew out a breath and walked to the leather sofa, falling onto it. "Isadora's dead, so it doesn't matter."

Maybe it did matter. Very much. "Tell me anyway."

"Mary Lou was diagnosed with a brain tumor. She told me before she was killed. No one knew except her husband, of course, and me. She told me she knew her mother had one, and her grandmother."

"Why didn't you tell me?"

"Because Mary Lou died on 9/11, and I certainly wasn't going to make Isa's life any worse by sharing the news. Periodically, I'd ask her if she got headaches, and she said no, then she joined the CIA, and I knew she would be undergoing rigorous health testing, so I thought it better not to tell her."

But someone better tell her. "Well, I'll tell her and…"

"Dexter." Her eyes widened, and she stood. "What did you say?"

"I said…I'd…I meant I should have…I…"

She put both hands over her mouth and stifled a scream. "She's still alive!"

Damn it. What the hell was wrong with him? He looked at her and slowly shook his head. "No, no, that was a slip."

But she had fire in her eyes now. "No, it wasn't. Tell me, Dex. Please, dear God, for once in your life tell me the truth."

He closed his eyes, defeated. "She went undercover for five years."

Blood drained from Anne's face as she made a strangled noise. "I cried at her memorial service."

"That wasn't her in the casket."

She drew back, pale now as the snow outside. "I…can't believe it." She pressed both hands to her chest. "I can't breathe, Dexter. It's too much."

Relief and regret roiled through him. "She's in the process of disappearing again, so please don't get too excited."

"I am excited!" She fluttered her hands and walked back and forth. "Oh my word, she's like another daughter to me. We have to tell the—"

"No!" He reached for her. "You cannot tell anyone. I'm a fool to have made a mistake like that. Her life is in danger, and no one knows where she is anyway, including me. That's what that call was all about. She and her son are in danger."

"Her son?" She clutched him. "Dexter! I need to go to her," she whispered. "I need to see her. You know how I adore her."

"You've actually seen her, Anne. She was at a dinner we had at the condo in DC a few years ago. A blond British woman by the name of Lila Wickham."

"A blond British woman?" Her voice rose in disbelief.

"She's undergone a complete physical transformation." Anne could never understand the world of intelligence, which was clear by the look of incredulity on her face. "Technically, Isadora is dead and will stay that way. It's for her own good."

"But she's not," Anne said, shaking a little. "She's alive and, oh my God, Dexter, she has to know about her mother. Otherwise, she could fail to recognize the symptoms and get help. She could die, Dex."

She might die anyway if she wasn't careful.

"I'll talk to her," he promised.

"Dexter." She squeezed his arm. "I'd give anything to see her. Anything in the world. You can trust me."

He shook his head. "That's not going to happen, Anne. I'm sorry."

Chapter Nine

Back inside her villa, Gabe couldn't help but interrogate her.

It was Gabe's nature to analyze every word and consider every angle, like any decent spook. And the angles of Lila Wickham had just thrown him a curve.

She wanted to leave her only child? Why not take him along? Not that he'd let her; he'd fight her to the end. Did she know that and give up in advance? That didn't seem like…

Well, he didn't know Lila Wickham. So he set about fixing that in his usual way—by asking questions.

"You're one hundred percent certain of this decision?"

She shot him a look. "Not a hundred, but I believe it's better this way. Safer." She shifted on the sofa, squaring her shoulders as if she expected a fight from him.

Better to leave her son?

"Is that the only reason?"

She closed her eyes, and he watched pain leave its mark on her features. "I suppose I feel guilty for taking him away from you for almost five years."

"Another good reason. Are there any others?"

She sighed. "Not really."

Lies. Lies. And more lies. Weren't they? New doubts mixed with old doubts and churned in his belly with every inch he moved closer to believing this crap.

"Of course, I don't *want* to leave him, but I know so much, too much," she said quickly. "And I've put so many people either in prison or in the grave, and those bad people are related to other bad people. When I took this job, I didn't know I'd have a son I care about so much it literally hurts."

She pressed two fingers to her forehead as if her maternal love had her temples throbbing. "It's what's best for him, a life with someone who I know will be sure he's safe. Someone who will love him like I do. Better than I do."

Shit. She was rambling. Gabe sat back, remembering everything he knew about spies who went hell-deep undercover. Those bastards got effed up hard in the head. Maybe she was worried she'd go off the deep end. Hell, maybe she *had* gone off the deep end.

"You've never, uh, hurt him, have you?"

Her head shot up with a gasp. "God no! He hurts me."

"How?"

"Because I…I love him so much, sometimes it hurts."

What the jumpin' jack shit crap did that mean? "Listen, we'll figure something out," he said. "Something that will be safe for both of you. I need some time to put together a plan and then execute it."

She turned to him. "I've already figured something else out. I have a plan. You want to hear it?"

"Sure. What's your plan?"

"I'll stay here for a little while, and you and I will…pretend to be a thing. In a little bit, I'll bring Rafe here. You'll fall in love with him, of course. And I'll…disappear. I can die or run away or just break it off with you, and you'll keep him and raise him."

Holy fuck, she *had* gone off the deep end. "*That's* your plan? That suckfest of stupid is your plan?"

A smile pulled at her lips. Isa would have smiled at that, too. The thought tweaked his heart, startling him. "More or less. You have anything better?"

"Don't have anything *dumber*, that's for sure."

"Well, it's something of a plan."

"Actually, I do have an idea," he said. "How about you bring Rafe ASAP, and he and I get to know each other, and you take a job in the area, and we both have perfectly healthy, normal roles in our son's life?"

She sighed with so much longing it sounded as if he'd just offered her a full-body massage with warm oil. Naked. "No. They'll find me."

"Let them. Whoever it is will have to get past me, and I'll mess them up so bad they'll wish they hadn't been born. I *want* them to find you, but only if you and Rafe are under one hundred percent constant supervision."

She let out a soft groan. "I *almost* believe you."

"Now you know how I feel. I *almost* believe you."

She squeezed his hand. "Gabriel. You really are my angel."

He flinched and caught himself. "I'm sorry, but it's weird to hear you…and look at you. It's like I don't know who you are, but I do."

"You don't know me," she agreed. "This experience, this life, all these decisions and surgeries and the constant pressure of living a lie *have* changed me. All the way, deep inside. You just can't understand what it's done to me."

He took a long, slow breath. "I think you need to fix your problems, not run away from them. See a shrink if you have to, get help, let me get you safe and secure, and set you up *here* with a job and a life."

"Oh God, you make it sound so easy."

"It's a helluva lot easier than pretending we're dating, faking another death, and handing our kid off to yet another new life."

"I just need to..."

Just again. Her Isa tic. It did something to his gut, knowing she was *in there*. But not out here.

He ran his fingertip over her knuckles, then spread her hand over his. "You hated nail polish."

"I still do," she confessed. "But I had to change in every imaginable way. I'm the opposite of the woman you loved so much. I know that. I'm flat-chested, too skinny...not pretty like she was. I don't think like her or sound like or...or...*feel* like her. Sometimes I don't feel anything. It's just"—she took their joined hands and pressed them to her breastbone—"empty in here. And that's the way I want to keep it."

So she wasn't in there. It was *empty*. "Wow."

"What?"

He shook his head, not quite able to put his sadness into words.

"What is it?" she asked.

"If you're telling the truth—"

"I am."

"Then what a damn shame. Isa was passionate. She was the opposite of empty. She was full of heart and life and feelings. It's where we connected."

"And why we fought."

The statement slapped him, like someone knocking sense into him. Or the truth.

"Kind of. You might be who you say you are, but she's still dead."

She made the softest little grunt in her throat, as if the truth of that hurt. But how could it, if she felt nothing?

"And you're wrong," he added. "You're very pretty."

She gave him a look. "You hate blondes."

"Hate is a strong word."

She pointed to him, a knowing look in her eyes. "Your grandfather says it's the curse of Italian men to want every woman to look like Sophia Loren. Dark hair, wide hips, and nice big bosoms."

Oh man. He remembered the moment he'd shared that with Isa, crystal clear. It was in DC, a few weeks after they'd met. In the shower, with her wet hair and slicked against her skin, her gorgeous breasts and generous hips on display.

And then the truth hit him. Clobbered him in the head and heart and dragged his unwilling corpse to the other side of common sense.

She was telling the truth.

Maybe not completely about giving up their son; he'd get to the bottom of that. But Isadora Winter was alive and sitting one foot away from him. And just like that, something clicked in his brain. The angles lined up. The facts couldn't be denied. He had to stop doubting her.

"Hair color can change back," she mused, unaware of his lightning-bolt moment. "But the bosoms are gone, baby, gone."

Gabe blinked at her, maybe because he'd stopped fighting, or because that statement was so…Isadora.

Was his passionate, funny girl still alive and kicking, deep inside this narrow, cool woman? "Whatever," he said, picking up the thread of the conversation. "I assume they still function the same."

"I was done nursing by the time I had that operation."

Another thing he missed—his son being nursed. Now that he would have liked to have seen. "I meant feelingwise. I remember that as a pretty erogenous zone for…" Isa. "For you."

He saw her swallow and shake her head.

"No feeling?" he asked. What the hell was left of her?

"I don't know. I mean, I can feel my own hand, but no one…I haven't…" She let her shoulders drop. "I have been alone, Gabe. For five years."

"Alone…like nothing? No one? Not even a quickie to relieve stress?"

"Never. It's not a life that invites…intimacy," she explained, studying him for a moment. "I'm guessing you haven't been celibate for five years?"

"Not celibate," he replied with a soft laugh, then grew serious. "Not exactly *intimate*, either. Just, you know, getting by."

Her whole body seemed to soften. Then she reached over and stroked his hand, which felt ridiculously natural. And intimate. "Yeah, by the way your housekeeper-turned-asset tried to matchmake us, I figured that there's no one in your life."

"No one special," he confirmed. "How did you figure out Poppy works for me?"

She rolled her eyes. "The general desire to walk through fire for you. You get that out of people."

"Yeah, I guess…" His voice trailed off as he looked at her. Really looked at this all-new model of his very favorite person. She was definitely wrong about not being pretty.

A man could get lost in those eyes, and even her strong nose had an exotic quality that reminded him of Cleopatra. Her body was thin but toned to perfection, and her mouth…man, that surgeon had done a helluva job there. A nice lower lip that begged to be bitten and—

She drew back. "Don't," she whispered.

"Don't what?" He released her hand and held his up. "I'm not doing anything."

"You are. I know that look."

"You know my looks? Well, I'd say that gives you an unfair advantage." He went for light, pushing away because, damn, this was way too complicated already to add sex into the mix.

"Anyway," he said quickly. "Pop Star definitely works for me and...what were we talking about?" Besides her mouth.

"Your love life."

He snorted. "Nil. And here in Bareass Bay, the best I can find is the occasional bridesmaid at a destination wedding."

"Ah, I see."

Actually, she didn't. She didn't see one single bit. He closed his eyes and made a quick decision that ran counter to the need-to-know philosophy that guided his life. But she'd shared a lot, and as much as he despised the thought, he believed her.

So he owed her a little honesty right back.

"The fact is," he said quietly, "I never got over Isa. Over...*you.*"

"You're the one who left without saying good-bye."

In the scheme of things, that sin didn't match up to hers, but who was tallying the score? It was all a mess. "I was pissed," he admitted. "Went to Miami needing to pulverize someone."

"I heard you did."

He laughed softly. "Okay, I may have blasted a few too many bullets into the bellies of some Cuban gang members who were stealing little girls and selling them to the highest bidder. I *mighta* gone a little crazy."

"Might have? I heard the price on your head in the Cuba Mafia could have fed a family of four for five years."

"You heard right. And I didn't care because it felt so fucking good to kill those dickbags, because I was so mad because…because…" He put his hands over his forehead, pressing on his eyes like he always did when he was trying to smash out a thought that wrecked him. "I never should have let her…you…*Isadora* go."

"You couldn't stop me," she said.

That didn't help. He kept his hands on his eyes. "I left CIA contract work completely, which wasn't hard, because they didn't love me much anymore for the crap that went down in Miami. I went up to Boston and started working for my cousins' security firm. Hung out with Nino and…tried to forget…Cuba."

"And me."

"But I couldn't." He finally met her gaze. "It just got worse. I dug around old contacts, and no one ever told me you'd died, just that you'd disappeared. A few people said you'd been seen in Cuba. When I decided to start this hide 'n' seek business, I happened to find this godforsaken island, and it fit every need—secluded, protected—and I had a friend in Luke McBain, a guy I'd met on an assignment when he was in the French Foreign Legion, and he offered me a cover. But mostly it was…"

"Close to Cuba."

He nodded. "And I started the search for you. Mal heard rumblings through his contacts about Radio and TV Martí in Miami, so I went there and stole some files that supposedly had your name in them."

"One of the things I did while I was pregnant was act as a distributor for Martí," she said. "Handing out flash drives of real news."

"That's where I found your name, listed as deceased." Damn it, his voice almost cracked. "And then my sister found out about...the baby." And everything changed. "She and Mal went to Cuba to find out what they could, and what they found was...a continuation of my personal shit show under a grave marker."

"I baptized him Gabriel Rafael Rossi Winter," she said. "And when we put that fake headstone in Alana's yard, we added her last name because she'd adopted him."

"It wrecked my sister when she found it." Not to mention him.

"I'm sorry," she whispered. "I made a lot of mistakes, but I made them for the right reasons."

They both made mistakes, even if hers were bigger and badder.

And right that minute, all he wanted to do was make another big bad mistake and kiss this woman. He wanted to kiss Isadora, and she was...sitting two inches from him, the scent of her perfume torturing him, the sight of that plump lower lip calling to him.

But she wasn't the same.

Still, he put his hand on her cheek and drew her closer, holding this stranger's gaze but somehow seeing, deep inside those bottomless eyes, the soul of the woman who mattered to him more than anyone.

"For the record, I would have waited for you," he said just before he put his mouth against hers.

He felt her suck in a breath and tense, but he angled his head and relaxed into a real kiss, opening his mouth enough to taste her, to feel her tongue and hear a sweet, soft whimper catch in her throat.

Her lips were soft and warm, pliable and delicious, and he slid his hand under her hair to grasp her head and tilt her to get closer and deeper into the kiss.

With his eyes closed and his heart open, he could taste

Isadora. Sweet and salty, a kiss that always made him hard and hungry and ready for more.

And this one was no different.

He pulled her closer and wrapped his other arm around her, tucking her into him as he finally ended the lip-to-lip but was already kissing his way along her jaw, headed for her sweetest of sweet spots. Under her ear, right beneath her lobe, where a kiss was guaranteed to make her—

"Stop."

He instantly drew back, more at the sharp note than the word itself.

She pushed him away and stood, holding her hands out with fire and agony in her eyes. Real agony, like *torture*. Anyone from any country could read that body language: Do not make another fucking move, or I'll kill you.

And the woman was armed, he remembered.

He reached to touch his lip, to dry it from the kiss and relive the touch of her mouth for one second. "Too soon?" he joked.

Her eyes grew darker, and threatening. Way more threatening than just a woman who wanted to slow down. She turned away, pressing her hands to her head. "It's…no, Gabe. We can't. I won't."

"Why not? If you're really Isadora, we have nothing to hide from each other."

"It hurts," she whispered.

"What hurts?"

She visibly dug for composure and turned back to him. "You need to leave." Her words were strangled, tight. "Just…leave."

But he didn't move, staring at her, trying like hell to figure out what was wrong. What hurt?

"Leave!" She pointed to the door, and he realized her

hand was actually trembling. Why? It was just a kiss, and she was totally—

"I mean it, Gabe, get out."

He stood slowly. "Cool your jets, blondie."

She shook her head, almost like she was trying to clear it. "Just don't...*don't*."

"Don't kiss you?"

She pressed her fingertips to her temples, squeezing hard enough to leave tiny little white spots under her blood-red nails. "Don't say you would have waited or that you loved me or anything like that, ever. I can't handle it."

He reached for her, but she backed away, skittish.

"All right, all right," he said. "I'm going to get my stuff. I'll send someone from the security team over here to watch the villa in the meantime and—"

"What are you talking about?"

"You're a *client* now," he informed her. "You're under my protection. Isn't that why you came here? I'm not leaving you for any length of time until we know you're safe, since you think you're not. And there is the matter of our son."

"You're going to take him."

Was that a question or a statement? He couldn't tell. But something was seriously up right now, that was for sure.

"I'll be back in a little bit," he said.

"Okay." The fight had gone out of her, along with the heat in her eyes. She turned and left him, and he heard the first sob escape right before she closed her bedroom door.

So she was still a crier, just in private.

Chapter Ten

Shame.

Pain and shame.

Lila's constant companions were out in full force today, strangling her, torturing her, and making her waking hours a living hell. Everything in her ached to tell Gabe about the headaches and what caused them. To share how utterly debilitating they were and how they'd made her certain she could never be the good, loving mother her son deserved.

How do you explain to someone that it hurt to feel love? That the only time she was pain-free was when she visualized herself trapped in ice, alone. Away from anyone who made her feel emotionally attached. Or when she was deep undercover taking on a new persona, again, but feeling nothing, only concentrating on work.

That's what changing her identity had done, and even if Gabe understood, he'd blame her. And she'd deserve that blame, and the shame that came with it. The godawful humiliation and disgrace of giving up her own child—because loving him made her head feel like it was going to explode—would never go away, even if the headaches did.

It was obvious he thought she was off her rocker. She

knew Gabe so well she could still read the subtext in his probing questions and decipher his expressions. She knew him, and she still loved every inch of the man.

And that feeling cracked her skull in two. In fact, it was so bad after that kiss that she figured why not steal another hour or two with Rafe? One Rossi man had wrecked her, so she might as well finish the job with the other one.

Slipping out of Casa Blanca Resort & Spa unnoticed wasn't difficult, at least not for a woman trained in the art of spycraft. Lila knew Gabe would be true to his word and would waste no time planting bodyguards around her villa, so she watched him disappear into the gardens, headed toward the bungalow where he lived.

Then she bolted.

The last time she'd been at this resort, her "assignment" had been to find Malcolm Harris, but he was already in Cuba by then, on his own mission for Gabe. That left Lila to spend her time at the resort exactly as she pleased, and she'd done plenty of homework that week.

She'd known the Lila Wickham undercover gig was coming to an end. So while she'd been here, she'd mapped out her short-term plan to come back and secure a safe house for Rafe and started moving toward…good-bye.

Her head throbbed at the thought, and her heart didn't feel much better.

She stopped at a four-way intersection in Mimosa Key's quaint town, using the car mirrors to do a three-sixty scan of anyone who could possibly be following her. The streets were relatively deserted, although the convenience store was open, she noticed, with an older woman with a bad blond dye job sweeping the entryway.

On Christmas Day.

Oh, Lila, that could be you in a few years. Alone, alone,

alone. Without a single attachment that would cause blinding pain. She'd live without love, but she'd live. If she had to continue this way, she could easily end up taking her own life.

Wasn't there any other way out of this mess? What if she just bit the bullet and followed Gabe's plan to live a normal life and raise their son?

She gave up normal the day she said yes to her last assignment.

The light changed, and she glanced around again, but this time, she didn't look for a tail, but at the little town itself. Cute, but not in a kitschy way. An authentic Florida beach town with sun-washed stucco low-rise buildings and sweet little stores like a florist called Bud's Buds and an ice cream parlor called Miss Icey's.

Could she live in a place like this? With Gabe and Rafe?

Right on cue, sunbursts of pain shot through her head, forcing her to stop thinking about the two people who made it the worst.

She drove south into the lush residential area that made up the lower half of Mimosa Key. Here, Florida ranch homes with emerald lawns and graceful palms sat side by side in warrens of quiet, peaceful streets. Finding a safe house to rent hadn't been difficult, and of course, Chris Sloane, her friend, nanny, and professional protection, had come along on this trip, thinking it was just another CIA assignment and Lila needed her most reliable employee on the road with her.

As she approached the beige stucco three-bedroom house where Rafe and Chris were staying, Lila's handbag hummed, which meant her secret phone that only Dexter Crain used was vibrating with a call.

She fished through her bag to unzip the virtually invisible

back pocket where she kept that phone, hoping it wasn't bad news.

"Merry Christmas," she said brightly.

"I wish it was."

Her heart dropped. "What is it?"

She listened to him relay information about a call he'd had with CIA Director Hollings, but the details were only partially processing. The only thing she heard was *credible threat.*

And that made her drive faster toward Rafe.

"Lila, they want you. I don't know why, I don't know who, and I don't know when they'll let up, but someone could know your role in the operation and make you pay for it. You need to get your plan to disappear underway, and fast."

She didn't know why or who, either, but she knew these people well enough to know when they'd quit: when they got the silence or vengeance or whatever whacked-out thing they wanted. Most likely they'd quit when she was dead, which was why her "suckfest of stupid" plan to fake yet another death wasn't exactly stupid.

She had to get Rafe settled and safe with Gabe and get moving.

"I've been released," she said, turning off the ignition and pressing the phone harder against her ear. "No one officially wants me. Anyone I worked for has made that clear. Who could it be, Dex?"

"I don't know. Someone rogue. Possibly someone associated with one of the cells. They know you, Lila. They know your face and name."

But did they know Rafe?

"No one knows where I am, Dex." She'd made sure of that. There was no trail. Cash for everything, even this house where her son and nanny were staying. She knew how to stay hidden, at least for a short while. "Not even you, and you wouldn't tell anyone if you did."

He was silent for a beat, then, "How are you feeling?"

Like I want to cut my head off. "I'm okay, really." The hallmark of a good spy was never to let anyone see you sweat. "Listen, can we possibly get some intelligence on an identity? I need to know who and what I'm dealing with." Not knowing the enemy was crippling; he could be anyone, anywhere.

"I'm trying," he said. "He's going to have to make a mistake and slip up somehow."

"The thing is, I'm safe. I'm surrounded by protection…" Or she would be when Gabe put a wall of bodyguards around her villa and planted himself next to her. "And Rafe is, of course, in a safe house with Chris."

"He's not with you?"

"Oh, no, I have him somewhere else." She dropped her head into her hands and rubbed, letting out a sigh.

"Are you okay, Lila? Healthwise, I mean?"

"Really good," she assured him, looking up at the house and aching to run in and hold her son, no matter the cost. "I have to go. Give Anne a kiss, just don't tell her it's from me."

"And give one to little Rafe. Tell him to make a good Christmas wish."

"I will." As she climbed out of the car and headed up a walkway tucked between six-foot hibiscus bushes, she made a wish herself. She wished her eyes weren't stinging and her heart wasn't so heavy. She wished her head didn't hurt and her—

A man's hand clamped over her mouth, yanking her backward into the bushes.

She instantly launched an elbow into his gut, which hit granite and got knocked away at the same second he managed to snag her weapon from the holster at her back.

Damn it!

She lifted her foot to find his toes but smashed on a boot, then jerked to the side only to get stilled completely by a powerful arm around her waist. She felt warm breath in her ear and the rock-hard chest of a strong man at her back.

"What the flippity fuck are you up to, Lila?"

Gabe whipped her around, easily balancing both of them against the bushes that had hidden him while she chatted on the phone. "You left without telling me."

That second, the front door popped open, and a bruiser of a man filled the space, aiming a pistol directly at Gabe, full attack stance, a grip that screamed experience and fearlessness. "Drop her and the weapon, or you're dead."

"Who's that?" Gabe asked into Lila's ear.

"The nanny. And he's not kidding."

He loosened his grip, and she squirmed away.

"The nanny…" Holy shit. That meant… "Rafe's here? In this house?"

Lila shot a glance toward the man in the doorway. "It's fine, Chris. He's…a friend."

The guy didn't budge. "I'll believe you when he hands you that weapon and gets five feet away from you with his hands in the air." He finished that with a blistering dark brown gaze as deadly as the Walther still directed at Gabe.

Lila managed to get her hand out. "Give me back my

weapon," she ordered Gabe. "You're done testing my vulnerabilities."

"And finding them." Gabe pointed her Glock to the ground and handed it back to her, ignoring the rest of the fathead's orders. "Finding…all kinds of things."

Like my son. He swallowed hard, not quite ready for this, but not willing to wait one more second. "Take me to him," he ordered her.

"No." She stepped out of the bushes away from him. "Close the door, Chris. I've got this."

The other man didn't immediately react but still scrutinized Gabe closely, as if memorizing every detail, a shift in his expression—if it could be seen under three days of scruff—showing that he did not like what he saw.

Normally, Gabe would slice and dice Hollywood Face with a few well-placed insults, but he had more important business than the nosy nanny. His son was in that house, and right now, that was all that mattered. After a moment, the man disappeared behind a solid wood door with at least three locks clicking in his wake.

Each dead bolt shot a new arrow of anger through Gabe. "You and your lug nut manny can't keep me from Rafe."

"Gabe, you can't march into the life of a four-year-old and announce you are his father." She spoke in a hushed whisper, glancing around as if a neighbor might be lurking.

A whole new wave of pissed-off splashed through him, white-hot and ready to fight for his rights. "You can't lock me out of the house where my own son is living."

"Shut up! This is a safe house, unless you scream it out to the world."

He leaned closer, right in her face. "Why did you come here alone, without telling me? Did you really think I wouldn't follow?"

"How did you?" she asked.

"I waited in the garden and saw you leave, which I fully expected you to do." He swiped a hand through his hair and glanced at the house, impatience rising. "Then I ran to Nino's car, took the back road out of Barefoot Bay that you probably don't even know exists, and I beat you to the four-way intersection. Watched you check out the old bag at the Super Min, then I tailed you here."

"Damn it."

"You can't out-spy a spy, sweetheart." He stepped around her, closer to the house. "I'm not leaving until I see him."

She huffed out a breath.

"And tell your boyfriend to put his biscuit back in the bag and out of my face."

"Christopher Sloane is not my boyfriend. He's a former Secret Service agent who happens to be great with kids and is willing to kill anyone who comes near Rafe."

For some reason that didn't take a shrink to understand, that just pissed him off ten times as much. "I'm his *father*, Lila. I'm the one who should kill for him." He eyed the house again. "And believe me, I will."

She let out a long exhale. "This isn't what I wanted."

"You think it's what I wanted?"

"This isn't about *you*." She poked him with a finger to the chest, a gesture that was so Isadora, it stole his breath and sanity for a minute. There she was, deep inside this blond cover, the woman he loved and missed and moved to this hellhole in hopes of finding. "This is about Rafe and how to manage this…situation."

"A situation we wouldn't be in if you hadn't—"

"Stop it!" She balled her fists, sparks shooting from her eyes. "I know that. I was going to introduce you to him, once I was certain…of you."

"Once *you* were certain of *me*?" he asked, dragging out the question so she understood just how inane it was. "I look the same. I *am* the same. There's nothing to doubt where I'm concerned."

"For one thing, I have to be sure you believe me and back my plan."

"I do." Tiny white lie, because while he believed she was telling the truth, he had zero intention of letting her dump and run. At least not until he knew why. But fighting her bad idea would just delay what he wanted most in the world…to see that kid.

"And I have to be sure you're going to be a good father."

He closed his eyes and let the need to howl pass.

"Seriously, Gabe. It's a huge commitment."

"Do you think I don't know that?" He leaned closer to her. "If you know anything about me like you claim you do, you know that family is the *only* thing that matters to me. And that boy in there…is family." The truth of that kicked him like a steel-toed boot in the gut. "And I'm not standing out here discussing your dumb-as-dirt plans or uncertainty for one more fucking minute." He turned from her and started to the door, but she grabbed his arm.

"Gabe!"

"I'm serious." He shook her off.

"Watch your mouth."

He choked a laugh. "*That's* what you're worried about?"

"No, I…I…" She put her hand back on his arm, her touch much gentler this time. "I had so many fantasies about this meeting. And it wasn't going to be like this, with you furious and me scared and him…"

Something cracked in his chest as he reached for her, pulling her closer. "It's okay. Really, it's going to be just fine."

She pressed her cheek against his shoulder—another full-on Isadora move. And he did what he'd always done. He kissed her hair, which felt different under his lips but smelled very much the same as he remembered. Old feelings stirred in him, making his arms ache and making him realize something.

"You know, I had a lot of fantasies about this meeting, too." At his admission, she stiffened in his arms, and he kissed her head again. "And it wasn't going to be anything like this, with"—a stranger in his arms—"you shacked up with some beefcake waving his stick around. Come on." He gave her a tug. "I'm anxious to meet this kid."

"Okay, but take it easy."

"I promise I won't pounce on him and claim him as a Rossi, and I won't pepper him with f-bombs, and I won't fall on my knees and tell him that his mother is horrible for keeping us apart for four and a half—"

"*Mummmmyyyyyy*!" The door launched open, and out came a bullet of a boy, vaulting his whole body right into Lila, leaping in the air to wrap skinny arms and bare legs around her. "You came back!"

"Rafe!" She seemed unaffected by the whirlwind, holding him easily and planting kisses on both cheeks.

"I saw you in the window!" he squealed, kicking his legs against her in a way that had to hurt. She didn't even flinch, but she did ease him down to the ground. "Mister Chris said I could..." He looked up at Gabe, suddenly aware of him.

And whoa. *Whoa*.

"Who are you?" he asked.

"I'm...your..."

And then words just evaporated, along with every promise he'd just made. He wanted to pounce. He wanted to claim. He wanted to scream his favorite word in pent-up fury. And he wanted to fall on his knees and thank whatever power had a hand in this miracle.

Instead, he crouched down slowly, staring, dumbstruck, completely unsteady as he looked into distrustful blue eyes, a chin jutted in a silent challenge, and a cunning smile that kicked up a little higher on one side than the other.

The picture hadn't told the whole story. This was…a replica. A carbon copy. A *son.*

Chapter Eleven

Lila's whole body vibrated, and not because a forty-five-pound Category 5 hurricane just hit her body and soul. But because the look on Gabe's face was truly stunning.

She'd wanted to plan and prepare for this moment, but, really? Had there been any way to do that? It had to happen and, she supposed, the sooner, the better.

"Rafe, I want you to say hi to Mr. Rossi. He's my friend."

Gabe flicked her a look, but he obviously couldn't spare a second of staring at anything but Rafe. His jaw loosened a little, and his eyes were wide as he drank in the sight of his son.

Chills rose on Lila's arms as she stepped into his shoes and tried to imagine what he was feeling. Amazed? Awestruck? Overwhelmed?

Very slowly, Rafe took a step closer to him. Rafe was never one to hide in Mum's skirt or shy away from a stranger, but he seemed uncharacteristically tentative in the face of this man.

"Hello, Rafe." Gabe's voice was thick with emotion, and the sound of it squeezed Lila's chest along with the vise at her temples.

"I got good Christmas presents," Rafe said simply.

"Yeah?" Gabe smiled, and his face lit up as he lifted one hand as if he was going to reach out, but then he changed his mind and lowered it. "I got a good one, too."

"Santa found us here in this house."

"He's a top-notch search-and-gift guy."

"I got Snap Circuits, a fire truck, a Zoomer dinosaur, and a Matchbox Adva…Ada…Ad…"

"Adventure set," Lila supplied.

"With twenty cars." He put his hands on his little hips, unfazed by the fact that he wore nothing but a rumpled Lightning McQueen pajama top and red-trimmed cotton underpants, his afternoon-nap attire of choice. "Did you get anything like that?"

"I got a…" Gabe looked up at Lila, and she saw the awe and amazement she expected, but there was something else, too. *Anguish.*

She'd done that, she thought with a stab of self-loathing. She'd put that look in his beautiful blue eyes.

"You got a what?" Rafe demanded.

"I got a…big surprise." Gabe sighed on the last word and lost that battle with his right hand, reaching out to put it on Rafe's shoulder.

"What *was* it?" Rafe's voice rose with innocence and curiosity. "A car or truck? Legos?"

"Something I didn't even know I wanted."

"Like the Zoomer Dino! I didn't put it on my list, but Santa knew, and I *loooove* it!" He jumped up and down on the last two words.

"Dude, I know exactly how you feel." Gabe shook his head as he straightened, like he couldn't even believe what he was looking at.

"You like Zoomer Dino?"

"I live for him. It. That."

"Come here!" Rafe snagged Gabe's hand and gave him a good yank.

"Rafe," Lila chided. "Mr. Rossi was just leaving."

Rafe's eyes popped. "No way. He's playing Zoomer Dino. C'mere!" He pulled on Gabe's hand, who, of course, put up no fight whatsoever.

"Rafe, you can play with him another time, but he has to get home." No way he was infiltrating that house and that room and that child's heart…yet. Lila wasn't ready for that, and her head was already searing with pain.

"No!" Rafe stomped his foot in a textbook temper tantrum that Lila had seen a million times. It escalated fast.

"Bro, you can't say no to your mother."

Rafe, openmouthed, ready to fight, blinked at Gabe, clearly surprised by the stranger's reprimand.

"Play with me," he insisted, his full weight clinging to Gabe's arm as he lifted his legs to swing.

Of course Gabe would fold and go tripping into that room for hours of dinosaur fun. This was it. Her time was over; it was his turn.

Gabe easily lifted his arm, bringing Rafe up to dangle a foot off the ground, making him squeal with pure delight and ecstasy. "Not today, little man."

"Yes, today, little man!" Rafe screamed, kicking his legs uselessly in the air.

"Tomorrow. I'll be back."

"*Todaaaaayyyyy*!" He was in high gear now, and Lila felt the heat rise, as it always did when her child had a meltdown.

"Rafe, this is going to get you in time out," Lila warned.

His voice shot up an octave. "*Noooooooo*!"

Gabe tossed him up, making him airborne for a split

second, then caught him by the waist, the move shocking Rafe so much, it silenced him.

"To. Morr. Ow," Gabe said. "Got it?"

Rafe blinked, stunned. "I got it."

"That's what I'm talking about." He stared at Rafe, nearly nose to nose, their profiles like mirror images of each other.

"Who are you again?" Rafe asked, no small amount of wonder in his voice.

"I'm…your…"

Lila bit her lip so hard, she tasted blood. *Don't say it, Gabe, please don't say it. He can't handle the truth yet.*

"What?" Rafe demanded.

"Behavior control specialist. Sent from the North Pole to monitor your every move and make sure you toe the line."

Rafe looked a little horrified, then lifted his foot in the air and practically stabbed his captor with his toe. "I have a toe. It's in a stupid line."

Gabe bit back a laugh.

"Rafe, don't say stupid," Lila said.

"Stupid!" He kicked harder. "Stupid, stupid, stu—"

Gabe flipped him sideways, twirling his body in a full circle, landing him right back in his hands upright, making Lila gasp and leaving Rafe open-jawed and speechless.

"Evidently, *stupid*"—Gabe got right into his face again—"is a bad word."

Rafe just stared and nodded.

"Then put a cork in it, little guy, or I gotta go all the way back to the North Pole and report to my boss that things did not go well down here."

Rafe's eyes grew wide, then instantly narrowed, peering through thick black lashes and looking exactly like the ones gazing back at him. "You don't really work for Santa," Rafe finally said.

"But you don't know for sure." Gabe slowly put him down. "So you're taking chances with your Zoomer T-Rex by saying things like stupid."

Rafe backed up. "Okay," he said, not sure what to make of this new arrival.

Oh, honey, it's only going to get worse.

"I'll take you inside, Rafe," Lila said quickly, needing to end the exchange and sensing, somehow, that Gabe and Rafe needed a chance to breathe and regroup, too. "I want to talk to you, and you"—she looked at Gabe—"wait here."

He put a hand on her shoulder as she walked by. "I will. But the game has changed. I'm calling *all* the shots from this minute on."

She swallowed her fight and fear, knowing there was no way to talk him out of that now.

The minute they disappeared inside, Dick on a Stick came back outside, his weapon gone but probably not far. No doubt he wanted to piss on the doorstep and mark his territory.

Gabe looked at the guy with what he imagined was the same version of the Who the Fuck Are You? look he'd just gotten from a four-year-old. Only Gabe would back it with an uppercut to the scruffy jaw if he had to.

"I don't know who you are or what your deal is," the man said, "but I do know my job, and that is to protect Rafe."

Was that an apology or a gauntlet? Gabe nodded slowly. "Good. Do it. I'm not going to hurt him."

"And Lila."

Irritation and protectiveness and something that felt like

an ugly bout of jealousy stomped all over his insides. "I got her covered, man."

"You got her covered?" He lifted a dark brow that matched his hair and eyes and bad beard. "You jumped out of the bushes and scared the shit out of her, then you manhandled her son and mocked her rules."

Son of a motherhumping donkey. Seriously? He had to have a pissing contest with this dickface two minutes after the most gut-wrenching moment of his life? The only thing that kept him from pummeling pretty boy was respect for the woman and the child in the house.

"I actually don't recall any rule-mocking," Gabe said through gritted teeth.

"Stupid."

"Yes, you are."

"I'm inside doing my job. You're skulking around the bushes. Which one of us is stupid?"

Gabe's fist itched. Bad. But just then, Lila breezed out and looked from one to the other, uncertain of what to make of the exchange.

"Everything okay?" she asked.

"I was just talking to your friend. Gabriel Rossi, did you say, Lila?"

Gabe seared him with a look, his dislike for the ballbuster so thick he could taste it. But right now, he had more important battles to fight than a turf war with Mrs. Doubtfire.

"Lila's coming with me," Gabe said, taking her hand. "She'll leave her car here, and we'll be in touch." He guided her away. "Let's go before a fight breaks out in the nursery."

She turned and said good-bye, but there was no second temper tantrum on the front porch today, thank God. As they walked toward the driveway, he nodded at a car on the street. "I'm parked right there."

"I didn't even see you." She sounded disgusted with herself.

"You're battling with the best, babe."

"I have to have a car, Gabe. I can't just leave my rental here."

"You can. You will." He steered her toward the street, to the nondescript compact car that Nino usually used to run his errands, knowing she'd have spotted a bright purple 1968 GTO with white leather interior. "Right here. Right now."

"And just like that, Gabriel Rossi has complete control."

"Just like every day on this planet."

She tried to stop, yanking backward. "He has two parents, and I am not giving up complete control."

"Really? A couple hours ago, you were ready to hand him over to me to love, feed, and send to college. What changed?"

"Nothing, but..." She exhaled but stayed with him. "I still have a say in what we do and how we do it."

She could say all she wanted, but any decisions that were made would be his. He crossed the street and opened the passenger door for her. "And that asshole better do a good job of protecting him, or he'll be eating my fist and his balls."

"I totally trust him."

Gabe looked skyward and held the door open for her. And she froze, getting right up in his face.

"Listen to me, smart mouth," she said, poking him with that Isadora finger again. "I've protected that kid from any kind of harm for almost five years. I carried him, birthed him, worried about him, and loved him, and that includes finding a nanny who happens to have been trained in the Secret Service. You may not blow in, flip my child around, make a few jokes, and go all Daddy on me. You have to give me some damn credit, Gabe."

He stared at her, a little overwhelmed by how much she turned into Isadora when she got passionate about something. Even with her fake English accent and fake hair and fake face and fake name. When something mattered, the real woman surfaced.

And, son of a bitch, he liked it.

"I give you plenty of credit for all that," he said.

"Then don't threaten me with calling the shots. There are two of us here."

"Actually, three. Four if you count Mary Poppins."

She threw herself into the car and instantly dropped her head into her hands. "Just stop it, okay? That wasn't easy. Nothing about that was easy." Her voice cracked, which had the intended effect of kicking him in the nuts.

He crouched down the same way he had with Rafe, instantly regretting his role in the misery that seized her. "Hey, I told you it's going to be okay. We'll figure this out. I already have a plan."

She turned to him, disbelief and doubt shadowing her eyes. "There's only one plan. I'm going to leave. How we figure that out is up for discussion, but I can't stay…with him. Or, God, with you." She dropped her face into her hands again and moaned. "Shit," she whispered. "This one's a brain-racker."

"You get really bad headaches, don't you?" He didn't remember Isadora suffering from anything worse than a hangnail.

She nodded, then lifted her head. "I'll be fine. They come and go."

He searched her face for a moment, not seeing a woman who looked like she'd be "fine" anytime soon. But he backed off and closed the door, rounding the car to get into the driver's seat.

By the time he sat down, her eyes looked a little clearer, which surprised him.

"Did Chris guess you're Rafe's father?" she asked.

"You didn't tell him?"

"I haven't told anyone, anywhere. But a blind man could see the resemblance."

"Not even your pal Dex?"

She shook her head. "I mean, Dex knows I have a child, of course. He was the first person I called when I found out I…" Her voice trailed off when Gabe clenched his jaw. "I'm sorry."

"Stop apologizing." He twisted the key in the ignition, hard, and whipped into the road. "Am I ticked off that I didn't get to see him pop out and scream, or piss in the bathtub for the first time, or shove his first Cheerio up his nose, or whatever other Daddy milestones I missed? Yeah, but it's done, and we have to move forward and do what has to be done for that kid."

She smiled. "He's never pissed in the bathtub."

Gabe snorted. "Oh yeah, Mom? Has a little wiener, doesn't he? He's pissed in the tub."

But she repositioned herself and put a hand on his arm. "He is awesome, isn't he?"

"Hell yeah. He's a pistol. I can't wait to…" *Raise him. Know him. Love the shit out of him.* "Figure things out."

She dropped her head back on the headrest with a noisy sigh. "I'm tired of that euphemism. Tell me your plan."

The adrenaline of his anger dissipated as he threaded through the streets and made his way back to Barefoot Bay. "Look, you don't need to make up for all that time I missed by leaving him completely. And you can't beat yourself up for your mothering, 'cause that kid would test Mother Teresa." He threw her a grin. "That's some robust DNA right there."

"It's not just guilt over you or him that's driving this decision," she said. "I am definitely in danger because of my role in that operation. I don't know who and I don't know why, but as long as someone wants me for whatever reason—vengeance or retribution or whatever—I am a liability to him."

"So let's find out who wants you."

"Easier said than done."

He shot her a look. "Not at all. If he knows where you are, he'll show up. I say let's draw the em-effer out and cut his heart into small pieces. Then you're not a liability, just a plain old mom with a handful of a kid who has a father willing to help. And I will not teach him my way with words."

She laughed softly. "That might be genetic, too. He just hasn't learned all the words yet."

He stopped at the light and put his hand on her leg. "I'm serious. It's a little risky since we're in the dark, but without knowing who or what you're up against, we don't have a choice."

"I have a choice," she said. "I can get a new name and new home and a new life."

He eyed her for a long time, then turned back to the road. "I thought this new model came with lady balls."

She shot him a look. "She does."

"Then use them. Let's bait and break."

"You make it sound easy."

"I make everything sound easy. That's one of my many gifts." He pulled into the convenience store parking lot to set his plan in motion, but she didn't notice because, once again, she had her eyes closed and her hands on her temples.

"It's not that easy," she admitted. "You can't imagine how I've changed. Inside and out, all the way through."

What the hell did that have to do with fishing for a freak who wanted to hurt her or the kid? "But you love our son, right?"

"Of course I do!" She pushed at her head like she could squeeze the pain out of it. "You don't understand…" She lost her voice, the words strangled in her throat.

"Then explain it to me."

She took a few slow breaths, and he could practically see the discomfort easing up. "It's too hard to explain, but…" She turned to him and reached a hand up to touch his face. "I'm really starting to remember why I loved the holy hell out of you."

"Then work with me. We're professional spies, baby. If we can't do this, who can?"

She looked at him for a long time, her dark eyes wide, that sweet lower lip trapped between perfect white teeth. Isa used to bite her lip, too, when she was uncertain about something. "Why are you doing this for me?" she asked on a whisper. "You have every reason to hate me, to want me gone, to keep Rafe for your very own."

"I'm doing it because it's the right thing to do and because he's our son."

"Gabriel, my angel." Those eyes filled, and when she closed them, a tear meandered down her cheek.

"Let me be that for once." Using his thumb, he wiped her cheek, lingering over the soft, creamy skin of a prominent cheekbone that she hadn't had before.

"I want to," she whispered. "I want to so much."

"Then let's start. Right now." He nodded toward the store where he'd parked. "First thing we want to do is let the world know where you are. And this is the best possible place to start."

"At the local convenience store?"

"Not your average 7-Eleven. This is the Super Min, and you're about to meet the equivalent of the town crier. If you want your name spread around, Charity Grambling is the old bag for the job. Let's go."

She gave a shuddering sigh, then pressed her fingers against her forehead.

"What?" he asked. "What's the matter?"

"I don't want to fall back in love with you, Gabe. I can't take the pain."

"That makes two of us." He lifted her chin and brought her face closer. "Are we doing this or what?"

"Doing what? Falling in love again?"

"Baiting the baddie."

But she just searched his face, her expression as ragged as if he'd answered the other way. Were they falling in love again? Not as long as she wasn't being straight with him about why she'd leave Rafe. He might believe her, but that didn't mean he trusted her. She still wasn't telling him everything.

"I'm not sure it will work," she finally said.

"If it does, and we get your guy, you can stay with Rafe. Isn't that what you want?"

She swallowed, silent. And all his red-hot alarm bells went screaming again. But he wasn't going to get it out of her here and now. It would take some finesse.

"I want him to be safe," she whispered.

"Then get out your real ID, Mama. We're going fishing."

Chapter Twelve

Lila stepped out of the spacious villa bathroom, wrapped in a towel, her wet hair sticking to her shoulders after a long, hot shower.

She stopped cold at the sight of Gabriel Rossi stretched on her bed, shirtless, dress pants on but not buttoned, bare feet crossed, an iPad on his lap and a Scotch on the rocks on the nightstand next to him.

Her breath trapped in her throat. "Oh, I didn't expect you here."

"What part of 'I'm staying in the villa' didn't you understand?" He looked up from the tablet, dropping his gaze up and down her bare-but-for-a-towel body. Heat rolled through her.

"The part about being on my bed, in my room, and not out there, waiting for me."

He looked back down at the tablet without lingering on her barely dressed body, and that heat cooled to something more like disappointment.

"This is more comfortable," he said. "And we can talk while you get ready."

Talk. Not that she wanted anything else—not that she wanted to admit, anyway—but it was a little tough to be reminded that she didn't look anything like the woman whose body and face he once adored to the point of distraction.

He, on the other hand, was in even better shape, with a six-, no *eight*-pack, ripped chest, and perfectly cut biceps that assured her he still started each and every day with a hundred one-armed push-ups.

Whatever he was reading on that tablet was more interesting than her nearly naked self. Okay, that was good, she rationalized.

She'd finally rid herself of the afternoon headache and wanted so much to keep the pain at bay. The solution was simple: feel nothing. And since he obviously felt nothing, she could do the same.

She walked to the closet, turning her back on him to study her meager wardrobe. "I wasn't planning on another holiday party," she said, pushing around hangers that mostly held beach cover-ups and sundresses.

"Gotta get you out there, blondie." He tapped the screen.

"I thought we did that pretty effectively with our twenty-minute Q&A session with the town busybody this afternoon." No surprise, Charity Grambling, owner of the Super Min, gushed over Gabe, and he'd had her lapping up everything he said.

And he'd said plenty.

"Oh yeah, Charity is probably over at the local newspaper filing a story as we speak. 'Former CIA operatives invade Mimosa Key.' Did you see her drool when I mentioned you'd done undercover work?"

She pushed another outfit aside. "But it was so weird. I'm so used to hiding, to staying low and deep and quiet."

"Not on this mission. You wave those CIA and MI6 colors like you're a freaking spook cheerleader. When they ask specifics, suggest they'd die a swift death if you told them anything. Then tell them some fake shit. People suck that crap up with a straw."

"So that's the plan for tonight at this Christmas party given by the resort owners?"

"Yep. Everybody who's anybody at this resort and the surrounding area will be at the Walkers' house tonight," he said. "Including my grandfather, sister, and…" He looked up. "Mal. You think you can handle that?"

She pulled a little black dress out and considered what jewelry might snazz it up. "I already ran into him last night, and it was fine. He'll never recognize me as Isadora. Trust me, I was in Roger Drummand's face for years, and he never once suspected I wasn't exactly who I said I was. Same will be true of Mal, and if he's inclined to check my story, Lila Wickham will show up in intelligence agency databases, saying exactly who I say I am—a former MI6 agent sent to the CIA to work on a task force who ultimately stayed in DC."

"You know he and my sister nearly died trying to find Rafe."

She felt the pain of that comment right down to her soul. "And you know that I can never apologize to them for that. Or thank them for ending my assignment by getting rid of Drummand. Or tell Mal how much I appreciate that he found my note to you. Gabe, they can never know the truth about me. No one can. Isadora is dead and will always stay dead, along with Gabriel Rafael, her son."

"Our son," Gabe corrected, glancing at the picture of Rafe he'd returned to her, propped on the nightstand again. "And be prepared: There will be questions and interest in us."

"Us?"

"Everyone will assume this is romantic," he said.

"Well, we better have our story straight, then."

"And as close to fact as possible."

That was the mantra of a good cover, she knew.

"So," Gabe continued. "We're ex-lovers from a former CIA gig, friends now. You have a son. When he shows up in the picture, they'll all know who fathered that child. Done, case closed."

But what about when she left?

She pushed the thought aside, not willing to feel anything that could possibly give her a headache. Any profoundly strong emotion would bring on the first thrum of pain at the base of her neck.

Still holding the black dress, she took a few steps closer to the bed, inching past the sheer netting tied to the four posts that gave the room a West Indies tropical feel. "What are you doing on the computer?"

"Research." He picked up his drink and raised the glass to her with his index finger extended. "I've been poking around a few classified sites that I can still sneak into. This operation you were part of was really deep. Not a word of anyone involved in anything like it."

"As it should be, and if you had asked me, I would have told you that."

"I was just checking." He held out his drink to her, a lock of his hair slipping over his forehead. "Want a sip?"

Heat shot up her spine as she fought the sudden urge to knock the Scotch to the floor. "Don't you believe me? Why are you checking up on me?"

He lifted a brow. "Careful, blondie. Your Isa is showing."

"You don't have to dig through files for information about me. Tell me what you want to know, and I will supply it."

"And the ice woman cometh back."

She narrowed her eyes at him. "Do you or do you not believe I am who I say I am?"

"I do."

"Then why?" She flicked a hand toward the tablet. "Why check my story?"

"Believing isn't the same as trusting."

She crossed her arms and lifted her brow this time. "Careful, your Gabe is showing."

"I'm not the one with a split personality."

"Neither am I."

He pushed the iPad to the side. "Really? Because, honestly, with a little light mining, I think I can find Isa in there."

Of course he could. He could find her and bring her out again. Because she was never so real or so happy as she had been with Gabe. Then she'd fall into his arms, his bed, and his heart.

"Please don't try."

"You can't stop me."

But she had to. The headaches…she had to tell him. She opened her mouth, the truth right there, ready to come out, but then she closed it again. Too much shame and pain for that conversation, at least now.

"There's nothing about me to distrust," she finally said, purposely changing the subject. She held up the dress and tried for casual. "This is the best I can do on short notice. I'll put it on, and we can get going soon."

She turned, but he grabbed her arm and held her there. "Hang on a sec."

"What is it?"

"Would it be so bad to bring her back?"

"She can't come back to life, Gabe. The agency would

never allow it, and that was part of the release I signed to get—"

"That's not what I mean." He drew her closer, strong enough to bring her to the bed and force her to sit next to him. "Her personality. Her passion. Her…heart. That's who you really are."

"Not anymore." That much passion would make Lila's head explode in pain. "Have you tried?" He sounded so hopeful, it broke her heart.

"No. I'm not Isadora Winter anymore." Not that green-eyed, freckle-skinned young spy with a little overbite that made Gabe crazy when she used it anywhere on his body. Now she was a skinny, brittle, self-protecting brown-eyed blonde who got raging headaches when she felt anything like she was feeling now.

He studied her for a long, long time, caressing her face with his haunting, hot gaze, his lips parted, his whole body…too close. She had no idea what he was thinking or feeling, but something had a hold on him as he stayed stone still and let electricity spark in the air between them.

She lifted her chin in defiance and, maybe, in hopes of a kiss.

He dashed that hope and drew back. "My friends and family are going to tell you about how miserable I've been lately."

The non sequitur threw her. "Okay."

"You should know it hasn't been easy for me. I came here with one goal, to be closer to the place where I thought my former lover might be. When I found out…" He looked away. "I swore to God I would never let myself fall like that again. Never."

"I understand."

"No, you don't. Because I intended to keep that vow, but

now Isa's not dead. But she's not really alive, either. So I can't be in mourning, but I can't exactly be happy. It's the worst of both worlds."

"In other words, it would have been easier for you if I had stayed away. Dead. Out of your life." She could barely utter the words, they hurt so much. But the truth did sometimes.

He leaned closer to her, taking her chin in his hand and lifting her face to him. "I want to find her in there," he whispered. "I want you back."

She slowly shook her head and stepped away from the bed before her head, and heart, betrayed her.

For someone who had mastered the art of lying low and staying out of the spotlight, Lila's shell cracked wide open as Gabe waltzed her through the crowded hacienda owned by Lacey and Clay Walker and introduced her to as many of the forty-some guests as he knew.

Was that because she was playing her part so brilliantly, like a trained spy, or because the real woman was starting to emerge? Still so many unanswered questions. But now, he had to play his role, too. Which wasn't tough.

As a "consultant" to McBain Security, Gabe knew most everyone there. The adults, anyway. The party was overrun with rug rats who all seemed to have similar names: Evan, Emma, Eddie, Elijah, and one little wild child named Maya.

The place was rocking by seven thirty, with the spicy aroma of Poppy's Jamaican cooking wafting from an oversized kitchen, Christmas carols playing through a whole-house sound system, and the echo of kids' laughter.

Lila hadn't had a sip of alcohol, but her dark eyes sparkled, as festive as the twelve-foot Christmas tree and as warm as the fire that added to the holiday atmosphere.

She chatted up strangers, answered questions about her reasons for taking a holiday in Barefoot Bay, and stayed close enough to him to set so many tongues wagging he felt like he'd gone to a party at a dog kennel.

"Well, well, well, we meet again." Chessie sidled up next to Lila, but her pointed look was aimed directly at Gabe. "And this time you're with my brother. You didn't mention that you knew him last night."

"I didn't catch your last name and missed making the connection," she said.

"Not the first time that's happened." Mal stepped closer. "Right, Francesca?"

Chessie gave him a secret smile and then waved Nino over from a few feet away. "Nino, come and meet Gabe's new *friend*."

The older man glowered at her, elbowing his way closer. "Don't embarrass him."

"Gabe is unembarrassable," Chessie said, holding her hand out to Lila. "Sorry you couldn't stay at the dinner last night."

"As am I." Even with her clipped British accent firmly in place, Lila's smile shone like sunshine on Nino. "I'm sorry I missed your feast. I've heard about it and really wanted to stay."

His weathered face creased up, his thick brows drawing together as he checked her out. "You've heard about it?"

"This is an old friend of mine, Lila Wickham," Gabe said, smoothing over the introduction. "My gramps, Nino Rossi."

Nino engulfed her much smaller hand in his gnarled one. "This is the blonde you were talking about?"

"I hope so," she said, a tease in her eyes that reminded him so much of Isa. "But with Gabe, you never know."

With *her* he never knew. Which woman was he getting? This was a cover, of course, and if she were to be noticed, as they wanted, then she couldn't freeze them out, but still. This unguarded, natural version of Lila was…attractive.

"How do you know each other?" Chessie asked, so curious Gabe thought she might crawl out of her skin trying to find a computer so she could run a complete background check of Lila Wickham. But he'd done that already, and even his superhacker sister wouldn't find anything that wasn't legit.

"I'm a former agent, like Gabe," Lila said. "I've met Gabe on various assignments over the years."

"Ohhhh." Chessie drew out the word.

"Could you be any more uncool or obvious?" Gabe asked her.

"Oh, I could," Chessie said brightly.

"Just give her a minute and a little more eggnog," Lila teased.

Smooth. Perfectly silky smooth. Gabe couldn't help shooting a glance of pure appreciation at Lila, impressed by how she'd jumped into this plan and worked like the pro she was.

In fact, he wasn't even sure Isadora could have pulled it off. She might have wanted to, but her style was to let him shine while she sat back and did the translating. This woman wasn't going to cede power or play to anyone.

A new trait that was incredibly hot.

"The truth is," Lila continued, "after Gabe and I talked, we agreed his family has no secrets, so you might as well know I was in British intelligence and worked on a task force with the CIA."

"Oh, you have to meet some of these other people." Chessie threaded her arm through Lila's. "They suck this stuff up with a straw."

Lila threw a look to Gabe and winked. "She even talks like you."

"I taught her everything I know," he said.

"Be right back. Nino," Lila said. "Don't go anywhere, I'm dying to talk to you about that cacciatore recipe of yours. Gabe made it for me once, years ago, and I never forgot it."

Nino's jaw dropped as Lila headed off with Chessie to continue to spread the love. And Gabe watched her go. Damn.

"I like her," Nino said, gazing after her.

So do I. "This from the man who started the day with 'don't get taken in by this woman,'" Gabe teased. "One mention of your cacciatore, and you're ready to marry her."

"You didn't tell me you knew her already. And I was so busy talking you out of her. Sorry."

"Don't be." Gabe brought his drink to his lips. "I had to make sure she wasn't here for my help going undercover. She's not. And we're old friends," he said, then washed the lie with a little booze.

Nino turned to him. "She looks good on you."

"She's not *on* me, Gramps." But he sure as hell wouldn't mind, especially if that spark he liked so much was lighting up the bedroom.

Could that ever happen again? Not while she was hiding something, he thought as he glanced after her again. What was it?

"I mean her…effect." Nino grinned. "Maybe you've moved past bargaining and into acceptance."

"Oh, stuff your stages of grief, Gramps."

"Careful, Mr. Gabriel." A large hand shot between them, palm up. "I'm listening to you."

"I didn't swear, Poppy."

"But you will." She added a smile. "And then you will pay me and pay me."

"And Merry Christmas to you, Poppy." Gabe gave her a kiss on her coffee-colored cheek. "How's the live goat cooking up?"

"It's curried goat," she shot back. "And stewed oxtail in spiced rum."

Nino rolled his eyes. "You know, a traditional Christmas dinner."

She elbowed the old man. Hard. "We had enough fish to fill an ocean last night, and tonight's my turn. Keep your pie hole closed, Nino Rossi, except to eat *my* traditional Jamaican food that *the owner of the resort* requested I cook for her party."

Nino flattened her with a vile look. "You aren't happy unless you're driving me over a wall."

She laughed. "Who taught this man English when he came to the United States?"

"Speaking of coming to the United States," Gabe said, sensing this conversation was headed downhill fast since these two could not get past their differences. "Surely I've cursed enough to get those nephews of yours here."

Her face fell, and she shook her head.

"You gotta have a grand saved up by now, Popcorn. You get five bucks every time I breathe."

Her sigh was heavy and far too sad for a woman who normally exuded joy. "Isaiah's in trouble, I'm afraid. And I can't bring Ezra or baby Samuel without their older brother."

"What kind of trouble?"

"The worst kind."

"He missed Sunday school?" Nino mused.

"He's in jail."

"Whoa," Gabe said. "What'd he do?"

Instead of delivering her usual slicing remark, she averted her eyes. "Nothing, but the law isn't always on the side of a boy like that. 'Scuze me, I have to check my goat curry."

Nino backed off, too, letting her leave without a snide remark. "Damn shame," he muttered. "She lives for those kids."

"Wonder what he did," Gabe said, only half thinking about it while he scanned the room for Lila.

"I can find out," Nino said. "Chessie's teaching me more computer stuff than you can hit with a stick."

"Or shake one at." Gabe put a hand on his grandfather's shoulder. "Let's go find Lila."

"You go." Nino stepped to the side. "Poppy probably needs a hand with that goat. If I know her, she wrecked it with too much spice."

"There's the Christmas spirit." Gabe gave him a toast and a smile, because he'd long suspected that they didn't hate each other as much as they pretended to with their kitchen competitions.

Gabe took off, wending his way through the rooms, narrowly missing a few running mini-humans.

"Elijah! Here we come!" Two little near-matching blonds came barreling through the room, a boy who might be five or six with his Christmas button-down out of his pants and shoes long gone, followed by a twin sister who moved more slowly, holding a red velvet skirt out wide, at least forty sparkly bangles on her wrists, a tiara on her head, and enough beads around her neck it was a wonder she could walk.

"I am the queen!" she called out as she passed. "Make way for Queen Emma!"

"Long live the Queen of Too Much Jewelry." Gabe let her by and added a slight bow. He watched her jingle-jangle away, a weird, unfamiliar, not totally unwelcome ping in his heart.

It was his day to be with kids, apparently. Kids he didn't know. Kids he should have known. Kids he wanted to know so bad. The sudden desire to have Rafe right here, running around with these kids, having a Christmas, being a family, hit so hard he nearly dropped his drink.

He wanted to get him right now. Spring him from his little prison and his douchebag babysitter and bring him right here where he belonged. He looked around for Lila, spotting her on the other side of the family room in the middle of at least five people, chatting and laughing. After a second, she looked over the shoulder of one of the women talking to her and locked on his gaze.

And took his fucking breath away.

What had made him think she wasn't beautiful? Maybe not conventionally, no. Not the way Isadora had been. But she simmered with something under the surface that attracted him every bit as much as the luscious, bodacious woman she used to be.

Shit. What was going on here?

Holding her gaze, he crossed the room and came right to her.

"Do you all know Gabe?" she said, taking his hand and bringing him to her side. Like she was the one who'd been in Barefoot Bay all along.

Introductions, or greetings with people he already knew, were made, and Gabe tried to remember to get Lila's name and background out there, but he kept stealing glances at the woman on his left, mesmerized.

"Oh, here's my husband." One of the women, the one

who owned the hot-air balloon business at the resort, reached her hand out in greeting to a man who'd just walked in, a six-foot-plus male-model type in doctor scrubs. "He had an emergency at his clinic."

In a moment, the man was next to her, introduced to Gabe and Lila as Dr. Oliver Bradbury.

"What kind of medicine do you practice?" Lila asked, her complete ease in a group of people yet another thing that reminded him of Isadora. But different, still.

"I have a clinic that specializes in advanced cancer treatment over in Naples," the doctor said. "I do research and surgery."

His wife, Zoe, beamed. "He's a brilliant physician," she said proudly. "And a wonderful father. Oliver, Lila is an ex-MI6 agent," she added.

The doctor was suitably interested, as anyone was when they heard someone was a spook, making Gabe certain his plan to get the word out that she was here would work.

The only question he had was what he'd do when the someone who was looking for her landed in his lap, besides break his face. Then what? Would she stay here? Would she go—

"Right, Gabe?"

He blinked, realizing he was staring right at Lila, and she was asking him a question.

"The life of a spy isn't always as sexy as in the movies," she said.

"It has its moments," he said, taking her hand. She closed her fingers around his, a natural move that felt as good as it did right, and kept the easy conversation going. All through cocktails, all through dinner, and even during the kids' painfully precious performance of *The Little Drummer Boy*.

As the last song ended, Lila put her head on his shoulder. Just like Isa.

"Ready to leave?" he whispered.

"If you think we've done our job here and every single person knows my name and story."

"Every one. And someone will tell a cousin who will tell a friend who will put a post on Facebook or tweet about meeting a real live female James Bond, and bam. We'll get some company."

She closed her eyes and sighed. "I hope this works."

She looked so pretty like that, so feminine and sexy. He tipped her chin up and gave her a light kiss on the lips.

"What was that for?" she asked.

"So people talk more," he lied.

She reached up and put her arms around his neck, pulling him close. "Then let's give them something to really talk about." She kissed him on the lips, long, slow, and sexy enough that everyone had to notice.

And he had to get her home. Now.

Chapter Thirteen

The walk back to the villa was short; Rockrose was less than a half mile down the beach from Lacey and Clay Walker's house at the curve of Barefoot Bay. But Lila wanted it to last forever, because right that minute, she didn't have a headache. Not even the shadow of pain at the base of her neck.

It was always like that when she was concentrating on a cover, and she longed for the pain-free moment to last.

But one look at the man walking next to her, his shoulders broad in a white shirt, his hair tussled from the breeze, shoes in hand, a half smile in place…and she knew this bliss wouldn't stick around for very long.

He'd hold her hand. He'd make her laugh. He'd pull her close and kiss her and then…it would start. Affection. Warmth. Love. It all *hurt* her.

"You know what's weird?" Gabe asked.

That love had to hurt her. "This whole situation?"

"Besides that." He slowed his step and turned from the water to study her. "We have a history, but it feels like I met you last night. I don't know where that leaves us."

She looked past him, not wanting to test the headache gods, pulling on her shield of ice. "It leaves us right where we are, on this beach, with this plan, and those memories."

He gave her a look, dubious and narrow-eyed.

"What?" she asked.

"You confused me tonight."

"Confused? I couldn't have been more clear. Hello, world, here I am, Lila Wickham. Please report my whereabouts."

"So you were acting?"

"I was…" She stopped walking to think about that. "Working, yes."

"But you were a lot like Isadora," he said softly. "Only a little different. Even though you were Lila. See? Confused."

So was she. "In what way was I Isadora?"

"Oh…" He thought for a moment, then stabbed her shoulder with his finger. "When you do this. You poked me in the chest today. Twice."

"Because you want to be in charge of everything, and you're stubborn, and I…" She laughed. "I don't really poke anybody but you. What else?"

He touched his left shoulder. "You put your head here like you used to."

"It's just…the right height." The need to put her head right there, right now, made her stomach clutch a little. Gabe's shoulder was the safest, sweetest, sexiest place she could rest her head…but if she did, that head would start to hurt.

"But then you say something like that, or 'it leaves us right where we are.' And, wham. The ice maiden is back."

"And you don't like the ice maiden?"

"I like her enough to…want to melt her."

She threaded her fingers through her hair and pulled it back as the tingling started in her scalp. Damn it. Damn it *all*. "Of course I changed, Gabe. I'm not that carefree CIA translator who jumped on every chance to be on an assignment with big, bad Gabe Rossi so I could fall into bed with him at every possible moment."

"Is that why you took all those assignments? I thought it was because my creative language was such a professional challenge to your translating skills."

"It's true." She tipped her head, remembering one particularly dicey meeting in China. "No other agent made me say, 'Shut up, you hopeless pile of wankstain' in Cantonese. It's every interpreter's dream."

He put his arm around her, squeezing. "Now there's my girl."

Her smile faded as her heart dropped down to her stomach. "I can never, ever be Isadora again, any more than our son can be Gabriel. The agency made me give up every piece of paperwork that would prove I'm Isadora Winter. Birth certificate, social security card, passport, driver's license. Plus there's a death certificate with Isadora Winter's name on it in their files." She turned to him again and took his face in her hands and forced him to look at her. "And, honestly, I'm sorry I'm not the pretty, voluptuous girl you loved."

As an answer, he wrapped his arms around her waist and pulled her closer to him. "I'm starting to like this new you. A lot."

The confession warmed her, almost as much as the pressure of his body, molding right to hers.

"I miss the memories," he added.

"We still have them."

"Do we?" he asked.

"They didn't surgically remove my memory banks, Gabe. I remember everything—every moment, every touch, every kiss."

"Me, too," he whispered, closing every bit of space between them. "And it makes me want more."

She tilted her head back, ignoring the pressure that started in her temples, and half closed her eyes. "I don't care," she whispered to that demon of pain. "I want this."

"I do care. And I want this, too." He dipped down and captured her mouth in a long, sensual kiss. She lifted her arms to circle around his neck while he eased her closer to let her feel how the kiss affected him.

"Ooh, I certainly remember"—she rocked into his erection and sighed at an avalanche of good memories—"that."

"Do you remember the time"—he trailed his lips over her jaw and throat and slid his hands over her backside—"in the bathhouse in Beijing?"

"Under the bamboo cabana?" She arched into him, the memory vivid.

"And how about that night you came to my apartment in DC in nothing but a raincoat on your birthday?"

"To show you my birthday suit." She inched back and gave a soft laugh. "Do you remember I got pulled over—"

"For having a headlight out," he finished.

"I was so scared the cop was going to make me get out of the car, and the coat."

He grinned at her. "I got you out of the coat."

"With lightning speed."

They smiled at each other, lost for a minute, in the past.

"See? It's still me," she whispered, laying her head against his chest because it felt so good.

"I knew I could find you in there."

She opened her eyes, and her gaze landed on the shimmer of silver moonlight spilling over the water, instantly calling to mind another precious memory.

"Varadero Beach on the outskirts of Havana," she whispered. "Oh, Gabe. That night."

"Best water sex in the history of water sex."

She drew back and looked up at him. "We went in completely dressed."

"And when we came out, you put on my shirt and tied it into a knot right here." He reached for the spot just under her breasts. "You know what you did in that moment?"

"Ran to the hotel room soaking wet?"

"You pretty much killed any chance of me falling for any other woman. Ever."

She let the words roll over her and then asked the obvious question. "Even this woman?"

"I guess…it depends on who you are."

Wordlessly, she lifted her finger and crooked it, refusing to lose this magic because the headache had slipped from a shadow to a five-point-five on the pain scale. Hell, she endured worse when Rafe climbed into her arms and said he loved her.

She could take this pain…because it also meant pleasure.

She started slowly toward the water and broke into a run, dropping the shoes she held on the way, tossing her bag next to them, aware that he was right behind her, all in.

Just the thrill of it eased the headache enough to forget anything but Gabe for a moment or two. She needed this. She so needed this.

The December-chilled water shocked at first, but adrenaline and the knowledge that he was right behind her warmed her up. She waded in, the sand soft, the water lapping around her ankles and calves.

He came up from behind, wrapping his arms around her, his mouth on her shoulder and neck.

This is perfection. As close to perfection as Lila could

know. The moon, the man, the madness of it all. She felt…unstoppable.

She kept going deeper, waist-high, then turned to find he'd ditched his shirt on the sand but still wore pants. Her dress grew heavy with water, the salty spray tickling her arms as she got deeper.

She flattened her hands on his bare chest, caressing like a blind woman who needed to feel everything, every angle and cut, his hard nipples and sweet pecs. She kissed his mouth and bowed her back to give him silent permission to touch everything, everywhere.

Finding his footing in the sand, he easily lifted her up, her body buoyed by the water. Each kiss grew hotter, crazier, and more desperate. He held her with two hands on her backside, her soaked clothes dragging around them as she rode a gentle wave and let his hard-on rub exactly where she wanted it.

She moaned in ecstasy and leaned all the way back, her headache forgotten and replaced by a different kind of ache much farther down, powerful and relentless and taut.

"Look at me," Gabe demanded, pulling her back up to him.

She opened her eyes and feasted on his wet chest glistening in the moonlight, his dark hair sticking to his forehead, his blue eyes piercing her with determination. Gorgeous Gabe. Sexy, bad, reckless Gabe.

"Isadora," he whispered.

A chill danced over her, leaving goose bumps on all her exposed skin. "Don't call me that."

"I'll call you whatever I want." He rocked so that he rubbed her again, right on the sweet spot, right where she couldn't stand it. "Isadora. It's you. Isn't it? *Isn't it?*" His voice grew gruff with the demand and dark with doubt.

"Yes…with you, always with you."

"You like this," he rasped in her ear, reaching under her to slip his fingers into her. "You like this."

"I love that." No ocean could drench the white-hot sparks that made her gasp with pleasure.

"Isadora." He ground out the name.

She wanted to fight him, wanted to say no, she couldn't be that woman anymore, but her voice was trapped in her throat. She couldn't think or talk or reason with a man who knew her every weakness. He spread her flesh, curled two fingers inside her and, all the while, kept her rubbing over his massive, granite-hard erection. And then he nestled under her jaw and sucked the tender skin below her earlobe.

And that took her over the edge. Torture and pleasure crashed through her, an old and familiar cocktail of sensations washing over her like the warm gulf waters. He wouldn't stop. Sucking. Touching. Finding her sweet spot.

She opened her mouth to say his name, but all she could manage was a low, long cry of delight as her body spiraled into a long, exquisite orgasm that rocked from her core to her fingertips. Shock waves of delight melted into rolling thunder of pleasure and finally quieted to a gasp of…pain.

A hatchet whacked through her brain, stealing every ounce of pleasure and the ability to think straight.

"I don't care what your name is," Gabe whispered, dragging his lips over her eyes and cheeks and, finally, her mouth. "We're perfect together."

The memory of the last time he'd said that to her punched its way through the agony in her head. It hadn't hurt to hear him say it then. Why, oh God, why did it torment her now?

Because now, she was inside a prison of pain that made love impossible. The only way to survive was to encase herself in ice or lose herself in work. There was no chance to be a normal, loving partner to this man or a normal, loving mother to his son.

"Let's go in," she said, finding her footing on the silty bottom of the gulf. "I…have a headache."

He inched back, searching her face, no doubt winding up for a snarky response about the cliché rejection for sex. But he didn't fire any sarcasm or humor, just took her hand and waded through the water with her.

She would always be a prisoner. Always. Even Gabe couldn't free her with his touch or kiss or love.

Chapter Fourteen

Early the next morning, Gabe slipped away to his office, confident the villa where he left Lila was secured by a couple of men on Luke McBain's security force. With a hot cup of coffee, he sat down at his desk to tap his way through some semiclassified shit that he could still access and face a simple and obvious fact: Lila Wickham was holding something back. Something big. Something important. Something he had to know before he let himself slip and fall in love again.

Because the more he discovered Isadora inside, the easier it was to slide right back to where he was five years earlier.

So what was it? What really made her carve up her face and body, fake her death, give up all ties to the past, and become a new person without telling him?

Because I have a chance to save someone from enduring the pain I did.

Her speech drifted back to his memory from that last morning. He could see the glint of determination in those green eyes and hear Isa's voice rise with passion for her cause. He knew what mattered to her…but he wanted to matter more.

If I can save one life, one single life, and prevent one

human being from going through that helpless, horrible feeling of being told some lunatic with a cause *killed your parents while they walked down a hallway, then I will. I* have *to. It's why I joined the CIA.*

Dexter Crain had dragged her into the CIA, as Gabe recalled. He'd planted the idea when he took the position as the chairman of the Senate Intelligence Committee, and he'd convinced her this was her way to use her language skills to take down the baddies.

I crossed that lobby and stood on that insignia so I could do that, not to meet a man who makes me feel weak.

There it was, the crux of what had broken them apart. She would always, always choose duty over love. For all he knew, that's why she wanted to give up her son—for a new assignment so dark and deep she couldn't tell him. Maybe he was a pawn in it.

Who knew? She knew.

And he just couldn't seem to get inside that head and really understand her. Whenever he got close, she backed off with a look of pain and the claim of a headache.

Something didn't fit.

He stabbed his fingers through his hair and pushed the laptop across his desk with a grunt, wishing like hell he hadn't felt the need to leave at dawn and figure out the woman who slept alone in the bed while he'd crashed on the sofa.

"Most people take this whole week off."

Gabe looked up to see Luke McBain standing in his office doorway. "When are you going to figure out that I am not most people, McBain?"

"Heard you never left Rockrose last night," Luke said.

"Crackerjack security is on point today," Gabe shot back.

Luke shrugged off the dig, long used to it since the two of

them met years ago on a mission in Somalia. "I have three men up there right now, per your request, and all of them reported you left at sunrise."

. "I only counted two lurking where they couldn't be seen, so one of those goons is really good."

"There are three," Luke assured him, taking the seat across from Gabe's desk. "And they are some of the best in the business. But, man, I need a woman."

Gabe lifted a brow. "Uh, dude. Your wife, Ari?"

"A woman on my security team," he corrected. "I hear that she's former MI6."

"Kinda makes your mouth water, doesn't it?"

"Makes my payroll water. Your mission, Rossi, is to make that badass blonde stay in Barefoot Bay and work for me."

Luke had no idea how much their "missions" aligned.

"Tell her to set up a meeting with me," Luke urged.

"Not yet." Because she sure as hell wasn't protecting someone else when her own life was in danger.

"She's not a client of yours, is she?" Luke asked.

"No, just…a friend." But he could tell Luke was fishing for more than that. "Why?"

"Well, I mean if she were a client, you'd keep her on the DL. When you have someone hiding out here, even my staff doesn't think it's anyone but a resort guest. You sure as hell don't drag them to a party and introduce them to everyone."

"She's not hiding," he replied.

"But you need a top-notch security team to watch her, and you're there all night long, even though you didn't get laid."

Gabe gave an indignant snort. "You got one hiding in the closet? Damn, you're good, McBain."

"Nope, this is pure brilliant deduction." Luke crossed his

arms, hazel eyes direct and clear. "You're in a shitty mood, and you're here and not in a nice warm bed playing spy games."

"You're not in your nice warm bed with Ari," he shot back.

"But I'm in a good mood." Luke propped his feet on Gabe's desk. "And this is my business, so showing up the day after Christmas is to be expected. Along with straight answers from you. We have a deal, Gabe. Honor it."

The deal was that Gabe would play "consultant" for Luke's security business, providing Gabe a great cover to do his wit-sec work. But, in return, Gabe had promised to always be straight with Luke about clients. The head of resort security had a right to know if there were any potential threats on this property.

But he couldn't be honest about this woman. Not completely. "You have enough answers, straight or otherwise."

Luke put his hand to his ear, pretending to listen. "What's that I hear? Oh, the howl of the lone wolf." He gave Gabe a hard look. "Sometimes the whole pack is more effective."

"I know that," Gabe said. "Look, she's not in hiding and isn't using my services, but she's got an asshole former boyfriend who might want to make her life hell."

"Who is he? Give me details, and we'll watch out for him."

Shit. Details he couldn't provide because there was no asshole ex. He angled his head and looked hard at his friend. "Luke. MI6. CIA. Shit gets…classified. *Capisce*?"

"So why are you telling every Tom, Dick, and Harry on the island what her name is and still insisting on protection?"

"Okay, look, it's not an ex. We don't know exactly who the threat is, or I"d go after him myself."

"You're baiting the guy," Luke said, no surprise in his voice. "So security can help."

He couldn't argue that. "Okay, watch every new face at the resort," Gabe said. "Run IDs on anyone who registers, secretly take copies of passports and licenses, and alert me if anyone shows up without a reservation."

"Done. Anything else?"

"No." Gabe stood and so did Luke. "And thanks, man. This one's complicated."

"They always are when you're in love."

Gabe groaned. "Is Oprah running your security detail now?"

"Joke all you want, Gabe. But I've been there, and I know when you're involved with someone you want to protect, you…" His voice faded as Gabe shook his head. "No? Then I sure misread you two last night."

So had he. "We were…" Gabe turned and busied himself with the open laptop. "We had a thing years ago."

"A thing?"

"That's what the kids call mind-blowing sex now. Haven't you heard?"

"But you're not having that thing now."

He made a point of typing and ignoring Luke. "How do you like it up there in my business, McBain?"

Luke chuckled, pulling a cell phone from his pocket and glancing at the screen. "Just so you know, she's on the move."

"She left the villa?"

Luke nodded. "Yup. Follow her or not?"

"She can't get far. Which direction is she going, toward the beach or the main building?"

"Toward the main building, currently on the path, passing Artemisia right now."

Gabe spun through the options, thinking about where that villa was located. He could get in his car and take the back road to the parking lot and beat her there or maybe get there at the same time.

"Tell them to keep a distance but watch. I'm driving over there." He didn't wait for an answer, but took off toward the front of the cul-de-sac, hustling to the classic GTO parked in his own driveway a few doors away.

He pulled out the keys, jumped in, and gunned it down the back road that led to the front of the resort. Just as he turned into the main entrance, he was cut off by a black SUV with shaded windows.

Was that just a prick in a big car…or someone driving a fairly classic government vehicle?

As he got farther into the lot, Gabe scanned the area, looking for a familiar blond head. He spotted her a long way off, still coming down the path, walking at a brisk pace with a handbag slung over her shoulder, loose light-colored pants and a thin top draped on her narrow frame like a runway model.

What was her deal, really? This woman who would give up everything when duty called.

The cold grip of mistrust, a familiar and never welcome old enemy, squeezed his chest just as the SUV blocked his view of her for a few seconds, then he saw her slowing down as she was in front of the first villa on the right. She paused for a moment and took out her phone, tapping the screen.

Gabe checked his, expecting a text that said, *I'm going to breakfast*, or *I have an appointment in the spa*, or…something.

None came.

As she waited, the SUV did the same, not moving so Gabe could get by, not taking a parking spot.

"Come on, you ball bag, get out of my way."

Then Lila started walking again, and the SUV started moving. At exactly the same time.

The hairs on the back of his neck woke up, and so did everything in him that had ever learned how to tail someone. She paused again, reading her phone and typing something, obviously texting with someone who wasn't him.

And the SUV slowed down.

What the hell? He studied the vehicle, a big-ass Tahoe with black-out windows and Florida tags, which he memorized out of habit.

She started walking toward the large overhang that shaded the entrance to the main building, a bit of a bounce in her step, like she was feeling great. Whoever she was texting put her in a damn fine mood.

Irritation danced on nerves already frayed from a shitty night with a relentless boner and even more relentless questions.

She slowed again, and the Tahoe in front of him almost came to a complete stop. From his place behind it, Gabe could see the passenger window slide down. Everything in Gabe went white-hot. Lila turned and looked right at the car, and Gabe's heart shot into his throat.

Without thinking, he threw his door open and dodged toward her, praying he'd take that bullet before she did, shoving her so hard they both went toppling toward the concrete.

She squawked. He covered her. And the SUV screamed out of the lot, threading other cars as it took off.

"Gabe!" She pushed at him, sitting up, a small crowd of valets and guests stopping and forming a circle. "Are you okay?" he asked, tearing his attention from the car to her. "Was he armed?"

“Are you okay, miss?” one of the valets asked.

“Do you need help?” someone else called.

Two of McBain’s goon squad came running from their distant protective positions.

A full-fledged gallery of looky-loos had surrounded them. Gabe got to his feet, bringing Lila with him, a protective arm around her. “We’re good,” he said, holding up a hand. “All good. I’ll just take her inside.”

She jerked out of his touch. “I’m fine.”

Gabe looked at her, stunned at her response, aware that a few of the onlookers got a little closer, like he was the perp here.

“That guy could have killed you, Lila,” he ground out, urging her inside to get away from the crowd. “Maybe you didn’t notice since you were texting, but he followed you around this parking lot and kept up with your every step.”

“I did notice, since I was texting the driver.”

He drew back. “Who was it?”

“That was Chris in a bulletproof high-security SUV with Rafe in the backseat. They were coming to pick me up for breakfast. So thanks for ruining my plans.”

Damn it. “You didn’t tell me you had plans.”

“You disappeared and left security professionals all over the place. I figured they told you.”

“You could have just called or texted me, and I would have known.”

“I was going to, but they were early, and I was anxious to see Rafe.” She looked past Gabe and sighed again. “He won’t take that well.”

Seeing his mom knocked on her ass would probably not sit well, no. Shit.

Gabe looked outside where his GTO was still running,

the door open. "Come on," he said. "Let's go get him and take him to breakfast."

"I'll go. Alone."

"Like hell you will." Gabe nudged her to the frosted-glass resort door.

She shook her head and stood stone still. "No, Gabe. You're not going." She pressed her hand to her forehead. "I can't take that."

Why couldn't he go? Was it really Chris and Rafe in that car?

Distrust prickled his skin.

"You just have to control everything and do it yourself." Shaking her head, she walked right past his car.

"No, I don't." He went for her arm, but it was as if she sensed his move before he made it, dodging to the side to avoid his touch.

"This was a bad idea," she muttered.

"This? What this?" He got very close to her face, speaking through clenched teeth. "Showing up claiming to be one woman but looking like another? Dangling my son in front of me and then denying me a chance to be with him? Or is it your whole story that's a bad idea, Lila?"

Her eyes flashed. "What the hell does that mean?"

"Excuse me, Mr. Rossi? We need you to move your car."

He turned to the valet, and almost instantly, Lila slipped away. This time he did grab her. "You're coming with me."

She relented, but her muscles were taut under his hand. "We are not going to see Rafe," she said through gritted teeth.

"No, we're not. Not now." He guided her to the passenger door and opened it.

"Where are we going?" she demanded.

"To meet..." He almost couldn't say the words, but he

knew he had to. Twice in one morning he'd been reminded he had to give up at least some measure of control in order for this to work. And to prove to her he could. "The team."

As he rounded the car to get to the driver's side, he took out his phone to do the one thing he hated most in the whole world. He called in backup.

Chapter Fifteen

Nino could hear Poppy fussing around cleaning the back bedrooms and bathroom that really didn't need to be cleaned. Any minute she'd start tsking and getting all judgmental and holy and better than everyone else, especially if she realized Gabe hadn't slept there last night.

Not that it was any of her business, but that never stopped Poppy Washington from having an opinion.

Nino wiped the kitchen counter with a loud exhale, counting the minutes until she finished chores they didn't need to do but she insisted on doing. Nino could clean his own toilet, thank you very much.

"I hear you puffin' out your noisy sighs, wishin' I'd be gone, Mr. Nino." Poppy's voice floated through the small bungalow, coming from Gabe's room now.

"I'm not sighing," he said. "I'm just letting out some wind."

A hearty chuckle came from the room, then Poppy appeared in the doorway to the hall. "You might be letting out some *air*, but wind is altogether different." She flashed a big strip of white teeth, a smile he wanted to ignore, but, damn it, he couldn't. It was just always there. Smiling. But today's wasn't quite as bright as usual.

"English isn't my first language." He casually flipped his mopina toward one of the stools at the counter. Not that he welcomed her and her know-it-all self in his kitchen, but…anybody at his counter was better than nobody at his counter.

Even her.

"It's not really yours, either," he reminded her.

"We speak English in Jamaica, *mon*," she said, layering her thick accent to make the point that it was a certain kind of English. "And *patois*. That's a little French, a little Creole." She came closer to the kitchen counter, a can of Lysol in one hand, a sponge in the other. "It's pretty in Jamaica, Nino. You should go sometime."

He snorted. "I got enough damn palm trees here in paradise."

She put the can down and held her hand out. "That's three dollars."

He plucked an olive from an open jar and dropped it in her palm. "This should cover me. Put *that* in your children's fund."

She popped it in her mouth, then made a face as she sat her wide load on the seat. "What did you put on this po' olive?" she asked, fighting with the pit.

"It's cured in oil and dressed with a little hot pepper. The way an olive should be."

She spit the pit in her hand and worked to swallow the rest. "That does not cover the money you owe to help me get my nephews to the United States."

He gave her an open hand to take her olive pit and throw it away. "You mentioned things weren't all peachy back at home."

It was her turn to sigh, settling in for a chat, which…he didn't mind. She was annoying, judgy, and knew the answer to everything and anything better than all other people, yes. But Poppy amused him, too. "My Isaiah has some problems, that's for sure."

He waited for her to say more, and when she didn't, he pointed to the coffee maker and lifted his brows.

"No, I…" She stopped herself. "Sure. I would love a cup. Strong, rich, and black, like a good man."

He smiled at that, turning to make her a cup. "You forgot Italian, who can cook."

She harrumphed and leaned over the counter, reaching for his bowl of dressed-up olives. "If you call this cooking."

"Can't be all bad if you're eating a second one."

She helped herself to two. "I need to figure out how you did this so I never make the mistake with my olives."

He couldn't help it—he smiled, placing a steaming cup in front of her. "You'll drown them in curry and nutmeg."

She spit out her pits and set them on the counter. "Did you fight with your wife about food, Nino?"

He drew back, surprised. He and Poppy bickered regularly, but rarely shared anything personal. "Not about food. Not about much of anything, truth be told. My Monica knew that I was always right."

"No wonder she's in the grave. Died of exasperation."

He ignored the dig. "And your husband? Died of goat poisoning?"

She rolled her big brown eyes. "I noticed you had two helpings of my goat."

"The curry was…interesting."

"And to answer your question, I never had a husband, Nino. No husband. No boyfriend. No lover."

Nino closed his eyes and held up two hands to stop her. "No more, please."

She just gave her hearty laugh. "I'm the bride of Jesus,

my friend. Problem is, He is just not listening to me these days. Doin' things His way, which isn't always mine."

Nino leaned on the counter and took a wild guess. "Is this about your nephew? The one in jail?"

She nodded and sipped her coffee, then inched over the counter to look longingly at the olives.

He picked up the whole bowl and put it in front of her. "They do cure what ills you."

"Ails you," she corrected, taking one. "I'm afraid Isaiah is guilty and will be staying in jail for a long time."

"What did he do?"

"Other than be forced to take care of little ones when his mama died and his no-good rum-swilling drug-dealing liar of a father took off with the entire savings that was supposed to keep them alive until I could bring them here with me?"

Nino took a breath for her.

"He robbed a convenience store outside of Kingston. Not armed, but he might have been high." Her voice cracked, and she closed her eyes. "Lord Jesus, save his soul."

Nino considered the charges and took an olive. "Does he have a lawyer?"

"Someone who doesn't care if he does five years or twenty-five."

"What about the kids, his brothers?"

She dropped her head into one hand and moaned. "Living with a neighbor. It's a mess, Nino, really." She shifted on the stool, uncomfortable.

"Maybe you should go visit them."

She didn't answer for a long time, then gave him a harsh look. "And who would do my job around here? And who would be Mister Gabriel's eyes and ears at the resort if I left?"

"If you *left*?" Gabe popped through the open back slider to answer the question. "You better not leave."

"Mr. Gabriel!" Poppy pushed off the chair and instantly picked up her Lysol can.

"Chill, Pop Off. You can take five and chat with Nino. Especially if you're not killing each other." He looked from one to the other. "*Why* aren't you killing each other?"

"Poppy was just telling me—"

"Holiday spirit, Mr. Gabriel!" She bounced off the chair—as much as a woman her size could bounce—and gave a look that Nino could read no matter what language was behind it. *Shut the hell up.*

"Chessie and Mal are on their way over, Gramps. Staff meeting. Poppy, put your Lysol away and help Nino make us all some food. I'm going to take a shower, and we'll start when they get here. We have a job to do."

When Gabe disappeared into the back, Poppy came around the kitchen counter and put her hand on Nino's shoulder, looking down at him since she had him by at least two inches. And fifty pounds. "Please don't tell him what I told you," she said.

"You already mentioned it to him last night," he said.

"He's got enough on his mind and can't worry about me, too."

Nino lifted his brows. "Don't underestimate my grandson."

She just shook her head. "And I shouldn't have gone unloading my troubles on you."

"It's fine, really." He almost admitted to her how much he liked it, how much he missed his family in Boston and their business and their problems, but then she'd go telling Gabe, and he'd send Nino home, and that boy would be here alone. "Set the table for five."

"Set the table? And let you ruin some omelet by putting ground-up basil in it? I'll cook."

He fried her with a look, and she stared right back at him. Then gave him a slow, genuine, bright Poppy smile. "Okay, you win. You cook. I'll"—she slid a look at the table—"set it for five."

She snagged a few olives and walked across the room to the table. "I have to say, these things are tasty."

Nino snorted, opening the refrigerator. "They're good for your soul."

"You know what's good for your soul, Nino?"

He inched out from behind the door to look at her. "Let me guess. Reading the Bible and saying your prayers?"

"That. But also friendship." She grinned at him, folding a napkin. "Friendship is good for your soul."

He wanted to argue, but couldn't.

Lila looked around the table at the crew that had assembled in Nino's kitchen. A wrinkled old man who called a certain social-media platform *Instantgram*, a foreign-born housekeeper whose entire experience with the CIA came from watching reruns of *Alias*, an ex-con who was on his way back to work for the CIA along with his girlfriend, Gabe's sister, a hacker whose résumé included exactly one assignment in the field.

And they all had one thing in common: a willingness to do anything Gabriel Rossi asked. For some reason, just the thought of that made the very first rumble of a headache begin at the base of Lila's neck.

But it was Gabe who pushed his hand through his hair and looked around the table again. "So let's wrap this. You all understand what we're doing here and why we're doing it?"

Nods, mostly. Except Nino, who was frowning. "Basically, it's the opposite of anything else we've done. Instead of hiding someone, making them a new identity, and slipping them out the back door, we're trying to shine a spotlight on her so that whoever is after her will show up in Barefoot Bay."

"Exactly," Gabe said. "Does everyone know their jobs? Everyone understands that they have an 'audience' to get this message out to. Poppy?"

"Yes, sir. I've got the current guests. I'm going to tell every single one I come in contact with that Miss Lila Wickham, a genuine female James Bond, is staying at the resort," Poppy said, folding her arms and looking smug. "I won't mention which villa, but I'll be sure to say her name and describe her in great detail. It's a sin to gossip, but in this case, I'm fine."

"Points in heaven," Gabe said, holding the woman's gaze with his charming smile. As if Poppy wouldn't go straight to hell for the man.

"And Nino?"

"I have the staff and will be talking to all of them, spreading the same information." He shot a look at Poppy. "Just talking about a person isn't actually gossip, you know."

Gabe held up his hand. "No discussions. Chess?"

"I'll cover social media," she said, pen in hand, checking her notes. "I can work with the new PR person at the resort and feed her some pictures and posts that get the word out that Lila is here. I'll hit Insta, Twitter, Facebook, even Yik Yak, in case he's within two miles. I tap friends to spread the posts, and I'll be sure they're not obvious. I got this."

Lila studied Gabe's sister, a longing to connect with her so strong it was physical. Gabe might be a loner in the outside world, but his family—and in this case, she included

Mal and Poppy—were never far. That's what mattered to him, as evidenced by the fact that he'd turned to them for this.

"And I've got the CIA and all my old contacts," Mal said, reading off a list of names she, of course, recognized. But what mattered most was that Mal didn't recognize her after all those months they'd worked together at Guantanamo, with Gabe flipping terrorists, Isa doing the translation and interpretation, and Mal undercover as a prison guard. He never even gave her a sideways glance as if she might not be who she sat there saying she was.

"This is a good plan, and it won't take long to get results," Gabe said, finally shifting his gaze across the table to Lila. "You and I will just be out and about and as visible as we can be. Your villa will have three extra men at a distance at all times. Luke McBain, as the head of security, will alert everyone in the front to be extra vigilant regarding strangers on the property, and he'll increase the level of identity and background checks for every new person who registers."

"Okay," she said, not actually trusting her own voice. Emotion, unexpected and powerful, sneaked up on her. "Thank you all, so much."

"Any friend of Gabriel's is a friend of ours," Nino assured her, putting an age-spotted and giant hand on hers.

"This is what we do." Chessie, sitting on the other side, made the same gesture, and Lila's temples tightened even more.

"Well, thank you," she said, her voice strained. "I'm so grateful for the help."

"Get to work, then." Gabe stood up, ending the meeting abruptly, sending them off on their assignments. She said good-bye to all, unsure if she should leave or stay.

Gabe walked outside with Nino, and they talked in the front for a few minutes while Lila stayed at the table and sipped her cold coffee, thinking about the plan…and the results.

"It sure would be nice if we knew who's after you."

She turned at the sound of Mal's voice, surprised he was still in the house. She'd thought he'd left with the others, but apparently he'd used the bathroom in the back.

She met his gaze with the confidence of having faced many people who knew Isadora Winter before they knew Lila Wickham. "That would make it easier," she agreed.

He came a little closer. "Mind if I ask you a question?"

"Not at all. I'm happy to go over that list of contacts at the agency again," she said. "I know most of them personally."

"Did you know Isadora Winter?"

The question froze her as effectively as if he'd dumped ice water on her, shocking her with how totally unexpected it was. "I've heard the name," she said vaguely. "Translator, right?"

"She's dead."

Not exactly. "Yes, I heard that, too. Why do you ask?"

He shrugged. "Just curious if your paths crossed when you were in the CIA."

"No, they never…crossed." *She died so I could be born.* "Should they have?"

"Well, you mentioned being in Beijing when Gabe was there. She was there, too."

Damn it. How could they have made that mistake? "We hardly talked to each other, at least not on a personal basis."

He glanced outside to where Gabe and Nino were talking. "They were pretty tight, Gabe and Isa."

Lila looked hard at him, wondering where the hell he was going with this.

"My guess is they would have gotten married eventually, but..."

She hoped he didn't see the chills that rose on her arms. "But what?"

He shrugged. "I don't know what happened, exactly. He went to Miami for an assignment, screwed up the job, and couldn't get back to Cuba. Before they ever saw each other again, she was killed in a car accident in Cuba. Had a kid, too, but he, well, he's passed as well." Mal closed his eyes as if even saying it hurt.

Oh God, she'd hurt so many people. She'd made decisions that she thought were right—and they *were* right because those decisions saved lives. But they'd cost people some happiness, too. And if these people ever found out who she really was, that she sat here at this table and lied to them...it would hurt them all over again.

Her head hammered, but she ignored it, staying in full Lila mode, not giving in to the emotional storm in her chest.

"Don't you agree?" he asked, making her realize she hadn't heard the question. She put her hands to her temples, desperate with the need to try to press her headache away.

"That it's sad?" she asked, taking a guess. "It's...unthinkable."

Mal leaned closer. "I mean, this has been good for him. To, you know, have someone new in his life."

Was it her imagination, or had he put an emphasis on *new*? "This isn't anything serious."

Mal lifted a dubious brow.

"It's just physical and meaningless. He's helping me out of a bind. Haven't you ever had a relationship like that?"

"Physical and meaningless?" A slow smile lifted the

corners of his lips, and his gaze shifted outside to where Gabe and Nino now flanked Chessie in conversation. "Yeah, once. Didn't last long, though."

"Exactly."

"Now she's my fiancée."

"Oh." She hadn't been expecting that. "And Gabe didn't kill you?"

He laughed and pointed at her. "You know Gabe pretty well. He got over it." Outside, the conversation was breaking up, and Mal stood. "And we all want him to get over the grief of losing Isadora and their son. So thanks for anything you do to help with that."

She searched his face and looked hard for a tell that he…knew. But Mal was too good a spy to give away a thing.

Still, they wouldn't be able to pull off this charade forever. The sooner this bait worked, the better.

Chapter Sixteen

"I'd suggest a nightcap, but somewhere between the tacos at the SOB and a scoop of rocky road at Miss Icey's, you started to go downhill fast." Gabe put the card key in the villa door and let her go inside, confident the little house had been secured and observed for the day and evening they'd been parading Lila around Mimosa Key.

Which had been a pretty damn good time until they sat down for ice cream, and that reminded him of a similar night in Cuba. When he started talking about it, she almost immediately began touching her temple and then the base of her neck.

He knew the headache tells by now.

She did it again as they walked into the villa, lingering on the temple a little longer than usual. "Yeah, this one's a bell ringer."

He slipped his hand under her hair, pressing the nape of her neck. "I can get rid of it."

She snorted softly. "On the contrary, you cause it."

"What?"

"Just a joke," she said quickly, stepping out of his touch. "And you can't fix and control everything, including my frequent headaches. Excuse me while I overdose on Advil, okay?"

Not okay. She walked toward the bedroom, and he waited a moment, replaying the conversation and feeling like something was *not okay*.

It wasn't really fair to move in when she was weakened by pain, but if he was going to get some answers, this was as good a time as any. Maybe better.

He followed her and walked in on her pouring some ibuprofen into her hand.

"Before you take it, let me try my personal magic." He angled his head toward the bed. "Lie down and let me fix and control things." He added a smile, but they both knew he wasn't really kidding.

She sighed and set the pills on the dresser, then climbed on the bed, facedown, arms out, fight finished. "At this point, I'll try anything."

"Anything?" he asked, playfully rolling up his sleeves and settling on the bed next to her.

She turned her head so she could see him, no smile. "*Anything*."

Promising. Still, she was in no shape to break the bed, so he started with a gentle rub on her neck and shoulders. "When did they start?" he asked. "I have no recollection of you having such frequent headaches."

"Don't talk," she commanded, closing her eyes. "This could work. But, please, don't make me talk."

"Okay, just relax." He situated himself next to her, getting a better angle to use both hands, controlling his touch carefully. Almost immediately, he could see the tension slip from her shoulders.

A soft moan confirmed that his hands were doing the trick.

He brushed her hair away and leaned a little closer, a whiff of Chanel No. 5 wending its way straight to whatever brain cells screamed for sex. He flattened his hands on her back, dragging them over her narrow frame and sliding them under her hair, making her sigh again.

"You like that?"

"Mmm." Her eyes fluttered with another sigh, and he studied her profile, barely seeing the tiny scars he now knew were there. Another, right under her earlobe where he used to flick his tongue to make her lose control.

He could almost see her former face at certain angles. All that did was make him want to dig more Isadora out of her.

He concentrated on the massage, pressing his fingers into the very top of her spine, eyeing the few freckles that somehow didn't get lasered off in some surgery center in Cuba.

Now *they* were familiar. Completely recognizable, he thought with a jolt. They dotted this skin around yet another scar, that one more obvious than others, like the surgeon got tired of all his artwork on the face and decided to stitch this last one in a hurry.

He rubbed the tiny raised flesh gently, one of her many hidden scars.

That's what she was. A woman of hidden scars.

"It's perfect, Gabe. Perfect." She whispered the last word, like she might have if he were on top of her, inside her, consuming her.

His body responded, of course, getting hot and hard and achy. He leaned over her and got his face a little closer to her ear. "Feel better?" he asked.

"A little, yeah. It's going away."

"You know what you need?"

She opened one eye and looked up at him. "I have a feeling I do."

"For the blood to flow in a different direction from your brain."

Very slowly, she smiled, then turned a little bit, some trepidation in her eyes. "I could try," she said softly, her words catching in her throat. "I want you so much, Gabe." Her fingers shook a little as she reached for him, pulling him down to her. "So much."

His blood hummed, definitely going in the right direction, filling him with need. He finished turning her all the way over so he could kiss her and slip his hand under her top.

"A bra tonight?" he asked, rubbing the lace trim. "What's the occasion?"

"It's a push-up. I thought you might like it."

The confession tweaked his heart and made him smile. "I like what you have, Lila. In and"—he unsnapped the front opening—"out of a bra." Pushing her top up, he kissed his way to her breasts, hungry to taste her and suckle her.

"Oh…" Her cry was sharp. Instantly, he lifted his head.

"Did I hurt you?"

She shook her head and bit her lip. "It's just…no. Don't stop." She pushed him back to her breast and arched her back, rocking her hips into him, a low grade of desperation in the move.

He liked desperation. But it wasn't…her. Not old her or new her.

He softened his kisses and trailed them down her stomach, adding little licks as she dug her fingers into his head. Hard.

Again, he lifted up. "You sure you're okay?" he asked.

She swallowed, a shadow of torment around her eyes. "I'm…okay."

"You're lying," he said, inching up.

She bit her lip. "I don't want you to stop," she said breathlessly. "I don't care if my head hurts, I want you." She reached down and closed her hand over his pants, squeezing his hard-on. "I want you and need you. Please."

Except there were tears in her eyes—tears of pain, not pleasure—which was a deal breaker for him, hard-on in hand or not.

Very slowly, he took her hand and removed it, forcing himself to sit up but never taking his gaze off of her. "Not like this," he said gruffly. "Not until you tell me what the hell is going on with you."

She took one long, ragged breath, shuddering the exhale and turning over on her stomach again, facing the other way.

"They started after Rafe was born," she finally said.

The headaches. "So it's hormonal? Can't they adjust that somehow?"

"Not so far, but they're easily triggered."

"Triggered by what?"

"Feelings." He barely heard the whisper.

"What kind of feelings?" he asked.

Slowly, she turned her face back toward him. "These kind," she whispered.

"Sexual feelings?" That didn't make sense. They were only talking about Cuba when he'd seen the headache start to really kill her that night. "Lila?"

Everything in the room grew silent and heavy.

Finally, she turned over to look up at him again. "Intense emotions like love. Any incredibly powerful emotional connection to another human being makes my head hurt in a way that I cannot begin to describe."

Her voice cracked and her eyes welled.

"Loving someone gives you a headache?"

"It's not quite that simple, but you're not far off."

He felt his jaw loosen in shock. "What a spectacularly crappy way to live."

She closed her eyes and nodded. "I guess I've developed some bizarre allergy to something like serotonin or another hormone associated with emotions. It happened during pregnancy, the doctors I've talked to assume. The headaches started when Rafe was really small but eased up when I was away from him. When I was deep into work and connected to no one at all, I lived pain-free. When I was undercover and pretending to be someone else, because by the very nature of that job you can't care about anyone, I lived just fine."

Holy, holy shit.

She put her hands on her cheeks, pressing into her temples, fighting the tears. "But the minute I was back with Rafe and my heart soared with love…" She closed her eyes and choked on the last word. "I just can't love him, Gabe. I can't love my own son. I can't love anyone." Tears rolled now, and his own throat thickened in sympathy. "That's why I want you to take Rafe. He deserves unlimited, intense, crazy love. I…" She shook her head from side to side. "I am not capable of it. It cripples me."

She wiped her eyes and tried to push up, but he eased her back. "We're going to fix this."

That turned her sob into a laugh. "You can't fix *everything*, Gabriel Rossi. You can't fix me."

"But you have seen a doctor?"

"More than one, certified and sanctioned by the CIA."

"Which doesn't make them the best in the business," he said dryly.

"They were excellent. They gave me MRI's and meds and therapy, and nothing helped. Finally, they sent me to a shrink who said it's another form of a migraine, just brought on by…what I've been through. The changes and stress. The surgeries and constant lies. Getting close to someone or feeling love is a trigger, like chocolate or coffee for other people."

Except you can live without chocolate or coffee. "Those bastards will wreck your life, send you undercover, and then wipe their hands of you." He stroked her cheek, pushing her hair back. "They should have told you this could screw up your whole life when you signed up for the job."

She snorted softly. "I didn't even know there was surgery involved."

"What? Dexter didn't tell you?"

"He seemed surprised when they wanted to go that deep and undercover, but he didn't tell me not to do it. I was all in at that point, Gabe. I thought I'd lost you and my parents and anyone else I'd ever love. What difference did it make what my name was or how my face and body looked? You know how much I wanted to make a difference in the world."

He lowered himself closer to her, desperate to comfort her, to change this horrible side effect unfairly thrown at her, ruining her life. "And you did," he assured her.

"Don't." She put her hand on him, frowning. "When you kiss me, when I start to feel…it hurts. I tried. I want to." She stroked his cheek with a soft groan. "There are no words for how much I want to, but I can't, Gabe."

He closed his eyes, sucker-punched. "I thought there was something you weren't telling me," he admitted. "I guess this is it."

"I hadn't told you because I'm ashamed."

He lifted his head up to look at her. "Ashamed of a bizarre side effect from something you did to save the world? Why the hell would you be ashamed of that?"

"Because I can't love my own son. Do you think I *want* to give him over to you and leave him forever?"

"Then don't."

She moaned in frustration. "It's not a normal headache, Gabe."

"I'm sorry," he said quickly. "I'm sorry."

"Don't be nice," she said, the slightest tease in her voice. "It only makes it worse when I like you. When I…feel. When I remember how much I loved you." The tears started again. "How much I loved sex with you."

"I loved sex with you, too," he said, wrapping his arm around her because he couldn't help but want her closer. "How's that for the master of understatement?"

She smiled and sighed. "I thought the same thing about my blood. That maybe sex would get all the blood out of my brain, and it wouldn't hurt just long enough to actually make love to you. Just once. But I can't make love to you without feeling things so intense and powerful and real that I want to die from the pounding that feels like it could crack my skull."

She couldn't live this way. "There has to be a doctor who can help you."

"No, not any doctor. They'll take a million MRI's and see all the work that's been done surgically and I risk drawing attention if I see a doctor who doesn't know what I've done and why. I can't tell that to just any doctor who could put it in some medical journal. I can't trust anyone to be discreet about this."

A shot of anger pushed him up. "So what if people find out you used to be Isadora Winter? Who are you protecting?"

"Everyone in the operation. The CIA. And, yes, Dexter Crain. If that operation became public, the fallout would be incredible. People would lose jobs, and attention or press coverage could potentially include Rafe or endanger him. No, I won't take that chance." She eyed him. "You need to know this, Gabe. You can never make another decision autonomously once you have a child. The possibility that it will affect him impacts everything you do."

"We gotta fix you," he said, too focused on that goal to even hear everything she was saying. "We have got to fix you."

She closed her eyes and reached for him, wrapping her arms around his neck and shoulders and pulling him into her. "I love that you want to, but it isn't going to happen."

"Don't love anything," he warned. "Yet. Until I solve this problem."

She relaxed a little, setting her head on its home base on his shoulder. He didn't know if that made her head hurt, but it sure did things to his chest. *This is what heartache is. This.*

Wanting. Needing. Loving. But not having…because *having* meant feeling, and feeling meant hurting yourself or the person you loved. What a spectacular shitshow.

"You want to know the worst part?" she asked.

"It gets worse?"

"This is why I'm so cold. This is why my whole personality is frigid. When I quite literally imagine ice around my heart, I get relief. It's the only technique that has ever worked. I learned years ago that if I don't let myself feel anything intense, whether it's happiness or misery, love or hate, I can ward off a headache. So I've developed the ability to control that. Mostly." She sighed, as if the loss of something so natural pained her as much as the headaches.

He stroked her hair, wondering if even that touch hurt her. Damn it. This was paralyzing. "What does it feel like?"

he asked, wondering if there was a way to pinpoint where they started.

She took his hand and pressed it right behind her ear. "It's like a knife slicing into my head, both sides, then up here." She guided his hand to her temple. "It's a blinding, agonizing, breath-stealing pain that honestly makes it impossible to function normally. I can even get confused or feel like I might black out." She bit her lip. "So the threat to Rafe isn't just some nameless guy hunting me down. It could be…me. The headaches make me an unfit mother." Her voice grew thick again.

"Shhh." He caressed her hair again. "Don't. Don't go there. You're not unfit. You're more than fit. And the kid has two parents now."

She curled deeper into him, pressing her body against him. "That's what I want for him. Your love. You and your wonderful family. Nino and Chessie."

He laughed. "There are so many more."

"Yes. Your brothers and cousins. Give him that love, Gabe. Give him that for me."

He lifted up his head to look down at her. "He needs all that *and* you."

"Oh." The word came out as a whimper, soft and helpless, as she reached up and clasped her hand over his neck. "I…Gabe…I…"

Despite her different eyes and different face, he knew what was coming. The declaration. The three words. The bond they'd had before. Love. It was starting again, as if the emotion had a mind and power of its own and neither one of them could stop it.

Isa and Gabe. One thing. One…one.

"Please kiss me," she whispered. "Please. I want to feel it."

He kissed her lightly, holding back, certain that anything he did would only make her feel the way he did—attached and connected and hungry to get inside. And that would hurt her head.

One kiss was all he took. One long, sweet, perfect kiss, and while he tasted her, he swore to God he would fix this woman. He just didn't know how yet.

Chapter Seventeen

"Someone's having a meltdown."

Lila pulled herself from sleep and squinted into the morning light, seeing Gabe's silhouette in front of the partially closed plantation shutters.

"What?" She pushed up, remembering how she'd finally fallen asleep next to him and that…he'd stayed there. And it had been warm and heavenly, but then the headache got bad enough that he'd just left.

And that broke her heart. He held out her cell phone. "Your pal Chris keeps texting one word. Meltdown. That can't be good."

"Oh shit." She pushed herself off the bed and shook off sleep. "It's not good."

"What is that? A code?"

"Hell yes, it's a code. Code red. Rafe's having a meltdown. I have to go."

"We'll go. I can handle a meltdown."

"Defcon 1 from a four-year-old?" She headed into the bathroom, glancing down to see she'd slept in her clothes. Next to Gabe, a normal woman ought to sleep naked.

Well, she wasn't normal, and he knew that now.

"My four-year-old." He came to the door and handed her

the Casa Blanca bathrobe that had been tossed over the chair. "I know these meltdowns."

She took the robe, but he didn't let go, using it like a tug-of-war rope to pull her closer. "You okay?"

"At the moment. It usually takes an hour or so after I wake up for a headache to start. Don't push it, though. Please don't be nice to me." She shut the door in his face.

"I'll be a bastard," he promised through the wood. "A stone-cold bastard."

Unlikely, but to his credit, Gabe was quiet as they drove south on Mimosa Key.

She used the quiet to stare at the road straight ahead. Despite the graceful palm trees against a clear blue sky, she took her usual trip to the Arctic and visualized a sheet of ice, cold, thick, and impenetrable, closing around her chest. The technique, taught to her by a hypnotist—one of a several CIA-sanctioned "expert" doctors she'd seen over the past few years—sometimes protected her when feelings got too intense.

After the ice formed, she started a mental chant to remind herself that nothing mattered. Whatever it was that caused the sensations of love, whether it was worry for her son or an incredible longing to kiss the man who insisted on coming with her today, those feelings didn't matter. Nothing mattered.

Gabe put his hand over hers and gave a squeeze. "Kid's a pisser, isn't he?"

He thought she was clammed up thinking about Rafe's meltdown. Better to let him think that than know she was mentally icing down.

"Watch your language," she warned. "That pisser is going to be within earshot in a few minutes."

"Oh hell. Heck. I can do it. Poppy has me almost cured with her Jamaican orphan fund."

"Almost cured?"

"Yeah. Three months ago I would have said almost fucking cured." He gave her a heartbeaker of a Gabe Rossi smile and threaded his fingers through hers. She glanced down at their joined hands.

It doesn't matter. Ice over the heart. It doesn't—

"What happens during a meltdown?" Gabe asked.

"Temper tantrum times ten. He cries to the point of giving himself a broken blood vessel in one of his eyes. Makes life hell for Chris or me. Gets his way eventually." She held her hand up to stop the inevitable. "Believe me, I've tried discipline. He hates that."

Gabe laughed as he turned onto the residential street where Rafe was staying. "Who doesn't?"

"Well, nothing works."

"Something must work," he said.

"I'll call your mother and ask what worked on you."

"My mom prayed a lot. My dad yelled a lot. JP beat the shit out of me, and Zach just freaking scared me. Marc was the only nice guy in the whole family."

"Your grandfather was the magic elixir, if I recall what you told me." That made Gabe smile. "Nino could usually settle my ass down with a big glass of milk, assuming I didn't drink straight from the bottle, and some scraps from his stovetop, yeah."

She thought about all the stories of life in the big Rossi family that Gabe had shared with her, in the dark in bed, after making love. "That house sounded like a pretty fun place to grow up."

"Never a dull moment." He looked at her. "Maybe that's the problem. Kid's bored out of his gourd, locked in that box with the Pacifier."

"Don't knock Chris. He's been a godsend."

"What god sent him? The god of dickheads?"

"The one who took great pity on me when I was having a breakdown in an elevator one day and Chris walked in."

"The white horse and all that knight armor fit in an elevator?"

She squeezed his hand, alternately touched that he still harbored jealousy over other men and infuriated that he didn't realize Chris's true value. "He'd just quit the Secret Service a week or two earlier."

"Convenient." He made no effort to hide his skepticism.

"Trust me, he was thoroughly vetted by the agency before I hired him. He quit over a dispute with his boss after he was passed over for a White House assignment."

"So not good enough for the president, but good enough for my kid."

"Gabe." No small amount of irritation slipped up and down her spine. "He was burned out and sick of the job, anyway, and he's a natural protector. I was trying so damn hard to hold an undercover assignment and be a single mom." She blew out a sigh, remembering the difficult days. Painful, headachy days where she fell asleep drowning in doubt over her ability to do either job very well.

"And in walks tall, dark, and good with kids."

She elbowed him. "Stop it. He's great with Rafe and would die before he let anything happen to him. You should be thrilled I have someone so competent on the job."

"So, does he do anything to cause…headaches?"

"Oooh, I'm having a hard time seeing around all this not so thinly veiled jealousy. He's a great nanny and a terrific friend. I trust him with Rafe and with…"

"With what?"

"Secrets. He knows I've been deep undercover, so I suspect he knows I haven't always looked like this. It's kind of hard to spend as much time in my house as he does and not know."

Gabe hit the brakes a little too hard when they reached the house. "But he wants to sleep with you."

"And you know this, how?"

"Well, look at you. You're fucking gorgeous."

Did he really believe that, or was he suffering from a crippling case of blue balls? "Drop one f-bomb in front of my kid—"

"*Our* kid."

"And Rafe doesn't know that yet," she reminded him. "And you're not going to tell him until I say so, is that clear?"

He turned the car off and nodded.

"And as far as Chris, you're dead wrong."

"Lila, I saw the look in his eyes when he damn near killed me. That was a man protecting his turf."

"Exactly," she said. "His *turf* happens to be our son. And if he laid a hand on me, I think his partner, Daniel, would be devastated."

"Oh." He tipped his head and frowned. "Didn't pick that up."

"So you don't know everything. Now let's go and I'll show you what a world-class meltdown looks like." She reached for the door handle, but as she did, Chris stepped out of the front door, scowling a little at them.

"Oh, that's not a happy face," Lila muttered.

She climbed out and looked over the roof of the car. "Code red?" she joked, using their name for the worst of the worst.

Chris scowled. "He's still asleep, and I'd like to keep it that way. What are you doing here?"

"I got your text that he was having a meltdown."

As Gabe got out of the car, Chris took a few steps closer, and, yes, Lila had to admit, there was a defensive look in his eyes. But they were just two alpha dogs protecting the same kid.

"I never texted you," Chris said.

Lila's heart dropped, and she instantly looked at her phone. "Meltdown? About half an hour ago?"

Chris slowly shook his head.

Immediately, Gabe was around the car, a hand on Lila. "Get inside. Is Rafe secure?"

Chris gave him a withering look. "As of one minute ago when I checked him before coming out here, yeah."

But Lila's throat went dry as she tapped the phone to call back the number that had texted her. Even as she put the device to her ear, she knew she wouldn't get a person or even voice mail.

"Burner?" Gabe asked, ushering her into the house.

Nothing but dead air in her ear. She nodded. "I need to see Rafe."

"And we need to get him to another safe house," Gabe said, eyeing Chris like he was the person who'd used an untraceable phone to lure her here. "With a backup security detail."

"Gabe," she chided, hustling forward, more because she was anxious to see Rafe than to get out of broad daylight. "We wanted him to find me, remember? I just didn't know it would happen so fast."

Or that she would lead him right to her son. The thought made her damn near run inside.

"Who are you talking about?" Chris asked, blocking Gabe's way but stepping aside to let Lila past.

"None of your business, bro," Gabe said, muscling closer. "Let me by."

Lila threw a look over her shoulder as she rushed into the house. "You're both on the same team, gentlemen. Get in here."

She didn't stop to watch them face each other down, but only because she needed to see Rafe. She darted down the hall to the last door on the left. The room was dark, and he was curled on his bed with his thumb half hanging from his mouth, lightly snoring.

Wordlessly, she dropped to her knees next to him, whispering a prayer of gratitude.

If someone knew how to reach her with the one word that would get her out of the resort, then that meant…

"He found you," Gabe said softly as he walked into the room. He closed the door without making a sound, darkening the room even more. "And Rafe. And your cell phone number that only two people in the world have."

Yes and yes. She let the horror of that hit her.

But Gabe knelt down next to her, a strong hand on her back as he looked at their sleeping child. "He has to be safe, Lila."

"I know." She wanted to touch Rafe's back with the same protective touch as Gabe used on her. Wanted the three of them to be connected. She didn't just want it, she needed it in a primal, basic way.

And that one little move would probably bring on the mother of all headaches.

She didn't care. She lifted her hand and laid it on her son's tiny back, and then Gabe put his hand over hers. She turned to him, the world swimming as she looked through teary eyes.

"I love him already," Gabe whispered.

"Amazing how that happens." She closed her eyes and put her head on his shoulder, just like she used to when they were a couple. And they sat like that for a long, long time, silent.

This was what she wanted, all she wanted, ever. This moment. This man. This family.

And then the slow, brutal, relentless thrum of pain started in her head. All she wanted, but she couldn't stand the pain.

"Hey. *Heeeeey*! Play with me, man!" Weight dragged on Gabe's back pockets, pulling his jeans halfway down his ass. *Shit.*

Gabe pressed one hand to his ear, trying to hear what Michael Brady, his friend at the NSA, was telling him as a four-year-old monkey decided it would be fun to hang on Gabe's jeans and play "heavy pockets."

"Dude, chill out, okay?" he whispered to the boy. "What was that again, Mike?"

"*Heavvvvvvy* pockets!" He hung again, and Gabe tried to walk down the hall, away from the human pendulum swinging off his rear end and the bodyguards talking to Lila and her nanny. Anywhere to hear what the security analyst was sharing with him.

"I said we can get a fingerprint of when a phone went online and the total number of calls," Mike said. "With burners, we look for a pattern, but if it's been used and tossed, then—"

"Hey. Hey! *Man*!" His jeans damn near came right down his ass.

"Rafe!" Lila called out.

"I want to talk to the man!" Rafe hollered.

"Leave him alone." Lila came closer, apologizing as

Gabe hitched up and rolled his eyes, walking farther down the hall, listening to Mike.

"Now, if you have the number in the database—"

"Hey, *maaaaaan*!" The howl could peel the motherhumping paint off the walls.

Gabe whipped around and swooped the howling kid up in one arm, keeping the phone pressed to his ear.

"—then we can run a search to see if those patterns are there. This week's tough, Gabe, but I might be able to try to steal some computer time."

Little legs and arms kicked like Rafe was swimming through air, while Gabe held him tightly around the waist, pressed up to his side.

Gabe tossed the little bag of bones lightly on a Star Wars bedspread. "That's good, Mike. I'll text you the number and anything you can run would be great. I owe you, pal."

"Pick me up again, man!"

Even with the scream, Gabe could hear Mike's low chuckle on the phone. "Didn't know you had kids, Gabe."

"I—"

Rafe launched off the bed and into Gabe's arms, wrapping his legs around him like a spider monkey. "I am Magnet Man! I stick to you!"

"I gotta go, Mike."

The other man laughed. "Hey, enjoy them while they're young. My daughter just went to college, and it freaking killed me."

"Will do." College? He wasn't going to survive preschool. He popped the phone into his pocket and tried to back away from the force that was Rafe. Wasn't happening. "What is your deal, little dude?"

"You're my friend." He slapped two hands on Gabe's face and gave a baby-toothed grin. "'Kay?"

Gabe laughed. "Okay. But your friend has some really important sh…stuff to take care of right now."

"Lego Star Wars on the Wiiiiiiii!" He patted Gabe's face about a hundred times with sticky little candy fingers that carried a decent wallop.

"Not today."

"Yes, today today today today *todaaay*!"

Gabe grabbed his narrow waist and lifted him a little. "Holy…cr…crud, kid. If you just chill for one minute, one f…fine minute, I will—"

"Play air soft guns with me."

"Guns?" What moron let him play with guns, even the air soft kind? Fucking manny. "You're not allowed to play with guns."

"But you have one."

He shot back. "How do you know I have a gun?"

"Mister Chris told me."

Of course the prick was already trying to sell him down the river. "Don't believe everything you hear, bro."

"I'm not your bro." He twisted Gabe's ears.

"But you are an asspain, you know that?"

His jaw dropped and he gasped.

"I know, I know. I said a bad word. Don't tell your mom."

"Aaaaaasssss!" He squirmed out of Gabe's arms and went flying down the hall. "That man said *aaaassssss*!"

Son of a *bitch*. Gabe stuck his hand in his hair and huffed out a breath and swallowed another curse.

"He can be a handful."

He turned at the sound of a man's voice, coming face-to-face with Chris. Swallowing all his pent-up frustration and dislike for the guy, Gabe nodded. "I don't have your daycare expertise, that's for sure," Gabe started to walk out, having no desire to chat like a couple of moms on the playground. But Chris blocked him again, a sizable guy but no match for Gabe, especially when he was this pissed off.

"'Scuze me," Gabe said under his breath.

"We need to talk."

Gabe exhaled noisily. "I have stuff to deal with."

"I have stuff to deal with, too, and his name is Rafael Winter."

Actually, his name was Gabriel Rafael Rossi. Or should be. Gabe just stared at the other man, waiting for him to say his piece.

"I know that you're trying to draw someone out using Lila as bait, and I honestly don't want to get involved in that. Her business has always been something I don't ask about."

"Great. Then stay out of it."

The other man shook his head. "Rafe's going to a different safe house, and I don't want Lila to know where he is."

"*You* don't? You're the babysitter, pal, not the shot-caller."

He got right into Gabe's face, dark eyes narrowed. "And you're the absentee father who suddenly wants to play Daddy."

The feeling of his fist cracking this guy's teeth would be so *sweet*. So tempting. The only reason Gabe didn't was Rafe. And Lila. "I hate to break the news to you, dickbag, but you actually do not know what the ever-loving fuck you're talking about. Now, move away and let me handle this situation."

Fucker didn't budge. If anything, he got closer. "Nothing will endanger that child."

"Damn straight."

"Nothing," Chris repeated. "And if she knows where

Rafe is, I guarantee you she'll convince you to take her to him, even if it's for five minutes so she can put her hand on his back and know that he's safe."

Gabe didn't know what pissed him off more. That this asswipe knew so much about what made Lila tick, or the fact that he was dead right. "Then let's make sure she knows where he is and can put her hand on his back when she needs to. I'm taking that child"—he leaned right into his face—"*my* child to where I want to take him and you—"

"Will go with him."

They stared at each other, both of them doing their level best not to snarl.

Behind Chris, in the hall, he saw something move and knew damn well Rafe was positioned just close enough to listen. He knew, because it's exactly what he would have done as a kid.

"Chris, you're doing an awesome job in your role here." Gabe slammed a friendly hand on the man's shoulder. "A role model for Rafe and really in control of your feelings. I'm certain my...that boy is learning only good things from you."

Chris looked confused as hell.

"Rafe!" Gabe jerked to the side and called out their eavesdropper. "I know you're out there, dude." He threw a warning look at Chris. "If you really care about that kid, you will not go filling his head with anything that's only going to mess him up now."

Chris opened his mouth to argue, but Rafe came plowing into the room and launched himself toward Gabe again, but he stopped when he saw Chris, looking from one to the other, torn over who should be the recipient of Magnet Man's attachment.

As much as Gabe wanted to scoop him up and tell him

what's what and who's who, he couldn't. Shit. The kid didn't need to be any more confused.

Gabe stepped forward. "Hey, bro." He ruffled his hair, flashing back to his own childhood and his own baby-fine black curls. "Wanna meet your new best friend?"

He frowned. "Okay. Where is he?"

"I'm going to take you there."

He frowned and looked past Gabe. "Are you going, Mister Chris?"

Chris just waited, wise enough to know who would call the shots. And Gabe was wise enough to call the right shot, even if it pained him.

"Yeah, of course he's going with you," Gabe said, shooting a look at the other man. "You can both learn to make gravy." At Chris's look, he added, "It's an excellent domestic skill to add to your résumé."

Which he'd be needing soon.

Chris didn't even smile. "Why the change of heart?" he asked.

"My heart didn't change," Gabe shot back. "Lila trusts you. That's good enough for me."

Except, as soon as he said it, he knew that it was proof positive that something had most definitely changed. Was it his heart?

Chapter Eighteen

"I found her! Dexter, I found her."

Dex looked up from his desk, frowning as his wife bounded into his home office waving her cell phone.

"Who?" But he knew. Deep in his heart, he knew.

Anne shoved the cell phone up to his face. "Lila Wickham. That's what you said her name is, right? Though this woman looks nothing like Isadora."

He tried to focus on the phone.

"Well, here she is at a resort in Florida. I Googled her name, and got a thousand hits, but this one was near the top and it says she has a job like James Bond. She looks like the right age, too. Is that her?"

Dex took the phone and frowned at it. "Casa Blanca Resort & Spa in Barefoot Bay?" Not possible. Lila would never reveal herself openly like that.

"Look!" She tapped the screen again, and there was a second picture of Lila. In this one, she was walking hand in hand with a dark-haired man who looked vaguely familiar. "There's her name on one of those celebrity gossip sites. Plenty of rich and famous there, too. Some billionaire who owns a baseball team, and that woman who's on that new

TV show *Nocturne Falls*. They're all guests at this resort on an island."

Dexter peered at the phone, shaking his head. "Something isn't right."

She put the phone down. "You can say that again. Dexter, I want to talk to her, and now I know where she is. I'm going there."

"No, you're not." Anger and frustration propelled him out of his chair. "This is a breach of security even a rookie wouldn't make. She's way too smart for this."

He folded his arms, trying to decide if he should call Lila, text, or go straight to the director and have her pulled back in.

Or if he should—

"Dex, listen to me." Anne grabbed his shoulder and forced him to look at her. "Maybe she's not thinking straight. Maybe she has a tumor and it's growing. She has to be made aware of this."

"I'll get the information to her. Trust me."

She leaned back, agony in her eyes. "You really won't allow me to go to her? Even if you came with me?"

"You don't even know what you're talking about."

"Then call her. With me here. I want to hear her voice. I want to talk to her." She grabbed his cell phone from the top of the desk. "At least put it on speaker so I can hear her voice."

"Okay. I'll call her. But not…with that." He opened his drawer and pulled out the phone used exclusively to communicate with Lila. Anne leaned against the desk, waiting, skimming her own phone, sighing heavily.

"I miss Isadora so much," she said. "And I can't believe this is her. How did they do it?"

"Surgery, mostly. And she's a pro." The call went to

voice mail, and Lila's clipped British accent invited Dex to leave a message.

"Only you?" Anne asked. "You're the only person who calls her on that phone?"

"As a precaution for her safety."

She put her own phone against her chest. "I'm worried about her."

"I am, too," he admitted. "But let me get some work done, Anne."

On a sigh, she shook her head. "It's like mourning her all over again."

"I'm sorry," he said. "I'll let you know what she says when I talk to her."

She left, and Dex sat down again, picking up his regular phone and dialing the director. He had to let the CIA know where she was.

It took a few seconds as the call was forwarded and clicked through to the familiar voice of Jeffrey Hollings.

"I know where Lila Wickham is," Dexter said.

"So does the free world," Hollings replied. "We'll be paying her a visit, believe me."

"To do what?"

"Senator Crain, this isn't your problem anymore."

"It's my problem if she loses her mind, for whatever reason, and starts talking about an operation that was supposed to die and be buried."

"We'll handle her."

What the hell did that mean? "I have an excellent relationship with her, and I can—"

"Senator, we'll handle her. We're already on it. We appreciate your concern, but you have nothing to do with her anymore."

"I have plenty to do with her. She's like a daughter to me."

The director laughed softly. "I'm sorry. I have another call."

He disconnected the phone, and Dex picked up the other device, already planning his text.

But then he knew, the phone wasn't *that* secure. Not when the CIA was involved.

There are spies among us.

Maybe Anne was right. Maybe he needed to get down there and make sure Lila remained silent about this operation.

Holding Rafe's hand and walking up the sidewalk to the bungalow where Nino and Gabe lived seemed like the most natural thing in the world. Bringing him "home" was the easy, smart thing to do.

Especially since "home" was next door to the resort's security headquarters, and Gabe had already instructed Luke to put a hedge of protection around this bungalow that a bulldozer couldn't get through. Chris was part of that crew and was, in fact, talking to Luke about heading it up.

It made sense. Having a face Rafe recognized in this sea of change would be good for the kid, Gabe grudgingly admitted. But Rafe would stay safely ensconced in the bungalow with Nino.

Gabe was sure whoever was after Lila had sent the text and watched to see which villa they'd left from, pinpointing her location. But they would be in another villa, and all eyes would be on Rockrose to wait for their catch to take the bait, which could take hours or days.

The plan was in place, and it was smart.

But when Nino opened the front door and wiped his hands on a mopina, frowning at the child, Gabe realized that nothing about this handoff would be natural, normal, easy, or smart.

He should have warned Nino, but how could he? Better to let him be surprised.

"Well, what do we have here?" Nino said, opening the door.

"This is—"

"Your new best friend!" Rafe broke free and ran to Nino. Gotta give the kid mad props for no fear of strangers. Obviously, he didn't have Gabe's trust issues…yet.

If there was one thing he'd like his son to avoid, it would be that.

"Who are you?" Rafe demanded.

"I guess I'm your new best friend." Nino's voice was just a little shaky as he looked from boy to man and…saw the obvious. "Gabe…"

"This is Rafe," Gabe said quickly. "Lila's son."

"But he's—"

Gabe shut him up with a look. "Very young and very uninformed about"—he narrowed his eyes in a silent plea—"cooking. He needs to learn."

Nino backed up, his creases deepening with a mix of a frown and a smile.

"Rafe," Gabe continued. "This is Nino, your great…" Great-grandfather. "Great new friend."

"Yay!" Rafe plowed into the house like it held his next big adventure. And it kind of did.

"Be cool, old man," Gabe whispered as he brushed by Nino. "Where are Chessie and Mal?"

"They went to the mainland for the day. I don't know—"

"Get them back here to stay with you."

Rafe ran through the house like an F3 tornado. "This place is coooooool!" He jumped onto the sofa, then to the floor, then—

"Whoa!" Nino snagged his little body with a giant dinner-plate-sized hand. "There will be none of that."

Rafe stopped for a second, sized him up, and tried to start running, but Nino lifted him up by the shirt and his little legs spun in the air.

"Look at that," he said, scowling at the child. "You got egg beaters for legs. Let's put them to good use."

"Egg *beaterrrrrrrrrs*!" He flailed, but even in his eighties, Nino was still an ox and didn't give an inch.

Gabe couldn't help smiling. "I guess you can handle this," he said.

"Ya think?" Nino shot back, lowering Rafe to the nearest stool. "Oh, and I may be old, but I'm not dumb, Gabriel."

Gabe just looked at his wise and all-knowing grandfather. Hiding this was impossible, but who cared?

"I got eyes, son," the old man said. "And a memory."

Rafe started to spin on the stool, but Nino grabbed him. "Hey."

For a long minute, those two just stared at each other. Gabe braced for Rafe's reaction—running around, screaming, demanding something—but he just stayed pinned by the power of Nino's glare.

"I have to leave him here with you," Gabe said.

Nino finally looked up, and all threat was gone from his old brown eyes. Replaced, in fact, by an unmistakable dampness that he'd probably blame on the nearest onion. "Go do whatever you need to do, Gabriel. Me and young Rafe will be just fine." Nino leaned in closer to the child. "Bad boys don't scare me. You know why?"

Rafe shook his head.

"They make the best cooks. Can you cook?"

Another shake of the head, his eyes wide. "But I can eat."

"That's a start." He nudged him off the chair. "Come on, short thing. We'll start with something simple. You like eggs?"

"Yeah."

"We put peppers in ours."

"*Ewww.*"

"Can it, kid. You'll cook 'em, you'll eat 'em, and you'll like 'em. Right, Gabriel?"

Gabe just nodded, backing toward the door, almost unable to take the punch of emotion. He snapped a mental picture of the two of them and vowed to move heaven, earth, and hell to keep these two Rossi men together.

Chapter Nineteen

Lila smelled garlic. Onions. Tomatoes. *Heaven.*

She opened her eyes and realized she'd fallen asleep, tucked into an oversize bed in a resort villa that bore the name Saffron.

Maybe she smelled a little of that spice, too. She blinked into the darkness, judged the time to be…dinnertime.

Well past.

And no one had shown up yet to kill her. Unless Gabe was doing it with marinara sauce.

After a moment, she sat up on her elbows and did what she always did when she woke: stayed very still and waited for the pain.

Nothing.

That was too good to last long. But since a deep sleep left her headache-free for an hour or more, this could last at least that long. Those hours had always been her best times with Rafe, waking and knowing she had a little slice of time to love him with all she had before the pain started.

She sniffed again, picturing Gabe at the stove. A glass of wine in one hand, a wooden spoon in the other. Teasing, cooking, tempting. All the things Gabe did so well.

Might be time to love him with all she had, too.

She pushed off the bed, stopped in the en suite bathroom, and took a minute to brush her teeth and wipe away the smudges of makeup under her eyes. She wore the same simple cotton dress she'd had on all day.

She should shower and fix her makeup, maybe put on something pretty since Gabe was out there cooking for her, but she didn't have time for that. She had to beat this headache and get what she needed and wanted most in the whole world.

Him.

Opening the door, she was assaulted by the scents. And the memories. One whiff and she was transported to a "kitchen" that consisted of a hot plate, sink, and fridge in the corner of a studio apartment outside of Guantanamo Bay. There, they languished in lazy Sunday afternoons of nonstop lovemaking that ended with red sauce and pasta consumed while sitting on the floor and eating off the coffee table.

Gabe had navigated that pathetic kitchenette with the same ease and mastery he used in bed, using his skilled hands, clever imagination, and expert mouth to taste, test, and, ultimately, delight Isadora Winter.

She hesitated in the hall, lolling about in the memory. It wasn't that she wanted to go back in time and be that woman Gabe loved so much. No, that feeling slipped away each minute that they were together. She wanted him to love Lila, to want her with the same ferocity, to start something new, not just relive those halcyon days in Cuba.

Could she ever have that?

Maybe…tonight. Once. *Now*.

She padded barefoot down the hall, following the aroma…and her heart.

His back was to her as he worked at the stove, a simple white T-shirt and jeans still the sexiest thing Gabe Rossi could wear, if he had to have clothes on. And, yes, a glass of red wine was on the counter next to him.

"How was your nap?" he asked without turning.

She smiled, drawn to him like he was—what was that game Rafe liked to play? "Magnet Man," she whispered as she came up behind him and put a hand on his strong shoulder, physically incapable of *not* touching him.

"Don't make me pick you up and throw you on the bed," he teased, turning to her and letting his gaze slide up and down. "Although…on second thought. Make me."

Heat curled through her, tightening her tummy, quickening her breath.

She lifted his wine to her lips. "I don't have a headache."

A slow smile lifted one corner of his mouth. "Code word."

"Yep." Leaning over the onions and tomato sauce sizzling in a pan, she waved her hand to bring the aroma right to her nose, moaning with appreciation. "I love this dinner, by the way."

"I remember the last time we had it together." He stirred the ingredients but looked beyond the pan, his mind hundreds of miles away…back to Cuba, she guessed.

"It was about two weeks before you left," he said softly. "Only, I didn't know you were going to leave." He turned to her, all humor gone from his eyes, just smoky intensity. The way he'd looked at her in bed that day.

"I remember the day." Because she'd interviewed for the job the Friday before and had made the decision not to tell Gabe until she knew if she got it. But that whole weekend, she'd known they were coming to an end, and every moment had been bittersweet. "It rained," she said. "Poured, as I recall."

His eyes shuttered for a second, as though just

remembering the sound of the rain on the metal roof that cozy, cloudy, sexy day hit him as hard as it hit her.

"We spent the day in bed, all day." His voice was gruff and low. "Just me and...you." He swallowed.

He put down the spoon and pressed his hand to her cheek, looking hard at her, making her whole body ache and sing and hope for that impossible dream...a future.

"We set some records that day, didn't we?" He stroked her cheek with his thumb.

His words fried every nerve in her body. "We sure did," she agreed.

"I remember looking down at you that day. I was inside you. All the way."

She bit her lip so hard it hurt. *All the way.* That feeling. That insane, perfect, over-the-top feeling of Gabe in her body. She wanted it so much. It was all she wanted, everything she wanted. Right now.

All the way.

"And before it was over..." He leaned closer, as if he had to say the rest with his lips touching hers. "I realized that I could not ever be whole, happy, or sane without you."

But he still didn't have her. Not really. He had Lila. Could it be the same? Better? "Gabe."

He exhaled, pure resignation, and pulled back.

He picked up a wooden spoon, then put it down again, definitely not done. "I loved you, Isa."

She let the name slide, but mostly because emotion had her throat thick.

"I *loved* you," he repeated. There was no sentiment coloring the statement, no sweet admission. This was Gabe, pissed. "I fucking gave in and gave up and *loved* you." He sounded disgusted. "I loved you." Barely a whisper, and she could have sworn his voice cracked. "And you left."

"I loved you, too."

He shook his head. "But not enough to stay."

She took his shoulder and turned him. "You know what you would say if the tables were turned and you'd left me and I was still whining about it?"

"Ancient fucking history?"

"Exactly." She squeezed his arms and pulled him closer. "I know we have a past, Gabe, and I have no idea if we could ever have a future. But we have a present. A little sliver of sacred time when we're together, alone, and my head doesn't hurt."

He studied her for a moment, his eyes so deeply blue and intense, his lips parted, and took the first ragged breath of a man who was losing control. "No," he said. "I refuse to give you a headache."

"I'm going to get one anyway." She reached up and rocked her hips into him, letting out a tiny whimper against his growing erection. "Now, Gabe. Right this minute. Now."

"Lila, don't." He visibly fought for control. "It hurts you too much."

She closed her eyes. "I will take the pain of an inevitable headache for just one chance to have you inside me again. One time…all the way."

"No." He turned back to the stove, squeezing the wooden spoon so tight it was a miracle it didn't crack in his hands. "Too much pain."

She inched back, the rejection stinging. "For you or for me?" She turned around and started out of the kitchen. She'd take that shower now. Icy cold and—

He grabbed her elbow and spun her around with one hand. "You want to know what my pain is?"

He pulled her closer. "My pain is when I think about how much I loved you. How sure I was I wanted to spend my entire life with you. I wanted to marry you and have five kids with you and get old and wrinkled with you and end up in the ground next to you."

Oh God.

"But you wanted to do the Company's business."

The words smacked her, but she refused to look away.

"And then my pain changed. My woman died. My kid was buried. My hope was gone…until you showed up. You. Not Isadora Winter. *You. Lila.*"

The next breath nearly strangled her.

"And now?" He choked the question. "Now, every time I touch you, it hurts you. You cringe. You flinch. You rub your head and stifle a moan. I hurt you." She blinked at him, pressed back from the intensity rolling off him as he kept up the assault. "My pain starts with how much I want you." He pulled her all the way into him, his chest pressed against hers so close she could feel his heart hammer. "How much I need to get all the way inside you and stay there, pounding and grinding and dying until neither one of us knows our fucking name."

Her knees buckled, but she held on, reaching up and closing her arms around his neck. "No pain, Gabe. Just this. Now. Us. Now."

He answered with a kiss, a powerful, potent, openmouthed kiss. Without looking, he flipped the knob on the stove and gave the pan a push off the heat, then kissed even harder.

"Now." He growled the word into another fierce kiss, his hands already moving over her body, walking her out of the kitchen. He turned her around the corner and pushed her up against the wall. "And I mean *now*."

She kissed him back, as desperate and ready and real as he felt. He devoured her with his mouth, finding new places to kiss, searing her skin, branding her, owning her.

Smashing her against the wall, he dragged her dress up over her hips. His fingers scraped her thighs, spreading them to pound his mighty hard-on against her.

Her whole body responded, softening and opening and aching. Her nipples burned and her hips rocked, closer and closer to the only thing she wanted.

Holding her with his chest, he reached into his back pocket and flipped out his wallet. Wordlessly, he removed a condom, threw the wallet on the floor, and inched back to unbutton his jeans and free himself.

She closed her hands over his hard-on, fighting the urge to scream with ecstasy when she touched the stiff heat of him. Every inch familiar, but so shockingly sexy, she had to moan as she stroked him.

He grabbed the thong she wore by the band on her hip. "You want this thing?"

"Not on."

"Good." He ripped the fabric with one easy snap, letting it fall and forcing her legs apart. He bit the packet, staring at her. It was dark in the hall, but their eyes met and locked.

"Head okay?" he asked in a harsh whisper.

"Head's fine. But this"—she jerked her pelvis against him—"needs attention."

He sheathed himself, and she stood on her tiptoes. He lifted her up the wall an inch or two, getting her right where he wanted her, easily sliding in with a low growl and grunt of satisfaction.

She cried out with pleasure, and he jammed in again, full force. Deeper. Harder. Longer.

All the way.

The masculine, musky scent of sex she associated only

with him made her as dizzy as every other sensation. The sound of his broken, torn breaths. Dirty words and sexy promises all mixed with the exquisite fullness of Gabe thrusting into her over and over again.

Gripping his shoulders, heat and pleasure twisted up through her as he pounded harder and harder.

Their teeth cracked in the next kiss, his hips impaling hers, his body completely and totally inside.

"I can't stop," he rasped. "I can't."

"Don't stop." She clung to him. "Come in me, Gabe. Let me watch you come in me."

He gave up the fight, pressing her into the wall, dropping his head back with a howl of surrender as he plunged in and out, utterly lost to his pleasure. His face changed, his jaw loosened, his eyes closed, and his beautiful mouth fell open, incapable of anything but helpless sounds of satisfaction.

And, just like always, watching him come made her do exactly the same thing, falling and twisting into the fierce and mighty whirlwind of this man she loved so damn hard...she literally couldn't remember her name.

Just like he'd promised.

Chapter Twenty

"Lila." Gabe leaned back against the sofa, stretching his legs under the coffee table, utterly satisfied by good sex, good food, good company, and the possibility of a long night of a lot more.

"Mmm." Across from him, she swiped her fork across the just-about-empty plate, scooping up some red sauce, as the plebes called gravy, and closing her eyes as she slipped the fork into her mouth.

What the holy hell was he thinking when he first saw this woman and pegged her as average or…not his type? Types were for idiots, and Gabe was not an idiot.

"What?" she asked after she licked the fork and made his poor dick twitch back to life.

"Why Lila?"

"Why?" Her eyes opened as she dropped her elbows on the table, the two candles she'd lit for their floor picnic flickering shadows under her prominent cheekbones. "Why am I giving oral to this fork? Because you cook like a god, and I can't remember the last time I ate anything so delicious."

"Why did you pick the name Lila? Does it have any significance?"

"Not a bit." She put the fork down, reluctantly, and situated herself on the floor, tugging at the dress that rode up her thighs. Even after recovering from sex, eating a good meal, and letting the glow die down, she still looked very much like a woman who'd just gotten good and laid.

Best of all, they'd warded off the headache so far by avoiding any conversation too deep or personal. It worked, but he doubted it could last all night.

Her lips were a little swollen, her hair needed to be combed, and...he happened to know she didn't have much on under that dress 'cause he'd made scraps out of that thong with one hand.

"They gave it to me, essentially. I didn't have a lot to say about the background of the character they dreamed up, just that I had to memorize it all."

He considered that, lifting his wine glass to finish the dregs. "I've been undercover but never so deep I had to seriously change my personality. Was it difficult?"

She shrugged. "It was consuming. During the preparation, I was pregnant, then Rafe was born."

"You named him Gabriel."

She looked down, almost as in apology. "I knew that there would come a time when that name—and, to the world, the child—would have to 'die.' I knew it was temporary, and I just wanted him to have a connection with you. His middle name was another angel, Rafael."

"'Cause he's *so* angelic," he said.

She smiled. "You know, I considered giving him your middle name, Angelo, which I guess is ironic because you're both devils."

"Yup." Gabe locked his fingers behind his head, thinking of his son. "Hate to break it to you, Mom, you were just a carrier of those genes."

"I knew it the minute he came out that he was your clone," she said. "He looked like he was pressed in a mold with your name on it."

A few different sensations rolled around Gabe, a hot cocktail of longing and pride and regret and wonder. "What was it like, having him? I imagine that kid came out kicking, screaming, and whirling."

She tunneled her fingers into her hair, pushing it back and resting her face on her palms. "It was bad. I had to be induced because he was in no rush, and I was."

So the bastards had even decided when his kid would be born. "So you forced him out?"

"No, no. It's very normal to induce labor when you're past the due date, and I was, but the induction drugs make the whole thing…intense. It hurt, as you would probably say, like an em-effer. I actually blacked out for a while, and they even called in a second doctor."

His gut tightened at the thought. "Is that normal?"

"I don't know, but it turned out okay."

"And where were you? In Cuba still?"

"Yes, I had to have him there. That was the plan from the day the agency found out I was pregnant. They have facilities and resources on the island, so it made sense."

"A true CIA baby born in some agency-sponsored clinic."

She lifted a shoulder. "It was a legitimate medical facility, and I had a good doctor who was completely briefed on my undercover situation, which was helpful."

"Why?" he asked, thinking through what he knew about the agency. "With so few people who needed to know, why would your doctor need to know?"

"He was my doctor from day one, before the first operation. He knew my complete medical history." She angled her head and nodded. “I know the assignment was uncommon in its depth and breadth, but the CIA was thorough and fair to me. They recognized what I had to give up and didn’t want my life in danger. And I got paid a ton, which is all in savings to send our son to college.”

“I’ll pay for college.”

She nudged him with her foot. “You’re such a guy, Gabe Rossi.”

“You noticed?”

She rested her chin on her hand, giving him a loopy smile. “Flat-out most guy-like guy I’ve ever known. And your son is made of the same stuff.” Suddenly, she frowned and sat up straight. “God, I haven’t really even thought about him for an hour or so. I should call Nino and make sure he went to sleep.”

“He’s fine,” Gabe assured her. “He’s probably not asleep, but he’s with family. The best place on earth for him.”

But she shifted again, uncomfortable now, looking around for her phone. “It’s not too late. Do you think we could sneak out and go see him? Just to kiss him good night and pat his back?”

“You can kiss me good night and pat my front.” But he had to give mental, if reluctant, props to the bonehead manny for calling this one before it happened. Maybe he’d been wrong about that guy. “You’re not going anywhere tonight, except to bed.” He moved his bare foot to the left, tucking it under her dress and sliding his toe over her thigh. “With me.”

She put her hand on his ankle, nestling his foot against her. “Better be careful, Gabe Rossi. You’ll end up liking a skinny blonde with tiny boobs and an English accent.”

“I already like her,” he admitted. “Your hair is pretty, your little A-cups taste great, and the accent is kind of hot.”

She looked at him for a long time, those bottomless eyes slicing through him. Neither one of them spoke for a long time. A stupidly long time. Long enough for his body to react and not in the way it should—with a nice, masculine stiffy. No, his fucking heart went triple rate and his throat bone-dry.

What the hell?

She sighed, breaking the silence and slipping her fingers to her temples.

"Shit," he murmured. "I knew this was too good to be true."

"Mmm. I shouldn't have relaxed and let myself feel anything."

He moved out from between the table and the sofa, coming closer to where she sat on the floor. As he got closer, she put her hand on his cheek, still looking into his eyes. "I'm sorry, Gabe."

"For what? Getting headaches? Baby, you're looking at six feet of human aspirin." He took her other hand. "This floor is hard, though. Let's go to the bedroom, and I'll give you a massage."

She didn't move. "That's not what I'm sorry for."

"Then what? For what you said? For all the decisions you made? For saving the world?" He stroked her hair, pushing it behind her ear. "You made the right call, Lila."

"I'm sorry I'm not Isadora anymore. I wish we could just fall back into where we were five years ago and..." She squeezed her eyes shut, sucking in a tiny breath. "Ouch."

"Damn." He rubbed her temple with his thumb, pressing like he'd seen her do.

She kept her eyes closed. "I hate to say this, but these headaches are getting worse every day. The longer I'm with you, the more I feel..." She shook her head. "It's like punishment, you know? It's like God is punishing me for changing all His work into something He didn't create."

"I see the headaches make you dumb, too. That's not how it works."

"We don't know that, do we? My mother was pretty religious, you know. She collected all those rosaries."

"Fat lot of good it did her when that plane plowed into the Pentagon."

She cringed again.

"Sorry, sorry." He took her hand and stood. "Come on."

"I can't, Gabe. I can't make love again. It hurts my head." She looked up at him, her eyes wide and dancing in the candlelight. "You make me feel too much."

How the hell could he stop doing that? It was the opposite of what he wanted in every way. He gave her hand a good tug. "We're not going to make love again. You're not going to feel anything but comfort. Come with me, and let me take care of you."

She hesitated, then relaxed and let him pull her up, wrapping her arm around his waist and putting her head on his shoulder. "It really hurts tonight," she whispered, making his heart fold in half.

"Let me fix it." He snuffed the candles with two fingers and walked her down the hall and into the first darkened bedroom, laying her on the bed.

Thankfully, she didn't argue but rolled over on her stomach with a soft moan. He kept the room dark and climbed onto the bed next to her.

He rubbed her shoulders and squeezed the base of her neck. "Don't think about anything, Lila."

She stiffened. "You know, you asked me about my name. I never really liked it until now."

"Why now?"

"It sounds nice on your lips."

He leaned over and pressed his mouth against her ear. "You feel nice against my lips." He breathed and fluttered her hair. "Lila."

"Ow." The word was just a whimper, a tiny little single syllable that ripped his heart out. "That hurts, too."

Damn it, the pain made him feel so fucking helpless. "You're feeling things."

"No. That." She reached back and tapped the nape of her neck over her hair. "It always starts there, especially when you press it. Then shoots into my temples, but right there? It feels like fire."

"Where that scar is?" He pushed her hair to the side, squinting in the darkness to see the sickle-shaped mark he'd noticed before. "Your plastic surgeon got lazy."

"I don't have a scar there," she said. "They didn't do anything back there."

"Feel it." He guided her finger to the spot. "Right there."

"That's not a scar. I thought it was like a mole or something. I remember when I first noticed it when Rafe was a baby and I showed it to the doctor. He said it was just a growth that's caused by hormones."

"Like your headaches?"

"Yes…like my…" She stiffened again. Then, holding her hand over the spot, she sat up a little, blinking in the darkness. "Gabe." She put a hand over her mouth, her body suddenly vibrating. "What does it look like?"

He reached into his pocket and took out his phone. "Turn around," he ordered. "Hold up your hair."

She did, and he snapped a picture, the flash like lightning in the dimly lit room.

"It *is* a scar," she said, taking the phone to study it closer. "And that is not the handiwork of the man who did anything else on my body." She put the phone down and looked up at him, pain replaced by sheer terror in her eyes.

"What is it?" he asked.

"I didn't have any work done there, so why is there a scar?" The demand and fear in her voice took him back.

"You had a lot of surgeries, so you don't know..." But something in her eyes said she did know, and suddenly, with a jolt of shocking realization, he did, too.

An implant.

For a moment, neither one of them could speak, but they stared at each other in stunned disbelief, the unspoken word hanging between them.

An implant. Those cocksucking dogshit sons of bitches put an implant in her.

She pressed her fist to her lips. "To track me?"

"Possibly. You wouldn't be the first victim in covert intelligence."

"But they always knew where I was. I checked in constantly. I was infiltrating a CIA operation, so my location was no secret."

"But they want to control something."

"Me." She barely whispered the word, and he followed the logical conclusion of that thought. "My...emotions. As soon as I feel anything, especially something good, like love or a connection with another person, I'm in pain."

He considered that, hating that it made sense. "It guarantees you don't get too close to anyone, for one thing. Or too emotionally involved in anything, which, I assume, protects the undercover operation."

"How?" She put her fingers to her temples, lightly this time, as if she was scared to even touch herself. "How could an implant do that?"

"I don't know, but my guess is that it reacts to chemicals

released by emotions, juicing them up when they start, sending them to crazy levels, giving you blistering headaches."

"Oh my God." She struggled with a breath and, he imagined, the impact. "I feel so…violated."

And she had been. Those fuckers were as bad as rapists. "But it can be fixed, Lila." He reached out to her, optimism surging. "We can get it taken out, and no more headaches, no more prison, no more fear of feeling anything."

She flattened her hands on her cheeks, which, even in the dim light, he could see had grown pale as blood drained. "All that pain. All that time. All those frustrations when I loved my son or looked at a sunset or…or…thought about you."

Hating that he had any part in causing her pain, he folded her in his arms, pulling her closer. "It's going to end now. It's going to end."

She drew back, fire in her eyes. "Someone has to pay for this, Gabe. Whoever did this is going to pay."

"What about the doctor when you blacked out during childbirth? That's when they started. Who was this joker? He's next on my kill list."

"I never got his name," she admitted. "Oh, there are spies among us, Dexter used to say."

"That prick?" Gabe shot up. "He probably knew all about this."

"No. He would never let them. He would have told me."

"Like he told you the undercover job required a total change of looks and personality?" Gabe almost spat with anger. "I never liked that asshole."

"Stop." She put her hand on his arm. "Let me think. Let me remember the delivery room. The nurse went in and out. Then I blacked out."

"Who blacks out during labor and delivery?" he asked. "I've never heard of anything like that."

Neither had she. "Oh Gabe, do you think that's what happened? They planned it?" She was shaking a little, and each word caught in her throat. "They would do that to me? The CIA? Why?"

A million reasons. "This was a treacherous job, infiltrating your own organization. Like I said, what better way to be sure you didn't get too close and chatty with someone than to give you pain every time you risked that?"

"I considered giving up my son!" Her voice cracked. "You have to help me, Gabe. You have to help me figure out who did this and why and—"

"Oh, we will. But we have to get it out first." Relieving the pain was more important than retribution, though he wanted that, too. And bad.

She sat still for a few minutes, thinking. "I can't go to a doctor."

"Why the hell not?"

"I have to see someone the CIA has approved, someone who knows my real history, or it won't take long to figure out I've had a lot of…" Her voice faded as she read the look on his face. "That's exactly what they want, isn't it?"

"Of course that's what they want." Anger ripped through him. "To control you."

"No, but now we have an advantage, if we're right about this." She closed her eyes and wrapped her hands around his neck. "We're right. I can't believe I never thought of it."

"You couldn't see it."

"There's an actual bump there, though. I was an idiot not to figure it out. Every single time I had an intense emotion. It's like…I don't even know who I am."

He frowned, inching her closer. "What do you mean?"

"This isn't just headaches when some chemical or hormone level spikes. This changed me to the very core of my being, Gabe. Living with the pain, or the fear of the pain, and knowing it was somehow associated with how I feel has completely altered my personality. I told you I have a shell around my heart. They did that to me."

He eased her closer, kissed her lips, and stroked her hair. "You know what I'm going to do?"

"Kill the person who did this, I hope."

"Oh yeah. Right after I crack that shell and get my woman back."

Chapter Twenty-One

Lila woke to see Gabe pacing the room. "Any word from Luke?" she asked.

"Nothing. The resort is quiet."

She peered toward a window, which was dark enough to let her know it was still the middle of the night. "What time is it?"

"Two thirty. You crashed."

"You should sleep." She pushed up and realized he'd covered her. "I'm the one who should be pacing instead of sleeping."

Gabe checked his phone, then put it down. "I'm just thinking of all the different ways I could actually kill Dexter Crain."

"I don't think he's responsible," she said. "He's like a father to me, Gabe."

He fried her with a look. "Someone knew. Someone high."

"We'll talk to him, to the director of the CIA if we have to. We'll find out."

"Please tell me you're not that naïve. They won't tell you shit, Lila."

He was right. Even about Dexter, she feared.

"We need a doctor we can trust," he murmured. "And we need to go through the entire CIA chain of command and get back to what happened when you gave—" Suddenly, he froze and turned to her. "You don't think some fuckhead planted something in Rafe when he was born, do you?"

Her heart tumbled at the thought. "A chip that made him disobey everything I say?" Her humor fell flat, not even earning the slightest smile. "No, I don't," she assured him. "I know every inch of his body, and I have since the day he was born. There's not a scar on him, except for the usual nicks and bruises of an overactive kid."

Gabe blew out a breath and paced again, like a trapped man. "Still, I don't trust anyone anymore."

"Anymore?" She snorted softly.

He slowed his step and turned to her. "I trusted you." The low undertone of pain twisted her gut with shame. "I don't think you know what your leaving did to me."

"Tell me," she said. "I really want to know. I need to know."

"It made me realize…" He puffed out a breath. "It made me know I'd been right all along. No one is really what they seem to be, and the minute you let go and buy into them lock, stock, and big Italian heart, they smash you."

Oh God. "I wasn't the first to smash you, was I?"

He didn't answer.

"What happened to her? Smasher number one?"

He turned, averting his gaze, signaling to her that whatever he was about to say, it was both important and he didn't like talking about it. She really *did* speak body language. "Gabe?" she urged when he didn't say anything.

"I put a bullet in her chest."

She inched back in shock. "What?"

He stuck his hand in his hair and dragged it back, looking

from one place to another, turning a little, avoiding any eye contact at all. "I'm really not at liberty to tell you."

"Well, as someone I know quite well would say, you better get at liberty in a big damn hurry. I told you my secret assignment and you..." She let the words process some more. "You *killed* her?"

Finally, he looked at her. "I was a contract operative for the CIA, Lila. You know exactly what that entails. Don't act shocked that we had to kill people in our jobs. Even people we...like."

Or love. "So you cared about her?"

He inched closer to the bed, propping himself on the edge as if he needed to sit for this but didn't want to get too close to her. "I could have. I think the worst part was I trusted her, as an asset and as a person. And then I tried to help her, and by doing so, I nearly got myself killed."

She studied his profile as he spoke, listening to the words. Each one infused with that undercurrent of passion that seemed to emanate from Gabe's every pore.

"Who was she? What country? When was this? Can you tell me that much?"

"Russia. Late 2007."

No mention of who she was, Lila noticed. "Russia in 2007?" she asked, spinning through a mental review of the recent history of that organization. "What were you doing in Russia in 2007?"

"The *siloviki*. The power boys."

She knew a little about the unofficial circle of influence that had formed after the leaders of the KGB were either fired, reassigned, or forced into less important jobs with the FSB, the security agency that replaced the notorious spies. The *siloviki* were tight and nearly as brutal as the KGB but quite under the radar and informal.

As informal as anything in Russia could be.

"Were you undercover? Doing what?"

"Trying to get the names of every one of them," he explained. "To watch them and know what decisions weren't political per se, but as the chairman of the largest oil company or the head of a company that produces rockets, each and every man wielded incredible political power."

"And the CIA wanted to know who they were and what they were up to." She fully understood an assignment like that. "What was your cover?"

"Besides blown?" He looked skyward. "American businessman helping the personnel department of Sevtronics, an electrical components company in Russia. I was allegedly teaching them best practices of US media companies, but I was sucking their personnel and private files dry."

"And you were creating assets from the employee base."

"Of course. And one asset? Well, she was my best. The administrative assistant to a power monger by the name of Viktor Solov, the head of Sevtronics. She was giving me memos and files, information and schedules."

"And you were giving her…" She almost didn't want to know, except it had been well before he'd met Isadora, so she shouldn't be jealous.

"A lot of laughs and some pretty decent sex."

No, she *shouldn't* be jealous, but something was burning in her chest. "Laughs and sex. Your specialty."

But she didn't get a smile in response. "It was good."

Damn it. "Did you love her?"

He tipped his head, an angle of uncertainty. An angle of torture. "I knew I shouldn't."

Well, *that* didn't answer her question.

"But it's moot, because she fucking betrayed me, and it nearly cost me my life."

"So you shot her?"

He gave a dry laugh. "Yes. That's what 'nearly cost me my life' leads to when you're a spy, Lila. She was about to kill me, and I stopped her with my gun. In our line of business, that's kind of another day at the office."

"Except, in our line of business you're supposed to walk away unscathed," she said. "But it doesn't sound like you did."

"Physically unscathed, though I got a pretty severe dressing down when I got back to the US, which is par for the course with the CIA. Risk your life, get them information that can save lives, and receive the middle finger in return." He added a smile. "I punished them by not giving them everything I had on the company. Decided to save it for a rainy day or a bargaining chip, but I never got to use it because the *siloviki* lost most of their power when Putin took over."

"Was it tough for you, that first kill?" she asked.

"I was a pretty young agent," he said. "I realized I'd been naïve and trusting and that is deadly and stupid. I wasn't going to get involved ever, at least not emotionally. But a few years later, I walked into this sexy recruit…and broke that vow." He caressed her cheek with his knuckle. "Until she left me."

"I had to do what I had to do," she said simply.

His finger froze. "Funny."

"It wasn't meant to be."

"I just meant it was funny because those were actually her last words to me."

She inched back, surprised. "Were they?"

"And they've always been a red flag." He eyed her with that same slightly narrowed eye of suspicion she'd seen so often when she'd first told him who she really was.

"Don't look at me that way," she said. "I'm not lying to you."

"I know, but...what happens when 'you do what you have to do'?"

She frowned, pushing up. "What is that supposed to mean?"

"It means exactly what I asked. What happens when duty calls again and you feel you have to honor the memory of your parents instead of someone you love? What will you do?"

She snorted. "I'll make them eat this freaking implant."

He just gave her a look, because they both knew how fast you could be sucked back in.

"What about you?" she shot back. "You're still a man who a woman can't be sure of anymore. Especially when..." Her voice faded.

"When what?"

"When that woman, the one you loved and trusted is...dead."

He scowled at her. "Isadora is dead?"

"Isn't she?" She shrugged. "Look at me. Thin and blond and...crispy."

He gave a mirthless laugh. "Crispy?"

"You know what I mean."

"I sure as hell do not. The woman I enjoyed up against the wall was not some kind of dried-up cracker. What the fuck is crispy, anyway?"

"It means I'm cold and protected and...and..." She nearly dented her temples she pressed so hard. "I don't look like Isadora, and I don't feel like her, either."

"That's what I'm trying to solve," he insisted, reaching for her. "Get that fucking bug out of your head. Literally and figuratively."

She backed away. "It might be too late. She's gone, Gabe. And this…" She gestured toward her face and body. "This is what you get now."

"And you think that matters to me? You think the color of your hair and the size of your tits are important to me? Who the hell do you think I am?" He took her shoulders in his hands. "I wasn't in love with Isadora's hair or body. I was in love with her heart and soul and spirit."

She blinked, hating that tears burned behind her lids. "What if my heart and soul and spirit are all gone, too?"

"They're not," he assured her. "I see them every day. Every minute, they come more and more to the surface. Which is probably why you're in such pain. We get rid of those headaches, we get you back."

He pushed her down on the bed, hovering over her, then lowering himself on to her. "Then it'll be like falling in love all over again." He kissed her mouth, tunneling his fingers in her hair and rocking against her.

"Are you?" she asked as he feathered her neck with more hot kisses and sent shivers down her spine.

"Yes." He searched her face, looking into her eyes, his smoky blue ones intense as he took slow breaths and hardened against her. "I'm falling for you, Lila. For you, not the memory of you. You."

She pulled him into a kiss, but the vibration of his phone made him leave her instantly, reaching for his phone.

"Hang on, it's Luke," he said, reading the caller ID. "Let me see what's up."

While he answered, Lila pushed off the bed and touched her head, which, of course, hurt. But knowing why, or suspecting she did, changed everything.

"Who is it?" At the sharp tone in his question, Lila turned.

"Is Rafe okay?" she asked.

He nodded, reaching for her hand to bring her back next to him on the bed.

"Guy named David Franklin just walked in and took an available villa," he told her.

A guest registered at this hour?

"No reservation, but he's in African Daisy, one of the larger villas, and paid cash," Gabe reported. "His background is blank." He waited a second, listening to Luke. Then, "The clerk got a Maryland license. Luke ran the number, and it doesn't exist."

"Do we have his picture?" she asked.

He nodded. "On the security camera at check-in and the front desk got a photo copy of his ID. Luke, text me that picture and let me know when he makes any move out of that villa." He hung up and looked at Lila. "Does that name mean anything to you?"

She thought for a moment and shook her head. The phone dinged again, and Gabe tapped it and showed her the screen. "Here he is."

She squinted at the shot and sucked in a breath. "Yes. That's David Foster, not Franklin. He's a low level operative I knew him in the agency, to say hello, but only because..." She swallowed the rest of the sentence as it hit her hard. "He's a family friend of Dexter Crain's," she said softly.

"Big shocker," Gabe growled.

Her phone, on the dresser, lit up and buzzed.

"Don't tell me, there's the Dixter now."

She grabbed it and blinked at the screen. "Nope, but it is David Foster. He's texting me."

Gabe whipped the phone out of her hand. "'I have the answer you need,'" Gabe read. "What the ever-lovin'—"

"Stop it!" She yanked the phone back, reading the text

and instantly writing back. "What is the question?" she said outloud as she typed.

They looked at each other, silent for a second, waiting for the response, which showed up in less than five seconds.

Does your head hurt?

"Shit," Gabe mumbled, reading it. "I knew it. I fucking knew it."

"Oh, Gabe, we just figured it out," she whispered. "It's like they can read my damn mind." She choked on the last word.

"Then we're going to talk to him and find out more."

She didn't argue that one, but typed her response. *Let's talk.*

He answered immediately. *Meet me at the harbor in 15 min. If any of the bodyguards crawling all over this place are there, you'll never see me.*

"Who exactly is this guy?" Gabe demanded.

She scoured her memory for what she knew about him. Other than the fact that he was close to Dexter. "He was a tech guy, an analyst brought on not long after I was permanently moved to DC. Not a major player in any way."

"But a friend of Crain's."

She shut her eyes and nodded.

Gabe pushed off the bed. "You're not going."

She looked up at him. "Of course I'm going."

"With a team of—"

"Gabe, stop it." She shot up. "You can back me up, but not one single guy from Luke's team can be there. He has information I desperately need and who knows..." She touched the back of her head. "What they know about me."

He flattened her with a look, but she could tell he was

thinking the same thing. He knew how spying worked, and he knew better than anyone how to manage an asset.

"Maybe he learned something through his association with Dexter and he wants to share it," she suggested. "Maybe he was undercover, too, and has the same symptoms. Maybe there are other agents enduring this or being controlled this way."

"Or maybe he wants to kill you."

She sighed heavily at the truth of that. "All I know is we won't find out unless we go and play his game."

He didn't answer, thinking and figuring things out the way Gabe did.

"You'll be there, but you'll be hiding," she said quickly. "I have to talk to him. I have to know where to start so you know who to kill."

"Why not in the light of day with friends around? Ask him that."

Nodding, she typed on the screen. *Why can't we meet in the daylight, out in the open?*

"It's a fair question," she said while they waited for a response, which flashed back almost instantly.

Because there are spies among us.

Lila looked at the six words she'd heard Dexter say a hundred times, and her heart dropped. Good God. "We're going, Gabe," she said quietly, already looking for the right clothes.

"Fair enough. I'll tell Luke not to follow him when he leaves. Get dressed, and let's go. Duty calls."

"One last time, I hope."

"At least this time we're in it together," he said, texting Luke.

She scooped up a pair of jeans and a dark sweatshirt. "Which means one of us has to live, Gabe. For Rafe." She pulled the sweatshirt on, flipping her hair and eyeing him as she popped out. “You have to promise me that if one of us has to die, it will be me. You can take care of him.”

He gave her a withering look and held out her Glock. “No one’s going to die.” He gave her nudge. “Haul ass, blondie, we got work to do.”

Chapter Twenty-Two

The air at Mimosa Harbor was still, silent, and heavy with salt. Dim uplights along the wharf cast strange shadows on all the boats. Lila parked Gabe's GTO and peered into the marina that housed the locals' pleasure craft and some fishing rigs docked along about seven or eight wooden ramps. All the while, she took slow, calming breaths.

As planned, she waited in the spot long enough for Gabe to park Nino's car well down the street and get here on foot. She double-checked her clip, the weapon solid and natural in her hand. From the seat next to her, she grabbed her phone, checking for a message from either Gabe or David Foster.

Gabe would be following her by tracking her phone and she completely trusted him to stay close but out of sight. Her heart hammered at a steady beat and her body tensed in anticipation of the dangerous job.

But her head was deliciously pain-free, as it always was when she went into work mode.

Maybe David Foster had answers about that, too.

When Gabe texted *Go*, she climbed out of the car and walked across the parking lot to the harbor entrance, her sneakered feet silent until she hit the weathered wooden deck.

The gate to the public marina wasn't locked, but at nearly three in the morning, the place was deserted. In an hour and a half, some hard-core fishermen might show up, but by then she hoped to be long gone and full of information.

To incriminate who?

Swallowing hard, she stepped onto the main dock and looked left and right, her eyes as adjusted to the dark as they could be.

Her phone vibrated with a text from Foster.

Last dock on the left, all the way to the end.

She looked that way and considered the choice for a meeting place. As the docks went, it was somewhat open. That last dock didn't have any boats on the left side, as it was most likely used for people who wanted to moor briefly then go back into the gulf. It was more visible than she would have expected, which might be safer...but it would also make it hard for Gabe to hide close by.

She started off, stuffing the phone in her jeans pocket in case she needed two hands to brace and aim her weapon. She passed one dock jutting out, the only sound a few clanging masts in the very light breeze. A few air conditioners hummed, reminding her that there might be sleep-aboards around—innocent people who shouldn't be collateral damage.

"Put your phone down."

She turned at the voice that came from a boat that sat low in the water, a go-fast with a giant bow that shot out twenty feet from the cockpit.

A man stood at the helm, dressed in black head to toe, his face mostly obscured by the hood of a sweatshirt. "Put your phone right there, on the dock."

She inched her gun up. "Step out here, David, and let me see you."

"David's over there, waiting for you. I'm going to take your phone so no one can follow you."

And, if she actually lived after following that order, Gabe would kill her. "Not necessary. No one is following me. I'm not going there without the ability to communicate, nor am I going without this gun." She took a step closer, as curious about his voice as she was his face. She could recognize people by their voices, by vocal patterns and the most subtle language styles.

He had a barely there accent, but she didn't quite get the country. But she would, if she could get him to talk more.

"Keep your weapon. But you're going to leave that phone right there, and then you can go. If you refuse, David will leave and take his answers with him."

Arabic? No, something else, but he was well trained to hide it.

"Just come with me," she said again, even though it meant two against one. At least Gabe would know where she was.

"You'll go alone and he'll tell you what you need to know."

Maybe Middle Eastern, but he moved his head enough for her to catch a glimmer of pale blond hair, so that was unlikely.

"Who are you?" she asked.

"Just another agent who wants the truth out. And no one else can hear, including the person backing you up by using your phone to track your every move."

Bastards. "The truth…about what?"

He snorted softly. "As if we don't all know." He took one step closer. "Isadora."

Her heart fell so hard it should have bounced off the wood dock. She managed not to react, but now she had to know who she was dealing with. Gabe would find this guy, at least, when he came for the phone. And he was armed and ready for anything.

Slowly, she crouched down and set her phone on the dock.

"Go. Find out what they did to you."

She had to know. Clutching her Glock, she took off at a fast clip, staying as close to the tiny lights along the side of the dock. Likely solar-powered, since they were nearly out for the night, but she hoped they shed enough light for Gabe to see her from where he hid, probably the parking lot, so he would know she no longer had her phone.

Turning onto the last dock, she peered out, still not seeing anyone. Along the right, five or six larger boats were moored.

She walked slowly, weapon raised, eyes scanning the entire area. At the end of the dock, she stopped, turned, and seethed in frustration.

"Where are you?" she demanded.

Nothing but the sound of water lapping against the hull answered her. Had that yacht moved?

She peered at the vessel that took up half the dock, well aware someone could be hiding anywhere, on any of the three decks, with a gun pointed at her head. The boat rocked gently again, but didn't they all? Or was someone walking around in there…taking aim?

"David!"

Did he want her to get on the boat? Because she had given up her phone in slight desperation, but she sure as hell wasn't getting on board without it. And Gabe.

"I'm ready to talk, David. Ready to share information both ways."

Why? Why lure her here, take her phone, and then ignore her? She held the Glock steady with two hands, lifting high in the direction of the upper deck where someone would have the advantage over her, but knowing that anyone on the lower level of the boat could take a shot right at her.

The boat rocked again, this time with definite weight, and she backed up as far as she could, taking in every inch of the vessel, looking for movement inside or out, waiting for a sound.

And then a scuff, a movement on the upper deck, in the shadows, and suddenly something large and dark came flying through the air, landing on the dock with a loud thud ten feet from her.

Not something. A dead man.

As Gabe slipped from shadow to shadow, he listened. He heard Lila's voice a few times, unable to make out her words, but hearing her tone rise in a sharp question. Then she'd taken off toward the last dock? Had she met Foster yet? Why didn't he hear—

He saw a shadow move on the speedboat hidden between two large trawlers. Deep down at the helm, a man stood, weapon drawn, peering into the darkness looking for someone. Not Lila—she'd gone in the opposite direction. Her GPS wasn't moving, but Gabe had seen her darting toward the last dock.

No, this guy, wearing head-to-toe black and holding a pistol ready to fire, was looking for someone following Lila. Him.

Gabe hung back, assessing the situation, using the hull of a trawler to hide himself.

He inched out silently and caught sight of a phone on the dock right in front of the oversize drug runner's fizzboat.

She'd left it there?

Good God, who trained her?

They had. And they would know that she'd give up her phone, at least, for information. But Gabe couldn't get to her without their lookout seeing him.

Son of a bitch. So much for believing it was a standard little one-on-one info exchange in the middle of the night at the wharf. Those pricks always lied.

Gabe glanced around, sizing up the possibilities of how to get past this guy. There was one way.

Still hiding behind the chunky side of the trawler, he took a step to the very edge of the dock, crouching down and stuffing his weapon in its back holster. Five feet between the water and the dock. He could do this. He just had to hang off the dock and work his way to the other side of the speedboat, then run to Lila.

Or fall in the water and get a bullet in his head for the effort.

He released his other leg and hung, bending his knees to stay dry. The wood dug into his hands, but he heard Lila again, which was enough to ignore the discomfort and start moving his hands to inch his way past the guy on the boat.

He got a rhythm in seconds and started making progress, ignoring a burn in his shoulders until the whole dock shook with a thud of weight and he froze. Peeking over the dock, he was directly across from the guy in the speedboat.

All the idiot had to do was look straight ahead and he'd see Gabe.

But he'd heard the noise, too. Lowering his weapon, the man looked at a lit phone in his hand. Almost instantly, he revved the engine to life, making all eleven hundred horses scream with power and the dock shake so hard Gabe nearly fell off.

That boat and that man could get to Lila so much faster than Gabe hanging off the side of the dock. He waited until the boat backed away, then Gabe hoisted his legs up and got one on the wharf just as the speedboat howled toward open water.

No, toward Lila at the end of the last dock. Gabe jumped to his feet, snagged her phone, and tore down the dock just as a bullet cracked into the wood a few inches from him, fired from one of the boats.

Ducking and pulling out his gun, Gabe ran full speed to Lila just as another bullet hit, a foot away. He didn't care. He had to beat that boat.

Lila took a few steps closer, about to use her foot to turn the body over when the roar of a mighty engine cut through the night. The go-fast boat, she presumed. Probably with her phone in hand. It had to be the only thing with the horsepower to make that kind of noise.

It almost drowned out the sound of a gunshot, making her stumble backward and look up to the third deck where the flash had come from.

She ducked and took aim at the upper deck, and the shooter fired again. Way over her head and down to the other end of the dock. That shooter wasn't firing at her, unless he was blind and stupid.

"Lila!" She turned again, seeing Gabe's silhouette as he ran toward her.

He was firing at Gabe!

"Get down!" she yelled, shooting again at the upper deck.

But the next bullet came right at her, just as Gabe plowed into her, slamming her arm into the dock as he covered her whole body with his. He rolled her away, avoiding the another shot that ripped up the planks right where she'd been.

The motorboat roared around to the wharf and Lila looked up, just in time to see a man scrambling down the ladder of the boat to escape. Gabe held her down, covering her completely, his weapon raised. Lila lifted her head and saw the man for one split second, his face catching enough moonlight for her to know that wasn't David Foster, but a stranger with penetrating eyes.

Gabe fired, but at the same moment, the driver of the boat fired at them, throwing off Gabe's aim when he dove to protect Lila again.

The man swung himself over the side of the boat, landed in the go-fast, and it took off. Gabe fired three more bullets, hitting the fiberglass, but if he managed to shoot either of the men, it was impossible to know. The go-fast was nothing but a distant sound in a matter of seconds. Professionals, without a doubt.

Slowly, Gabe got off of her, and she crawled to the body of the man on the dock, squinting at the corpse as Gabe kicked it over and revealed the face of CIA agent David Foster.

If he'd really had answers she needed, they'd died with him, which was exactly how the CIA always worked.

In fact, the more she sought those answers, the bigger her chances of ending up exactly like this guy.

Chapter Twenty-Three

The sound of a shrill scream cut through Gabe's sleep, followed by the rapid tap of flying footsteps, the crack of a door popping open, and the sudden *oomph* of a lunatic child landing on his chest.

"*Duuuuuuude.*" The voice was loud. Too loud for this hour. "Mummy told me to tell you to get up."

He squinted one eye open, peering up at the tiny face, the sparkling blue eyes, the mop of soft brown hair, and a lopsided smile that was so damn familiar it was like staring in a mirror to the past. "She needs to pay for that."

"How much?" he demanded, his little fingers digging into Gabe's bare chest.

"Ouch! You little demon, stop."

"Gabe." Lila's soft voice came from the hall.

"He's awake, Mummy! I did it. Just like you said."

Gabe inched to the side to look beyond Rafe at the woman he'd held in his arms after they'd escaped the harbor under the cover of night.

David Foster was the CIA's problem now, and Gabe knew they'd swoop in and quietly handle the death, keep it out of the papers, and let residents think an indigent had shot himself.

And they'd succeed.

Gabe had never hated the CIA, or Dexter Crain, more.

They'd left and gone directly to Rafe, not bothering with the villa. Nino had made a bed for Rafe out of the living room sofa, so Gabe and Lila had crashed in Gabe's room, whispering theories and thoughts until they finally fell asleep in each other's arms.

She must have gotten up when Rafe did, because now she wore baggy sleep pants he recognized as his and an oversize T-shirt that also came from his drawer. No makeup, hair in a ponytail, the sharp lines of her face softened by a smile.

She was so fucking beautiful it hurt to look at her.

He put two hands around the narrow waist in front of him. "Off, beast. I have to talk to your mother."

"Noooo!" He pounced on Gabe's chest, knocking the damn wind out of him.

"*Ooof*!" Gabe shot up and whipped Rafe gently to the side, laid him flat on his back and hovered over him. "Don't say no to me."

"No! No! Nooo—"

Gabe put a light hand over his mouth. "You can't do it."

He blinked, momentarily silent. "*Mwha*?"

"You can't go all day, one whole day, without saying the word no."

He licked his palm, the little animal.

Gabe freed him and started out of bed, suddenly aware he wore nothing but boxer briefs and couldn't be trusted to climb out of bed and be acceptable at this hour. Especially with that beautiful woman staring at him.

"*Noooo*!"

Shit. Is this what life with kids was like? Hiding the chub and being treated like a human bouncy house?

As if she read his expression, Lila stepped into the room,

dropping a duffel bag on the floor to hold her hand out to Rafe. "Come on," she said. He didn't budge. "Rafe, would you please—"

"Rafael!" Nino's baritone boomed down the hall, and Rafe shot straight up to attention, his eyes wide. "I need my sous chef!"

He scrambled off the bed. "That's me," he explained to them. "Sous chef. It means 'under' in French." He stopped in the doorway and pivoted, holding up a finger and suddenly looking more like his great-grandfather than his father. "But the French can't cook like Italians. Nino told me that."

He was gone before Nino bellowed again.

Gabe fell back on his pillow and groaned, wishing he could blow out a few f-bombs, but those days were gone, too.

"Good morning." Lila closed the door behind her and locked it, eyeing him as she approached.

"Finally, someone with some common sense." He flicked the comforter aside and tapped the bed. "Get in here and take off anything that belongs to me."

"Gabe, I can't."

"You will." He reached for her arm but stopped at the sight of the bruising there. "Good God. I hope I didn't do that last night."

"If you did, it was for a good cause." She climbed in and slid under his arm, settling her head in that spot on his chest that Isadora Winter had once owned. He loved when she was there. "You need to get up."

He took her hand and guided it south. "I am up."

"No, you need to face the people in this house."

"People?" He turned over, frowning. "Nino? Rafe?"

"Plus Chessie, Mal, and Poppy." She gestured toward the

bag. "They brought me some clothes from Rockrose. And…they're all out there talking to Rafe."

And looking at him. "What did you tell them?"

"I told them he's my son and thanked them for the clothes and came in here."

"Chessie." He huffed a breath. "She knows the Cuba kid's middle name was Rafael and she can take one look at him and know he's mine. And she knows about Isadora."

"And thinks Isadora died in a car accident in Cuba."

His gut rolled at the thought, the mourning he'd experienced, and that his family felt just because they loved him. They *loved* him. She had to understand that. He lifted her face to meet his gaze. "They can be trusted."

"Gabe."

"You have to understand these are my people. Plus, Chessie's going to work for the CIA—a move we will have to stop as soon as humanly possible. But honestly, telling them the truth is not even a choice at this point. They are going to figure it out if they haven't already."

"We can't do that, Gabe. We can't do anything. Don't you see? Someone in the CIA does not want this"—she tapped her head—"to get out. Not out of my head and not out in the world. And they'll win, one way or another. We can't fight people that powerful."

"Like hell we can't," he fired back. "Once it's public, there's not a damn thing they can do. Our first order of business is to get that thing out of your head. Then we have proof, and they can suck a giant bag of dicks."

She blew out a breath and clutched him closer. "They'll kill me before they let me talk. And you. And…" She lifted up. "Anyone who knows. So, you may think you're just trusting your family, but if you tell them about this implant, you are endangering their lives."

He couldn't argue that. "The joker in the speedboat damn near killed us last night." He sure as hell had tried, but they'd managed to stay alive *and* get the phone on the dock. "I love outsmarting those pricks."

"But we haven't outsmarted them. They'll be back. Maybe we should all three get new identities and leave this place."

Gabe practically spit. "And let them win? No fucking way."

"But don't tell your family yet. Not anything. At least wait until we come up with some way to get the implant out first, so I can deal with all the emotion and maybe not get killer headaches."

Of course, he hadn't even thought of that. "All right," he agreed. "But they're probably going to figure out who Rafe is. They're all pretty smart out there." He pulled closer and kissed her. "And when those headaches are gone, are we allowed to have sex under the same roof as that kid?"

"No. Not yet, anyway."

He closed his eyes. "*Fuuuuuuuuck.*"

She laughed. "You sound like him saying no. And if you teach him that word, I'll—"

He silenced her with a kiss. "I won't. Can we have a place with a guest house, then, so we can get nasty morning, noon, and night?"

She inched back, blinking at him. "Gabe."

"Yeah?"

"What are you talking about?"

What *was* he talking about? Life. With his kid and his…his kid's mother. He pushed up. "I think I smell peppers and eggs."

She didn't move for a moment, then, as always, she put

her fingers to her temples and pressed, instantly making his heart ache.

"I got to get that thing out," Gabe said.

She rolled her eyes. "Even you can't take an implant out."

"Watch me." He gave her a little nudge to get out of the bed. "Come on, let's go lie to my family and friends. It'll be fun."

"Fun?"

"Don't you remember? Everything's fun with me."

She let out a long sigh. "That's the problem. It is."

Chapter Twenty-Four

Just listening to Nino and Rafe bantering in the kitchen made Lila feel like a jackhammer let loose in her head. She couldn't even stand that much of a tug on her heart. But this was all she wanted—Gabe and Rafe and being surrounded by family.

Losing her parents hurt. Possibly losing Dex, who'd taken their place, hurt, too. But losing the possibility of this family? No, she simply couldn't take it. And unless she found a way to fix her problem, she couldn't enjoy this life. Any life, really.

"So let me get this all straight again." Chessie leaned closer to Lila, planting her elbows on the kitchen table and resting her chin on her knuckles. Her eyes—so incredibly blue like her brother's—were intent and unwavering as she looked at Lila. "You were with the CIA in DC, and you knew Gabe…when? How many years ago?"

Gabe surprised her by suddenly appearing behind Chessie's chair and landing his hands on her shoulders. "We need a good surgeon. Anybody know one?"

That got Chessie's attention—and that of everyone else in the room. Nino turned the sink faucet off and looked at them. Poppy froze in the act of clearing the dirty dishes on the table. And Mal put down his coffee cup to frown at Gabe.

Only Rafe, drying dishes next to Nino and uncharacteristically quiet, didn't react.

"What kind of surgeon?" Mal asked.

"Who's sick?" Nino demanded.

"Why?" Chessie chimed in.

Gabe closed his eyes in disgust. "Trustworthy. No one. Don't ask."

Poppy slowly put down a plate and looked at Gabe. "Mr. Gabriel, can I talk to you outside for a moment?"

Gabe didn't hesitate, backing away from the table and reaching to open the sliding door to the patio. "Right this way, Popcorn."

Lila watched them walk outside and close the door, a little surprised that he dropped the subject of finding a doctor so easily. At the beat of uncomfortable silence, she turned to the kitchen, her heart hurting just at the way Rafe looked at his great-grandfather.

"Rafe, you're behaving so nicely here," she commented.

He grinned at Nino. "That's five points, right?"

Lila felt her brows rise. "Five points for what?"

"It's a little game we're playing," Nino said. "Points, not dollars, for good stuff. Some taken away for bad stuff."

"And at the end, I get to go help in the garden with Nino!"

Lila pushed her chair back, intrigued. "You have a magic touch, Nino."

Nino shrugged a thick shoulder, returning to his work in the sink. "I'm just doing what I did when Gabe was this age because he was the same *ragazzaccio* that this little guy is."

Lila felt the blood drain from her face but forced herself to keep a blank, pleasant expression, any Italian she knew eluding her in that moment of panic. Did he know? "*Ragazz*…"

"Bad boy," Chessie supplied. "And he was. If a Rossi or Angelino—that's our cousins who lived with us—was out of line, you could put good money on Gabe being the one in the middle of the trouble."

Lila turned to her, hoping nothing in her face gave her away. "I bet that made him the most fun."

"You got that right." Chessie rocked back on the chair's two legs and studied Lila. "Pretty sure all the bad-boy genes in the whole family went to Gabe. And maybe"—her gaze shifted to Rafe—"they pass on."

Oh, they were smart all right. Of course they would look at Rafe and see Gabe stamped all over him. And they could do math, and they knew where Gabe was when a child Rafe's age would have been conceived. Mal had been there, too.

Was that why he was looking so hard at her?

She looked around from Chessie, whose face practically begged for truth, to Mal, a man she'd once called a trusted friend, to Nino, who had a mysterious ability to connect with her son.

All three of them looked right back at her, waiting. Just waiting. She tried to swallow, but her mouth was bone-dry. Gabe was right. It *was* time to trust them but not about the implant.

She turned to the patio, seeking Gabe's help, but he was on the phone and talking to Poppy at the same time. She seized the possible change of focus.

"I wonder what they're talking about," she mused.

"Jamaica," Nino said, coming away from the sink to get closer to the table and peer outside. "Her nephew's going in the slammer, and the two younger ones might get shuffled off to whatever the government does to kids like that."

"I'll tell you what the government does with kids like that," Chessie said, an undertone of bitterness in her voice. "They give them to strangers and let them die."

Lila sucked in a soft breath, tearing her attention from the patio back to Chessie.

"Not every government, Francesca," Mal said, pushing back from the table. "And you're just looking for someone to blame."

"Damn straight I am." She stood, too. "Lila, has Gabe told you the whole story of what happened to us in Cuba?"

Digging into her training for every imaginable ounce of nonchalance, Lila shook her head, not trusting her voice. "Not everything."

"He will, eventually," she said.

"Maybe," Lila managed. "He's pretty secretive."

Nino snorted. "And the Pope's holy."

"Catholic," Chessie corrected. "But he will tell you, I'm sure. I would, but he'd get all over my case for telling stories that are not 'need to know.'"

"Then don't," Mal said, coming around the table to put his hands on Chessie's shoulders. "Don't interrogate people, at least not obviously, and don't spill secrets." He pressed a kiss on her head. "Let's go take a walk, and I'll teach you more about being a good spy."

Chessie softened a little, her eyes still on Lila. "I'm surprised he hasn't told you about the woman he—"

"Francesca." Mal inched her away. "Don't."

She blew out a soft sigh and reached out. "I'm sorry," Chessie said. "I know you're going through a tough time with baiting this guy and all, but you need to know that Gabe…had a…"

"A relationship?" Lila offered.

"Actually, a..." But it was Chessie who paled this time, as her gaze moved beyond Lila to Rafe. "I was going to say a..."

Lila actually saw the moment it hit Mal and Chessie at the same time. Chessie still looked confused, like nothing going through her head could make sense. But, behind her, Mal's jaw slackened slightly, and his whole muscular frame seemed to draw back as shock and realization hit him.

He started to say something, but was literally speechless. They knew Rafe was Gabe's son. And right at that moment, they may have figured out who Lila was. At least Mal had.

"He had a child," Chessie said softly, a subtle note of accusation in her voice. "That boy would have been five in a few months. When is Rafe's birthday?"

The sliding glass door opened with a noisy rumble. "Let's go, Lila," Gabe said.

Everyone turned to him. "Go where?" she asked.

"Just come with me. Now."

Without offering some explanation to these two people staring at her in shock?

"Mummy!" Rafe came running over, reaching for her, and she automatically picked him up. "Will you leave me with Uncle Nino?"

"Uncle Nino?"

"That's what the whole family calls him," Chessie explained. "Ever since our cousins came to live with us." She stepped forward and put her fingers on Rafe's cheek, her touch gentle and tentative. "Everyone calls him Uncle Nino. Even his grandchildren and great..." Chessie's eyes filled as she stared at Rafe. "Great kids like Rafe," she finished.

Gabe took a step closer, putting an arm around Rafe and Lila, no doubt making the father/son likeness as obvious as possible. "You can stay with Uncle Nino, little man. I think you'll be here for a few more days because your mom and I have to go somewhere on business. Is that okay?"

"Yayyyy! Ninooooooo!"

Lila turned to throw a grateful glance at the old man, who stood drying his hands on a kitchen cloth, looking proud. And then she caught a glimpse of Chessie and Mal, who were trying so hard not to react or respond to the fact that Rafe was the child they'd gone to Cuba to find. The child they thought was dead.

Oh, my friends. It gets worse…or better, depending on how they'd feel when they found out everything. Would they welcome her or want to kill her all over again?

A knife of pain sliced through her head, reminding her that until she took care of that agony, she couldn't love any of them, anyway.

"Let's fly, baby." Gabe grabbed her arm, planted a kiss on Rafe's cheek before Lila put him on the floor and Gabe pulled her to the door.

"We have half an hour," he said as they walked toward the street. "On the way, you can tell me what the hell was going on in that room."

"As if you don't know," she said, hustling to keep up with him. "Half an hour for what?"

He didn't even slow his step, but did tighten his arm around her shoulders. "They guessed."

"Maybe," she admitted. "Please tell me where we're going. Jamaica?"

Now he did stop. "Why the hell would we go to Jamaica?"

"Isn't that what you were talking to Poppy about? Nino said she's having trouble with her family."

"No, but I need to help her solve those problems. And I

will. She was helping me this time." He reached the GTO parked on the street and opened the passenger door. "Remember the doctor we met at the Christmas party?"

"Oliver? Oliver Bradbury? Isn't he a cancer specialist?"

"He is." He nudged her into the seat and bent down to plant an unexpected kiss on her hair, suddenly reminding her very much of the affection Mal had just shown Chessie. "And a surgeon. And he loves Poppy, but then, who doesn't?"

She sat in the car, feeling her whole body decompress for a few seconds while he darted around to the driver's side. The pain in her head was steady and strong, and so was the one in her heart.

Gabe slid into his seat and started the car in one fluid, graceful motion, glancing at her while he reached for his seat belt. "Did you really think they were all blind and couldn't do math?"

"You're happy about it, aren't you?"

"I'm not upset, if that's what you're asking. Chessie looked a little blown away, though."

As she should be. Lila turned to look out the window at the passing scenery, putting herself in Chessie's shoes, who'd found a gravestone with her nephew's name when she'd gone to Cuba expecting, or at least hoping, to find the child alive and well. And now…he was in the kitchen doing dishes with Uncle Nino.

"She's going to hate me."

Gabe just laughed. "Chessie doesn't do hate. No one in my family does. Well, JP, but he's just a douchebag. Don't worry. They might be a little perplexed, but my family has known me as a spy, in some capacity or another, for a long, long time. They won't question anything too much."

She shifted in her seat, thinking of Mal. "I stood there

and pretended I'd just met Malcolm Harris a few days ago."

"It's going to be okay. We found a doctor, and he's going to meet with you right now, at his home. If he agrees to help, we'll go to his surgery center. They are open and staffed, but because it's Christmas week, there are no other patients."

"Oh my God, that's perfect. Thank you."

"Thank Poppy. You can thank me later, because if I have anything to do with it, that bastard of a bug is coming out of your head today."

"Today?"

He squeezed her leg. "If I have my way."

"When don't you have your way?"

He just grinned at her.

Chapter Twenty-Five

Gabe had his way.

He paced the waiting room of an upscale medical center tucked into a swanky side street in Naples, less than forty minutes from Barefoot Bay. The place was called IDEA, an acronym for some overblown bullcrap like Integrated Diagnostics through Experimental Analysis.

The place could have been called Joe's Bar and Surgery Center for all Gabe cared, as long as the Ken Doll doctor knew his stuff. He certainly seemed to. In fact, Dr. Oliver Bradbury, husband of the pretty hot-air balloon woman named Zoe, turned out to be an exceptionally cool dude who liked to push the medical envelope and made his name by refusing to follow the rules.

Gabe liked that, as Poppy, the world's most unlikely super spy, knew the minute he'd mentioned needing a doctor.

Gabe and Lila had talked with the doctor in the living room of his home in North Barefoot Bay while a precocious toddler named Maya careened in and out of the room, followed by her mother, Zoe, who was also too cool to ask questions.

Gabe was straight-up blunt with the guy, telling him enough of Lila's backstory that no one with a brain would think they were making this shit up.

Bradbury was no stranger to the scalpel, and even though what they explained to him was obviously nothing he ever trained for in med school, he agreed to help them in his surgery center that very afternoon.

Despite its hip name and pricey leather sofas, the place was, essentially, a hospital. Maybe not a traditional one, but Gabe was, for all intents and purposes, alone in a hospital room while the woman he…

Oh hell. Did he love her? Or did he love who she used to be? Or did he love the idea of loving her? Or was he just—

His phone buzzed with a text from Chessie.

We gotta talk, bro.

Yes, they did. Who paced a hospital room alone, anyway? He needed his sister. And brother-in-law-to-be. And grandfather. And son. He tapped the screen, issuing orders he knew would get him another thing he wanted today: the people he loved the most right here in this room with him.

Forty-five minutes later, he heard Rafe squeal as the elevator doors opened and then a low-pitched warning from Nino, followed by a sudden hush. Who knew the old man was a kid whisperer? No wonder Gabe loved that man so much. Gabe had been getting the same treatment Rafe was his whole life and hadn't even realized it.

Chessie came around the corner, her eyes bright with expectation and the determination she used when she was facing an impossible computer bug that she fully intended to squash.

"Is Lila okay?" she asked, reaching to hug him.

"She's going to be." He hoped.

Mal followed close behind, giving Gabe a fist bump. "'Cept she's not Lila," he said under his breath.

Gabe gave a quick and silent nod. "Not in front of the kid," he said.

As if on cue, Rafe came running in and flew at Gabe. "Where's my mum?" he asked, using, as always, the British reference she must have taught him. Even poor little Rafe had a cover and didn't know it.

"She's talking to a doctor right now."

His eyes grew wide. "Does she have to get a shot? I hate shots. Don't you?"

"Depends on what kind." Gabe easily shifted him to his hip, catching Nino's eyes as the old man lumbered into the area.

"What kind of doctor's office is called IDEA?" Nino asked. "They're not supposed to have ideas. They're supposed to have answers. That's what I'd want my doctor's place to be called: Answers."

Chessie rolled her eyes, but Poppy came in next, looking around like she was on a White House tour. "Very, very nice, Mr. Gabriel."

For crying out loud, he wasn't *buying* the place.

But she kept nodding with approval, running a finger over the mahogany panels of an armoire that housed a TV he'd shut off when he walked in. "I heard Dr. Oliver's place was high class and now I see why."

Just then, Dr. Bradley came in, and they all turned to him, and Gabe fought the urge to lunge forward and demand to see Lila. Instead, he set Rafe down and walked toward the other man so they could have privacy.

"We've completed a battery of tests," he said. "Why don't you come with me, and we can talk with Lila."

Gabe signaled for his family to sit tight and followed the

doc behind closed doors to a small medical prep room, where Lila was in a bed wearing a hospital gown and a tentative smile.

"Is this good news?" he asked as the doctor led him in.

"Good that you are one hundred percent correct about an implant in the base of Lila's neck."

Good Lord. Gabe reached for her hand and shared a look with her. "Can you take it out?"

"I think so."

"Today?"

"Actually, yes. She's in excellent health, except for the headaches, and my partner and a special surgery nurse are on their way in if Lila gives the okay. They will have to be briefed on the situation."

Gabe gave a questioning look to Lila. "That's a no-brainer to me, but it's not my brain on the table. What do you think?"

"I want it out, Gabe."

"And that will end the headaches?"

"I don't know," the doc said. "The scans and MRI just tell us that there's a foreign object just under the brain stem. I can't tell what it's doing, although by the placement, I would say it's attached to a gland that secretes monoamines, like serotonin, melatonin, dopamine. Could a certain neurotransmitter spike something in the nerves near that to cause pain? Yes, I suppose that is entirely possible. We have to go in and find out."

Go in. Gabe swallowed hard and squeezed Lila's hand. "So, brain surgery?"

"Not technically," Bradbury replied, flipping through a chart and studying a black-and-white image. "It's a surface removal at the base of her neck. I don't have to go under the skull, or it couldn't be done, not here and not by me."

"Is there a risk?" Gabe asked.

"It's surgery," he said calmly. "There are always risks, but the pain you're describing, Lila?" He shook his head. "No one should live like that, and I feel qualified to at least go in and take a pass at it. No guarantees this will work." The doctor lifted his file. "I'll give you two a minute alone, and then we'll take it from there."

After he left, Gabe turned to Lila, seeing how pale she was and immediately recognizing the shadow of pain around her eyes. "You have a headache now," he said.

"Like a Mack truck is plowing through my brain."

He lifted her hand in both of his, bringing it to his chest. "Why? What are you feeling? Fear? Uncertainty about this?"

She blinked, her eyes brimming. "Love. It gets me every time."

"You love this studly doctor and his sexy scalpel?" he teased. The words caught in his throat as he said them.

She smiled at him. "I love the man who will turn the world upside down for me, who fights and claws and takes risks for me, and who…" She squeezed his hand. "Who loves me."

He lowered his head to press his lips against hers. "Then let's try to make it painless for you to love me back."

She reached up and pulled his head closer to deepen the kiss. "You can tell your family," she said into his mouth.

"Good, 'cause they're all in the waiting room."

She laughed against his mouth. "I should have guessed as much." She eased him back. "Rafe, too?"

"Yeah, but I won't tell him anything, I promise. We can do that together. And when we do, it won't hurt." It might be one of the best moments of any of their lives, if this surgery worked.

The door opened, and Bradbury came back in, a question on his face.

"Let's roll, Doc," Gabe said. "And please let me see whatever you take out of her head, because it's evidence, and someone is going to pay for this."

With one more reassuring kiss, Gabe left the room and headed back to where his family waited.

He looked around and saw only Chessie, Mal, and Nino.

"Poppy took Rafe downstairs to look at the aquarium," Chessie said, coming over to him. "Then they're going for ice cream."

God bless that woman. "Perfect," he said. "Lila's going into surgery now."

Chessie gasped softly, and Nino and Mal stood, concern darkening their expressions. Gabe took a breath and closed his eyes, then gestured for them to sit back down.

"I have to tell you something." He crossed the room and took the seat next to Nino. "Stay near me, old man. If you have a heart attack, I can drag your ass right into surgery."

Nino's dark eyes narrowed, and his bushy brows drew together. "I already know that boy is my great-grandson."

"He's Isadora's child, isn't he?" Chessie demanded, not able to wait one more second. "Lila somehow got him and is pretending to be his mother. Right? Am I right?"

"Partially. He *is* Isadora's son. And Lila is…" Was he certain? One hundred percent absolutely certain? Not a shadow of a lingering doubt, right? Of course not. "Lila *is* Isadora."

Blue. Everything was deep, dark, endlessly, cerulean

blue. The color of night. The color of seduction. The color of eyes that made her happy, and hurt so much.

And everything was warm, deliciously, wonderfully warm and wet. In fact, water sluiced over every inch of her body and hair as she floated, helplessly suspended by the warm, blue water.

She was in the water with Gabe, wrapped in his arms. The moon hung over Varadero Beach as he turned her in his arms, whispered her name, and ran his fingers through her long, dark curls.

Isadora…I adore ya.

Euphoria engulfed her, warm as the water, drowning her in love.

"Lila, can you wake up?"

The words were muffled by the water, nothing but noise that made no sense. She let herself sink deeper into the water. It was calming and painless…bliss.

"Ms. Wickham, please try to open your eyes."

The voice, a stranger's voice, didn't register. Nothing clicked. Just the water and the warmth and the hand that suddenly, softly pressed against her cheek.

Isadora…I adore ya.

"Hey." A whisper in her ear, secret and sweet. "Come back to me, baby."

And everything made sense. The world was right and good. Gabe was there. Always, in the blue water, under the moon, laughing, kissing, promising. She would fight anything in her way, brave any pain, crash through any obstacle for Gabe.

Because he had done that for her.

The first finger of bright light jabbed at her eyes, pulling a moan from her throat.

"There we go." A woman spoke. "Time to wake, dear."

"Mmmm." It was the best she could manage. Plus, she didn't want to leave the warm water or blue world. She didn't want to leave—

"Lila."

Gabe. No, she wasn't Isadora. She was still Lila. She forced her eyes open again, the world a bright, cold blur with no water, no moon, no…

Blue eyes peering down at her. Beautiful eyes. His eyes. The eyes of Gabe, the eyes that matched her son's, the two men she loved. Her…family.

She loved them so much, and it always, always hurt.

But nothing hurt now. Not even her head.

Her eyes popped wide, an injection of hope rolling through her veins like hot, loaded morphine. "My head."

"I know, it hurts." The woman appeared over her now, all efficient and bright, the perfect nurse. "I'm Mary. Do you remember me?"

Mary. Her mother's name. Her mother who collected rosaries and prayed to a saint whose name she had. A lovely, sweet, solid name. A lovely, sweet, solid woman. She braced for the shot of pain that always came with that thought, with that poignant deep *love* she truly felt for her mother…but there was nothing.

"My head," she repeated, trying to sit up to make her point, but Mary put her hand on her shoulder.

"It's going to hurt for a few days where the incision is."

"That's just it," she mumbled. "It doesn't."

Suddenly, Gabe was in front of her again, nudging the nurse away. "It doesn't hurt?"

"Not on the inside." She closed her eyes for a moment and waited for the tap of the first pain in the base of her neck, and there was discomfort. A slight pulling of her skin. On the outside. Inside, it was just…soft. Blurry. Peaceful. Blue.

The way her head never was. Usually, it was edgy, harsh, and angry red with pain.

"What did he find?" She looked at Gabe, her brain fuzzy still but never so dulled that she would say anything she'd been trained not to say in public.

"We're waiting for the doctor. Mary just called me in." He put his hand on her cheek and caressed, the way he had in the dream. In the water. On the beach in Cuba. She remembered it all now, sighing softly, drifting in and out of the remnants of anesthesia.

When she opened her eyes, he was even closer, even more beautiful, and a surge of love electrified her whole body, waking her and making her brace for the…

"There's no pain," she whispered, feeling a smile pull at her face.

He leaned closer. "And no British accent. Was that part of an implant, too?"

"Oh. I don't…" There it was. "I just forgot. I forgot everything except…" She tried to lift her hand, but an IV was secured, and moving hurt. "You."

He smiled. "Good girl." Then he stood and turned at the sound of someone coming into the room.

"Let me see her." Dr. Bradbury stepped next to Gabe, who instantly made way for the other man. "Mary, we need privacy."

Mary disappeared at the order, and Dr. Bradbury gestured for Gabe to move around to the other side of the bed. "There was definitely an implant at the base of your neck," he said. "I've never seen anything like it."

Gabe snorted softly. "Because you don't know the CIA."

A dozen different emotions spiraled through her, ranging from fury to shame, and no small amount of disbelief. Why? Why would they do that to her? Did

Dexter know? How could they do this to one of their own?

One look at Gabe and she knew he was thinking the same thing, only with thoughts far more murderous.

"How do you feel?" the doctor asked.

"My head doesn't hurt. Not inside. Do you think this implant really was the cause of my headaches?"

He considered that, tilting his head, a handsome, movie-star type with kind but sharp eyes and what she imagined was a very successful bedside manner.

"I am no expert on how those work, but the device was planted exactly in a way to send a pulse through your hypothalamus when serotonin was secreted. Very much on the surface, which made it easier for us, but still situated in a way to do the job. I hate to say this, but the placement makes me think whoever put it there didn't want you to enjoy one moment of real happiness or the contentment that secretes serotonin. And, frankly, that's some of the most disgusting medicine I've ever heard practiced."

She felt her eyes shutter in agreement.

"I will say," he added, "whoever did this was an expert. I don't know much about secret-agent implants, but whoever inserted this knew what he was doing. My guess is you aren't the only spy dealing with this kind of…sickness." And he meant that on every level, she could tell.

"But she's better?" Gabe asked. "No aftereffects?"

"None that I'm aware of, and I'm really not the neurologist you need to see."

"Who we need to see is the head of intelligence in this country," Lila murmured. Even if they let her live long enough to do that, what would she do? Sue? Spill it to the media? Ruin Dex's life or whoever ruined hers? How would that give her back these pain-inflicted years?

"Do you have the implant?" Gabe asked.

"Yes and I cleaned it." Dr. Bradbury stepped to the side and slid a rolling tray over, lowering it so Lila could see. There, on a white piece of gauze, was a square no bigger than half her baby fingernail. The bastard that had made her head hurt.

Gabe leaned close, not touching, but examining it. Slowly, he stood and shot a fierce look at Lila, his gaze full of something she couldn't interpret.

Dr. Bradbury stepped away, wordlessly handing the issue and problem to Gabe and Lila. "I'll keep you here for a few hours. After that, you can go home, but you have to rest. Bed rest. Nothing strenuous, nothing physical. I'll see you in three days, and if you're willing, I'll refer you to a neurologist for further testing. Right now, avoid anything that could cause a headache."

The only thing that ever caused her head to hurt was…love. She glanced at Gabe, who'd picked up a long pair of tweezers to turn the device over for closer examination. How could she avoid loving him? She more than loved him, with every breath. "I'll try," she said.

Satisfied, the doctor left, and Gabe straightened again, his eyes wild with emotion.

"We'll get to the bottom of this," she assured him. "I won't let anyone get away with this. No matter how much I think they care about me."

"Don't blame Dexter for this," Gabe said.

What? "The director, then. Someone in that damn agency is going to pay. The United States of America cannot inflict torture on its agents." Her voice rose with the rage that rocked her.

"The United States of America did not inflict any torture on you," Gabe said, his voice nearly a whisper.

"Are you kidding? Those headaches were—"

"The Soviet Union did."

She just stared at him, speechless.

"Trust me, I know those bastards. This implant is Russian. It's made by the same company I was spying on, Sevtronics. Largest electronic device manufacturer in Russia."

"Wha…how? What?" She barely mouthed the word. "They may have made it, but that doesn't mean they implanted it. Only CIA had access to my medical procedures."

Gabe gave her a look, and she immediately knew.

"There are spies among us," she whispered. "Dexter always said so."

He lifted a shoulder. "Someone infiltrated your operation and your operating room. You heard the man. You're likely not the only one. We may never find out who did this to you, Lila."

She shook her head and cringed when the move hurt her, but she lifted her hand to her mouth as something clicked in her newly cleared brain. "It was Russian!"

"That's what I just told you."

"No, no. The accent of the man who made me put my phone down at the marina. The one driving the speedboat."

Gabe frowned. "No, he didn't have an accent."

"You wouldn't hear it," she countered. "It's my training, and I can hear accents."

"Are you kidding? I can spot the slightest bit of a dialect and pinpoint it immediately."

"An American dialect, yes. But there was just something sort of under his language. It's hard to explain to someone who hasn't studied linguistics, but Gabe," she grabbed his arm. "You know what this means? It isn't Dex. It isn't the CIA. We can't blame them."

His lip curled as if he realized they were back to square one.

"I have to talk to Dex now. He can help us, get us back into the intelligence community and go through the names of every person who was in a surgery center with me, and we—"

He put his finger over her mouth. "As soon as you're better, and not a minute earlier. First, you heal, then we'll track this down, Lila."

Lila. She gently set her head back on the pillow. "Am I Lila? That thing has been inside me, changing me as much as the surgery that broke my nose and the chemicals that made me a blonde. Who is Lila, anyway?"

He frowned at her. "You want to be called Isadora?"

"That's my name, Gabe, but I can't be Isadora. She's dead. And Rafe would be confused."

"He's four. He won't remember what name you had when he was a kid. You're his mum."

"With an English accent and blond hair." She reached to a lock that had slipped out of the special surgery bonnet on her head. "Which reminds me, I'm really sick of being a blonde."

He grinned slowly, leaning close to kiss her. "And I was just starting to like you as a blonde."

She lifted her IV-free hand and inched him back. "You'll like me even better now."

He lifted a brow. "I think I've said this to you once before, Isadora…"

I adore ya. She waited for the rhyme he loved, hoping she didn't feel disappointment as he leaned into her ear to whisper the rest.

"Whatever your name is," he whispered. "I love you."

She closed her eyes and let the words she'd heard in her head echo over her heart, and there was no pain. Only love. Sweet, painless love.

Chapter Twenty-Six

"You just rest, child. I'll be back in the morning." Poppy tiptoed out of the bedroom, and Lila kept her eyes closed, hoping the fussing would end so she could be alone. With Gabe.

They were well past forty-eight hours, and she'd get cleared to be up and about tomorrow, but Lila felt like a new woman.

No, an old woman. The old woman she used to be. She was dying to test out this new head with Rafe and Gabe. Eager to let herself feel the deepest love and not suffer for it.

That problem was solved, but what about her safety and security? And Rafe's?

She hadn't been able to talk to Dexter yet. She'd sent a text about the death of David Foster, and the strangest thing happened: radio silence.

Maybe Dex was trying to find out more about David's involvement in what was happening before getting back to her.

She pushed her worries aside for now, tired of thinking about it all. Tonight, finally, she was free to be herself in the confines of this villa. Gabe had made her rest, let Poppy nurse her, and now she felt fantastic. All she wanted to do was be with the man she loved and not be in pain.

In fact, she couldn't wait to be in pleasure.

Certain Poppy should be gone by now, she threw the covers back and got out of bed, her every step strong and sure. She'd really had no idea how much she'd lived in constant pain, or the fear of it.

She stepped into the hallway to hear dishes in the kitchen sink, stopping to make sure that was Gabe and not Poppy. If the woman saw her out of bed, there'd be hell to pay.

"C'mere, Popcorn," Gabe said. "I have to show you something."

Oh, for heaven's sake, she was still there. Lila didn't dare move for fear Poppy would hear her.

"I only have a moment, Mr. Gabriel. There's a new guest at one of the villas, and my goodness gracious, she's demanding. Wouldn't even take the box of tissue I brought. Had to have a particular brand. And only a certain kind of sparkling water from France. As if the country the water comes from really matters."

"I know." But Lila could tell from his voice that he couldn't muster, as Gabe would say, two fucks about the difficult new guest. "Can you just look at my computer for a second?"

She heard Poppy hustle to the living room—of course. He said, *Jump*, and she said, *Through which roof?* Smiling at the loyalty, Lila stayed still, expecting whatever he was going to show her would last only a moment.

"You see this woman, Alyssa Fitzgerald?"

"She's pretty. Friend of yours?" She tsked loudly. "I don't know why you'd want any other woman than the one in that room I just left."

Lila smiled. *You go, Poppy.*

"She's a lawyer," Gabe interjected. "Based in Kingston. And she's taking Isaiah's case as a favor to me."

Even twenty feet away she heard Poppy gasp. "Really?"

"He's going to have to do some community service and pay a fine, she thinks, but I'll cover that."

No surprise, a wave of affection rolled over Lila. There he went again, saving the world all by himself.

"Oh, Mr. Gabriel!" She could practically hear Poppy squeezing the life out of Gabe. "Thank you, thank you. And thank you, Jesus, for putting this great man, named for your favorite angel, in my life. You are an awesome and wondrous Lord!"

I feel you, honey, Lila thought. She wanted to thank someone for putting Gabe in her life, too. The sheer joy she felt probably matched what was going through Poppy at that moment, and best of all, there was no pain in her head. Just happiness in her heart.

"But it's not free, my friend."

Lila inched forward, not sure she'd heard right. Gabe would make Poppy pay for this?

"I have a thousand dollars from the swear jar!" Poppy said.

He let out a soft hoot. "Shit."

"A thousand and one."

"I gotta stop that now," he said. "I seriously have to clean up my act."

Of course he did. Because he had a son now. Even more happiness sparked through Lila, making her want to leap into the living room and hug them both. But then she'd be sent right back to bed.

"Thank you, Mr. Gabriel," Poppy said for the tenth time. "Let me write down this lady's name and see if I can get in touch with her."

"Not necessary. I've lined it all up." Of course he had.

"You do like to do things on your own, don't you?"

"So I've been told."

Lila smiled at the wryness in his voice. At least, it sounded wry. Or was he just sick of being reminded that he was the ultimate lone wolf? Maybe he was just coming to terms with the fact that he wasn't going to be alone anymore.

Lila pressed her hand to her chest as if she needed help to keep her heart from popping out from an overdose of happiness.

"Mr. Gabriel, I'll work for free forever, but that won't be enough to pay for this. What does this good lawyer charge?"

"Nothing for you."

"But you just said it's going to cost me."

"Not in cash, Pop-Tart. In love."

"I don't think I'm your type, baby boy."

Lila had to cover her mouth to keep from laughing at the conversation. "You'd be wrong," Gabe said. "I like my women strong, smart, capable, and trustworthy. You are all of that and more."

"Aw, child. You make my heart flutter."

Mine, too.

"But you do have to do something for me," Gabe said.

"I will do anything for you, Mr. Gabriel." True that. She'd walk to Mars and back for the man, which only made Lila love him more.

"Would you live with a man you aren't married to?"

What? Poppy's stuttering reply sounded exactly like the one in Lila's brain. Why would he ask her that?

"I…I…no. I would not. I'm a virgin, Mr. Gabriel, the bride of Jesus Christ."

"I'm not asking you to sleep with him, just consider sharing a house."

"With who?" Good question. Her brows drawn, Lila took one silent step closer to hear the answer.

"Nino."

Poppy gave a soft hoot. "One of us might be dead before a week is out, and I'm afraid I'd be the one going to hell for the killing."

"He's not that bad, and you two have really been getting along better."

"I can tolerate him," she said. "Mostly. But why would I?"

"Because I think I can get you a nice big house to live in, right out here on Mimosa Key."

Lila took another step out of burning curiosity. What was the master controller controlling now?

"And why would we need a big house?"

"To live in."

"I live in a house over on the mainland."

"Alone. But you could live here on the island, with Nino."

The older woman grunted. "Or Satan. Take your pick."

"I need you to do this because Nino needs kids around. Lots of kids. Not just mine."

Lila leaned against the wall, sighing contentedly.

"And what about you, Mr. Gabriel?"

What about him, Lila wondered, biting her lip as she waited for his response.

"I'm not sure yet," Gabe replied, each word a little pinprick in Lila's heart.

He wasn't sure? She was. She was positive. She loved him. She'd stay here, and he'd have his business, and they'd raise Rafe, or…

Or was this still Gabe Rossi, the original lone wolf with a brick wall around his heart?

"Of course I would take care of Nino." Poppy heaved a sigh as though he'd asked the moon. "But I don't know why we'd need a big house, and who are these kids you are talking about?"

"The Bible boys," he said. "Isaiah and…what are their names? Moses and Methuselah?"

"My nephews? Isaiah's little brothers are Ezra and Samuel."

"Yeah, them. The lawyer I found you specializes in international adoptions, too, and she says arranging for those boys to come here and live with you, in a big house, would be relatively easy for her to arrange. But they'd need stability. Two adults. Two adults who don't want to kill each other."

Lila's heart softened at what he was doing for Poppy.

"My nephews? My boys? Here on this island? Living with me and Nino?"

"Isn't that why I've been swearing all these months?"

"Thank you, Mr. Gabriel."

"And Jesus," he added.

"And thank you, Jesus! Praise the Lord! Praise the—"

"Shhh. You'll wake up our patient. Hell, you'll wake up the dead."

"I'm not going to charge you for that, Mr. Gabriel, but when you are around that sweet little Rafe, you must stop swearing. You must."

"I will," he promised. "I'll do anything for that kid."

Lila let out a soft sigh, and not just because she couldn't love the man more if she tried. But because it didn't hurt anymore to feel that way. She could close her eyes and experience the bone-deep thrill of falling in love, and it didn't cause the burning, excruciating pain that had become part of her very being.

How could she possibly thank him for that gift?

She knew how she wanted to start. Now. "What's all the commotion about?" she asked, entering the room.

"Miz Lila! You need to get back in bed."

"I don't want to be in bed anymore." At least, not alone.

Gabe was already up and coming toward her. "You're supposed to be in bed." He reached his hands out and put them on her shoulders, a sweet light in his eyes that made her legs weak. "I'll go with you. I know how to keep you there."

"Oh my my. I best be leaving." Behind Gabe, Poppy hoisted herself to her feet and beamed at him. "Thank you for being wonderful and full of surprises, Mr. Gabriel."

He blew her a kiss, but his full attention was on Lila. "Did you hear that? I'm wonderful and full of surprises."

She looked up at him, studying his expression. "You certainly are." She took his hand and waited for the door to lock behind Poppy. "Come to bed with me."

"You need to rest."

She poked his chest. "Rossi, go put the security lock on that door and get your sweet ass in the sack with me."

His jaw dropped, and then he broke into a giant smile. "Well, well, well. The magic of medicine."

"What?"

He lifted her fingers to his mouth for a kiss. "Welcome back, Isa. I've missed you."

Chapter Twenty-Seven

When Gabe came into the bedroom, he expected to find Lila naked and under the covers, but she was sitting on the edge of the bed with a strange look on her face.

"You okay?"

"I guess." She tucked her feet under her and got settled on the bed. "It's just that when you called me Isa, it felt...wrong. Weird."

"You reminded me so much of her. She was pretty fond of my sweet ass, as you recall."

But she didn't smile. "I know, it's just such a strange sensation. The headaches are gone, but I feel like...like I just got out of four years in prison."

He sat next to her. "Yeah, you did. And you were essentially in solitary confinement."

She nodded, chewing on her lip. "And we know what that does to prisoners."

He brushed her hair back and kissed her cheek. "It's going to take time and patience and lots and lots and lots of sex."

Smiling, she nuzzled into his hand. "Lots."

"Epic amounts of sex." He kissed her head and stroked

her back as he urged her under the comforter. She wore nothing but a long T-shirt, making him want to strip off his clothes and climb in naked.

He pulled his own T-shirt over his head, eyeing her as she dropped back on the pillow, a troubled expression still on her face. “We’ll take it slow,” he said.

“I don’t want to take it slow. It’s just that when you called me Isa, something inside me slipped a little.”

“I won’t call you that if you don’t want me to.” He opened the button of his jeans. “You just reminded me of her. Of you.” He laughed. “It is you, right?”

Still chewing her lip, she stared at him as he unzipped and stripped down, but left the boxer briefs because he didn’t want to get all hard and distracted until he made one hundred percent certain she was ready.

“You still want me to get in there with you?”

“Yes.” He got under the covers and slipped his hand under the T-shirt, finding smooth flesh, his body already responding to the feel of her. “Let’s start with something really slow and easy that won’t make Doctor McDreamy mad at me.”

She fought a smile. “He is pretty cute.”

He found her breast and gave a gentle squeeze. “He can kiss my—”

“Gabe.”

“—astronomical bill for his services.” He thumbed her nipple, earning a little moan as it popped to life.

He kissed her cheeks and inhaled her hair and slid his hand slowly and carefully down her body. “We gotta take it easy,” he murmured into the next kiss. “Doctor’s orders.”

“My head doesn’t hurt, but…” She took his hand and dragged it between her legs. “This does.”

She wore nothing but a tuft of silky, sweet hair, and his

fingers immediately found their spot. He moved on top of her, kissing her mouth, tasting the sweet, familiar flavors of Lila.

"Lila...Lila." He whispered her name a few times, letting the sound of it really roll around in his mouth. "I love that name now. It fits you."

She pushed him up and searched his face. "Are you sure? Are you absolutely sure you're not disappointed that I'm not Isadora anymore?"

Seriously? They were going to go through this just because he made a quick joke about something she said?

"She's not gone completely. She sneaks out, and I hear her laugh..." He kissed her forehead. "And she says things that only Isadora Winter would say..." And her eyes. "And she feels things that can only be felt with me."

She sighed into the kiss on her lips. "She certainly does. So you're okay with that? Isadora is gone forever, and Lila is the woman you want."

He rolled his erection against her. "Does that feel like I'm okay?"

"Mmmh. Yeah." She put her hand inside his briefs and circled his hard-on with her hand, pulling a grunt of sheer pleasure from his chest.

"Then I'm yours, Gabe Rossi. Lila Wickham is yours."

She stroked him slowly with one hand, using the other to push off his underwear. Freed, he started tasting everything he could find, while she wrapped her hands around him and lovingly stroked, up and down, cupping his balls, every moan of appreciation making him swell with need.

"Lila...I love ya."

She laughed softly as he pushed her T-shirt up to suck and kiss one bare breast, licking it to a precious peak. He closed his eyes and tasted her again, not caring that the body was different, or her face, or her hair, even the slender hands that rode up and down his cock.

It didn't matter what she looked like. The essence was the woman he loved today as much as the day he lost her five years ago. More, even. She'd been toughened up by life and softened up by motherhood.

He lifted himself up, and she started to slide down to get her mouth on him.

"No," he said. "Stay still. We have to take it easy."

She gave him a *get real* look. "I'm fine."

"Maybe…for a minute."

She laughed, a throaty, sexy sound that was every bit the laugh he once loved to hear, pushing him onto his back.

"I'm in no pain," she promised him, kneeling and inching her way south. "I feel amazing."

"Good, 'cause I'm in a lot of pain and…" He stroked her skin and finger-combed her hair as she moved down. "You do feel amazing."

She laughed, but it was muffled as she took him into her mouth, and Gabe closed his eyes and gave in to the raw pleasure. Her body was different, her name, her hair…but she still made him want to cry with that mouth of hers.

She curled her tongue over the tip and drew him into the heat of her lips. All the while, she moved her hand over his shaft, pulling him closer and closer to the edge, filling his balls so he could spill into her.

Into her. He had to be in her. He eased her back up, grabbing a condom from the drawer where he'd put them in preparation for this very moment. "Come on, Lila. Let me love you."

She took the top, her silky blond locks falling over her shoulders. Very carefully, she slipped the T-shirt up, exposing her body completely as she took it over her head without touching the bandage at the back.

He reached up to cup her breasts, vaguely aware of the thread of a scar under her nipple, faded and barely visible.

"I love these, too." He assured her. "I love you. You. The strong, capable woman who makes me laugh and—"

She grabbed the condom from his hand. "Don't go all mushy on me now, Gabe Rossi." She sheathed him, her hands trembling. "I need you inside me."

He didn't argue, reaching up to bring her closer and put her right into place. She was wet, ready, hot, slick, and tight, taking him all the way in one thrust.

Nothing had changed there. He fit in her pocket like he belonged there, swelling as he plunged in and out, lost in her, lost like he always was and always would be.

She whimpered and moaned, clutching him, riding him, taking him completely. Forced to go easy, he slowed them down, kissing her mouth as they joined in perfect rhythm, a timeless beat of life and love.

Squeezing him with her hands and arms and legs, he felt her snap loose and give up, falling into her orgasm with ragged breaths, pulling him along with her.

"I love you, Lila. You are mine. You know that? Mine."

"Even if I'm not Isadora anymore? Are you sure?"

Why the hell did she keep asking him that?

"But I'm…"

"Mine," he finished for her, kissing her, feeling the electricity and vibration and need building to a breaking point. "Mine. And I love you."

She made a sound, acknowledging the phrase. "Yes, Gabe, yes. Yes, I do. I do love you, too. I'm sorry, I'm *sorry* I'm not—"

"Stop. Stop. Just…that." But he didn't have any brain

power to decipher her sex talk. He had to come. Had to. He pressed his lips against her jaw, losing the fight, losing control, and exploding into her like a cannon shot, furious and fierce no matter how gently he wanted to take it.

Each jolt to his body was electric, endless, exquisite. He couldn't stop. Couldn't stop slamming into her, over and over and over again until there was nothing left in him.

She fell on him, her body sleek with sweat and heavy with exhaustion. "I like when you call me Lila. It really turns me on."

"Could get dicey in the supermarket."

"It's just that I want to be sure you don't regret losing her and getting me."

God*damn*. Still, he wanted to be patient. She *had* been in prison, and he had to respect the aftereffects of that. "Clearly, Dr. Bradbury plucked the common sense out of you along with that implant."

"I'm serious, Gabe. I don't look like her, and I feel like an impostor. Isa is one thing to you, and I'll never *be* her again."

He inched her back up again to look at her. "How many times do I have to tell you that a body and hair and face don't make a person? It's you I love. I know you, and I know that tongue. Tongue's the same, right? You're no impostor. Okay?"

She smiled, her dark eyes dancing. "Okay."

"How's the wound?" he asked. "I tried not to accidentally touch the bandage."

"It's fine."

"And the headaches?"

She just sighed. "Blissfully, wondrously gone. The only thing that hurts my head is figuring out who did this to me and why and how. And when they're coming back."

"Luke's on the lookout, and no one is coming near this villa or that bungalow. They're going to have to draw you out, and next time, I won't be alone."

She nodded. "But since I'm better now, can we talk to Dex?"

He sighed. "I'm still not a hundred percent sold on him."

"You think he works for the Russians?" she asked.

The thought had crossed his mind, but she'd been in no shape to discuss it. And right now? He didn't want to ruin this and get into an argument.

"Shhh." He turned slowly, bringing her next to him so he could take off the condom. "Not now. You need to rest. It's late, get some sleep."

He pushed up and walked to the bathroom on surprisingly unsteady legs, closing the door to pee, which would take an hour after that kind of sex.

With one hand on the wall, he leaned forward, closed his eyes and tried—failed—to wipe the smile off his face. He *loved* her. And he was going to spend the rest of his life with her.

Behind him, a handbag she'd hung on the bathroom door hummed like a phone was vibrating in it. He frowned, because her phone was in the bedroom, he was certain of it. But the rhythmic hum was definitely a phone in there.

After a second, the sound stopped, and he washed his hands and opened the door, ready to tell her that something had buzzed in her bag, but she was conked out. He didn't have the heart to wake her, but then it hummed again…and he could see her phone right there on the dresser, dark and silent.

Maybe she had another one for Rafe emergencies? He closed the door and unzipped the bag, not seeing any light or sign of a phone. But he could feel it and discovered a well-disguised zipper in the back. Why would she hide a phone there?

He pulled it out and could see most of a text from Dexter Crain.

He automatically curled his lip at the name. Gabe just didn't like him.

Check in when you can. Anxious to know if he still believes you. I know this has been a tough one, L, but you've done an incredible job making

His heart stopped. Literally, he felt his chest grow ice cold at the words and unfinished message.

If he still believes you...

What the fuck? He started to yank open the door, then froze, his brain suddenly clear, crystal clear, like a sharp shard of ice was stabbing sense into his head.

She was lying. She *wasn't* Isadora Winter.

His very first instinct had been right—it always was. He tapped the phone furiously, trying to read the rest of the text, but he needed a passcode.

Four digits. A date, most likely. He tried her birthday, didn't work. Tried the anniversary of her parents' deaths. Didn't work. Tried 0629, Rafe's birthday. Didn't work.

So he tried his birthday and...bingo.

He closed his eyes for a second, not at all sure he could handle reading the truth about a woman he just damn near proposed to. A woman he loved.

I feel like an impostor.

Because she was?

He took a breath and read the text.

Check in when you can. Anxious to know if he still believes you. I know this has been a tough one, L, but you've done an incredible job making him think you're Isadora. Foster was an unfortunate loss, but necessary. I'm finally here, in Artemisia. Three villas away from you. See you tomorrow and we can finish this job. This time, Gabe Rossi will die.

Words—any words, bad, good, filthy, or indifferent—escaped him.

He considered going back and reading the rest of the texts, but he didn't need to. The words were there, proof that she'd lied. That she knew about Foster coming. That she expected Dexter all along. Was there any other way to interpret these words?

Maybe. But the last sentence didn't take any brains to figure out.

Gabe Rossi will die.

Instead of her sweet kisses, all he could taste was the bitter, metallic flavor of betrayal.

Everything made sense now, including why she said she was sorry a few minutes ago. Sorry for lying to him. Sorry for plotting against him. Sorry for betraying him.

Bile rose in his tight throat, but he forced it down. No time for emotions. Not now.

I'm sorry...I'm sorry *I'm not...*

Had she been trying to tell him just now? What about the implant? She just went along with the removal so he didn't suspect? Maybe she didn't know about it. And what about Rafe? Was he Gabe's child or did they just get an incredible look-alike for whatever this effed-up mission was?

He didn't know, but he'd find out. And the best way to get information, as any good spy knows, was to act like you weren't looking for it. If he was even capable of that right now.

He took a rough breath and replaced the phone, exactly as it had been. A close examination would show he'd read the text, but he'd watch her very closely. If she came into the bathroom, he'd be right next to her. He wouldn't leave her…or sleep.

Not tonight. She'd lie next to him, breathe on him, touch him, ask for more.

And all the while he'd hate her more and more and *more*. But he had to play the game and let her slip, and then he'd take her down so hard she'd have new scars.

Her and her fucking old senator.

He turned to the sink and splashed cold water on his face, looking up at the mirror as it dripped down his cheeks. Like tears.

No fucking way. He'd cried over Isadora. He'd never cry again, no matter how much this tore his soul to shreds. And he'd never trust anyone as long as he breathed. Ever.

Chapter Twenty-Eight

Someone's watching me.

The thought woke Lila with an unsettling start, making her blink into the early morning light with a hot shot of adrenaline in her chest.

"Oh," she whispered, frowning at the sight of Gabe in a chair, staring at her. "Hi. What are you doing over there?"

He lifted one bare shoulder and made a strange face. "Didn't want to wake you. You sleep like the dead, you know. Nino would say you have no sins on your soul."

She let out a soft breath, not quite a laugh. "I have no ache in my head and am still glowing from the best sex I can remember since…the last time we made love." She tapped the bed. "Get back over here, Rossi, and let's do it again."

He stood, revealing that he was not, sadly, naked, but wore long, loose shorts. "Gotta go work out."

Frowning, she pushed up on her elbows, eyeing every muscle in his well-developed chest and abs. "I'm not complaining about the results, but couldn't you postpone your exercise just a little bit today?"

"Can't. Have so much to do today."

She felt herself scowl. "Yes, I know. The doctor, the

beach with Rafe. We planned the perfect day, but it starts with sex. Remember? Epic amounts?"

His expression shifted, a slight shake of his head. "It's a bad day for…that."

"What?" She sat all the way up now, oblivious to the fact that the sheet fell, exposing her breasts. His gaze dropped to them, but didn't warm like it always did.

Didn't he tell her he loved her breasts last night? "Are you okay, Gabe?"

"Yep. Just have to get out there and start doing some push-ups."

She pointed to the floor. "Do them here. I'll watch, er, I mean, count." She tried a playful grin.

But he didn't play. Didn't approach the bed or kiss her good morning or make a joke. He just turned and grabbed his keys from the dresser and picked up his wallet and phone, absently studying the screen.

"What's the matter with you?" she asked.

"Nothing." He pocketed the keys and looked over his shoulder. "I'm not sure when I'll be back."

"Oh, okay." She fought back the disappointment.

"So you can go wherever the fuck you want. *Lila*."

She winced. "Gabe, what is wrong?"

He shook his head like he was trying to get a thought out of it. "We need to get on this implant thing. Let's fly up to DC." He finally looked at her, hard. "Let's go see your pal Dex."

Fly up to DC? Yesterday he wasn't even sure he trusted Dex. Hell, he'd never trusted Dex.

"I'll call him," she said. "No need to leave here."

"I want to see his face when we tell him. If he's in on it, I'll know immediately."

"I told you I trust him." She whipped the covers back

and climbed out of bed, trying to ignore the fact that he didn't immediately reach out for her naked body. "How many times do I have to tell you that before you believe me?"

He took a slow breath, a steadying breath. But why was he *un*steady?

"You know how jealous I get over that old blowhard," he said gruffly.

He dragged his hand through his hair and looked away, the morning sun highlighting bluish shadows under his eyes.

"You didn't sleep, did you?" she asked.

"Not much."

"Why not? It wasn't like we didn't exhaust each other last night."

"I don't know. A lot on my mind." He stared at her. Not heated, not curious, not affectionately…all the ways he looked at her. Right now, his expression was as blank as the wall behind him. "I just don't know," he said again.

But she did. She knew that look. The look of a man who trusted no one.

Maybe just one too many *I love you's* passed between them last night. Maybe he hadn't changed that much, after all, and his inner lone wolf was howling in fear.

"Hey," she said. "Can we talk about this?"

"No."

She inched back from the verbal slap.

"Listen." She reached out a hand to touch his arm. "We don't have to rush this. We don't have to make any decisions or moves or plans until you're comfortable—"

He shook her off. "I *am* comfortable."

"Really."

"Really…*Isadora*."

She blinked at the name, the way he said it like a cold

stab of a knife through her ribs. Five seconds ago, he'd called her Lila with the same accusation in his tone.

Why? Because, deep inside, he couldn't love this woman who wasn't Isadora? Or he couldn't really love *anyone*?

She tamped down the thought. "This is all going to take time," she said, coming close to him. "In some ways, we have to get to know each other all over again."

He nodded slowly, searching her face. "Yeah, we do."

She reached up and touched his unshaved cheek, rubbing her thumb on the whiskers. "I don't want to go to DC," she said. "I want to stay right here with you and Rafe."

"Don't you want to find out who put that implant in you? You're the one who's been so anxious to get started."

"Of course I do, and we will. But today? I just want to live one normal day with my son and my…"

"Son's father?" he suggested, the slightest challenge in his voice, which sliced her.

"Yes, with you."

"I'm going to be gone for a while," he said, backing away. "Will you be here?"

"Yes, why wouldn't I be?"

"I don't know, just wanted you to know you're free to go."

"So you said. What should I do? Spring Rafe from Nino?" she asked, trying to be lighthearted and ignore the weirdness that hung between them. "I'd break both their hearts."

"Well, I have stuff to do." As if he realized that stuff had to be done fully dressed, he turned and yanked a T-shirt off the back of the chair, pulling it on. "I'll see ya."

She just stood there, not even trying to hide her dismay. "That's it?"

He chucked her chin and kissed the air, as if…as if it would somehow pain him to actually kiss her.

She stayed standing there after he left, staring at the empty room, trying to figure out what in God's name just happened. She wasn't sure, but she needed to wash it all off.

She took a shower long and hot enough to leave the bandage on the back of her neck hanging from a single string of adhesive, so she tugged it off and dried her hair. Dressing quickly, she sat on the bed for a minute, dropping her head into her hands.

Heartache definitely hurt worse than a—

A footstep on the side deck pulled her attention and made her swing around to peer out the French doors.

Gabe came back. He felt terrible, realized he'd been a jerk, and came back.

Lila pressed a hand to her heart as if she could soothe it, standing and walking toward the doors. But there was no sign of Gabe. She stepped closer and inched back the sheer curtain, not seeing anyone, but she'd definitely heard something.

One of the bodyguards? She peered into the morning light, not seeing anyone. She knew Luke's men were stealthy, but this was like they weren't even out there.

Automatically, she opened the top dresser drawer and lifted out her Glock, only noticing then that Gabe's weapon was missing.

Why would he take his gun to work out? No, he couldn't have. She'd seen him with shorts on, front and back. He had no holster. Then where was his weapon?

Her spine prickled as she wrapped both hands around the pistol, straightening her arms, braced to fire if she had to.

Hearing nothing, she used one hand to silently unlatch the door and inch it open, lifting her gun, peeking around.

"Please, Isadora, don't shoot me."

She spun at the sound of a woman's voice, sucking in a

breath at the sight of dark, bobbed hair and wide brown eyes. A familiar woman and face but so out of place on the deck of a Barefoot Bay villa that it took a second for Lila to actually comprehend who it was.

"Anne?" The world tilted for a moment as Lila stared, a rush of shock and joy and disbelief swamping her. "Anne Crain? What are you doing here?"

The woman put both hands over her mouth, her eyes welling. "Isadora. Is that *you*?"

She lowered the gun, running through all the possibilities of how Anne could be here and why and how she knew Lila was Isadora. Whatever the answers, the charade was up with this woman who'd tried so hard to be a mother to her. She'd never succeeded, but Lila had appreciated the effort, although Anne had always left her sort of…cold.

"It is me," Lila said softly. "Dex told you?"

Gnawing on her bottom lip, Anne nodded, coming closer, her arms out. "My sweet girl. I thought you were dead."

Lila swallowed hard, kicked by guilt. "I'm sorry. I hope he explained that it was a very important undercover job. I never wanted to hurt anyone, but there were only a handful of people who mattered. You were one." She stepped closer, setting the gun on the chaise. "I hope you can forgive me."

"Of course." Anne closed the space between them and hugged her, and like it always had, the embrace was somehow chilly and forced. She backed up to examine Lila. "He warned me you look like a different person. I would never have known it's you."

Lila brushed back her hair, deeply conscious that this woman had mourned her death. "You know how many lives were saved because of this decision."

"Of course I do, honey. I'm married to Mr. Intelligence Committee, remember?"

"So he told you, then." She still couldn't wrap her head around that. "He's sensitive about the impact that whole operation could have on his future. On both your futures, in the White House."

"I admit I coerced it out of him, Isa." Her brows furrowed. "Or should I call you Lila?"

"I'm Lila now," she said. "Five years, and I've sort of grown into her."

"Well, you've done the opposite of growing." Anne slid an arm around Lila's waist. "You're terribly thin, dear."

"It's just...exercise and plastic surgery." And the headaches had destroyed her appetite. "I'm not so..." *Thin.* She frowned at the echo of Anne's word in her head. Had she said 'tin' or thin?

"And I hear you have a child."

Dexter told her that, too? Well, Lila Wickham's story was no secret, so if Anne knew that, she knew everything. She felt her whole being relax a little, so ready to drop the cloak of secrecy that shrouded her life.

"I do," she said. "A beautiful little boy named Rafe."

"Can I see a picture?"

"Of course." She gestured Anne inside, then picked up the gun. "Sorry about this. Training. How did you get past the bodyguards, by the way?"

"Bodyguards? Why do you have them?"

"Just...precaution."

Anne followed her inside. "Didn't see a soul."

Had Gabe taken them off duty? Did he not care about her safety anymore? Swallowing that thought, she put the gun back in the dresser drawer.

"Is this him?" Anne picked up Rafe's photo, and her jaw dropped. "What a gorgeous little thing. Who's the father?"

The question threw her so much, she hardly noticed the *th* mispronunciation happened again.

"Oh…he's…" She took a breath. "A man who lives here, as a matter of fact."

"On this island?"

"Yes." Years of training made her stop and think and gather her wits no matter how shocked this visit left her. Why would Anne Crain come to her out of the blue, without her husband? "Where is Dexter, Anne?"

"Home." She didn't look up, still holding Rafe's picture.

"Does he know you're here?"

"Of course." She shook her head. "This is like another grandchild to me, you know?"

Her voice hitched with emotion, but not enough to mask that very unusual subtlety that, now noticed, was the only thing Lila heard. Had Anne always had that undercurrent of an accent? The woman was as Midwestern as she was. She must be hanging around foreign-language speakers in DC, which, Lila knew, could slightly affect the way someone spoke.

The inflection was so…

Russian.

Lila sucked in a silent breath, the image of the implant flashing in her brain with almost as much pain as the device had caused.

"So he's met his father now?" Anne asked, yanking Lila back to the conversation.

How would she know Rafe hadn't met Gabe before this? "He has, but we haven't told Rafe everything. He's so young."

Her mind whirred. Why would Anne Crain have anything to do with Russians? The spy in her surfaced instantly, clicking through all the ways to handle this.

Information. Answers. Explanations. Anne had what Lila wanted. She just had to be crafty and cool to get it.

"Tell me about you," Lila said, dropping on the bed next to her. "I know Bethany is married and has a child. A little girl."

Anne smiled. "Lizbeth Anne, the apple of my eye." She lifted the picture. "But this little guy has a chance of taking her place."

Dis...little guy. Of all her languages, Russian was Lila's weakest. Chinese and any Arabic were second nature to her, but she'd had little use for Russian in her career. Staring at Anne, she rooted for a skill set she'd let go dormant: the ability to recognize the phonology and stress patterns of a native language.

"Tell me about Lizbeth," Lila said, trying to get her to relax as much as possible. "Is she walking yet?"

"Oh, she's as busy as a little beaver."

Forget the American idiom, the emphasis was ever so slightly on the second *as*...exactly like a Russian would say.

If Lila had had any hairs left on her neck after the surgery, they would have stood straight up as alarm bells screamed in her head.

Anne studied the picture one more time, then looked at Lila long enough for her eyes to grow moist. "I can't believe it's been so many years." She blinked, and one tear rolled, and she looked around, but Lila grabbed a tissue from the box next to the bed for her, handing it to Anne. "Tell me, Isa. Are you...healthy?"

Again, the *th* was slightly "folded," as a linguist would say. Or was Lila just imagining things?

"Isadora?"

She blinked at Anne, feeling the slow burn that every spy is taught to heed from day one. The fire in the gut that says *something isn't right*.

And something was definitely not right about this. "Of course," she said, recovering quickly. "I'm very healthy. It's hard for me to respond to that name anymore."

Anne leaned a little closer, examining Lila's face as if she didn't believe her. "Nothing's wrong at all?"

"Why would it be?"

"I wondered, when I heard you were alive, if you've had any problems with…headaches. Bad headaches."

Only the best CIA training kept any reaction off Lila's face, except for a casual frown as if the question confused her. "No bad headaches. Just the standard fare that comes with a very active four-year-old and a tough job. Why do you ask?"

"I have to tell you something, dear." She put her hand on Lila's arm. "It might shock you."

Right that moment, nothing could. Lila inched forward. "Go ahead."

"Before…the day. Before 9/11, your mother told me she had a brain tumor."

Lila's eyes popped open, nothing fake about the reaction. "What?"

"Obviously, that's a moot point now. But she learned it was…hereditary. And when I learned you were alive and staying down here, I decided I owed you that information, because no one knew but me."

Of all the lies Lila had ever heard, this was the most preposterous, and it was Anne's second real mistake, after the language slip. Because Lila and her mother had been indescribably close. They'd talked daily, sometimes more than once. There was no way Mom would have had a brain tumor and not have shared that with her daughter. No possible way.

"Well, I'm fine but thank you for telling me. I'm so sorry my mother had to endure that. And so glad she confided in you." Except that the only woman Mary Lou Winter confided in completely was her own daughter.

"She didn't have time to get very sick," Anne said.

Lila nodded, thinking of all the possible answers to that. "Maybe I'll visit a neurologist to be on the safe side."

Anne searched her face, doubt in her dark eyes. "You're positive you're fine?"

"Yes." She patted Anne's arm, thinking how to keep her here. Make small talk. Figure out her game. "Now tell me more about your family, Anne. How are the boys?"

"They're not boys anymore, and I don't want to talk about them." *Th*ey're. *Th*em. Oh yeah. A perfectly Russian *th* fold from a woman asking about...*her headaches.*

Somehow she got past the bodyguards, possibly by hiding out all night in the dark, and slipping onto the patio when they talked to Gabe. As tempting as it was to go screaming for help, that would ruin her chance to get information she had to have.

And what about Dexter? Wouldn't he have texted her to at least warn her that Anne was coming down? Or maybe he didn't know.

Or maybe he's in on it.

She refused to let the fissure forming in her heart show on her face. "You know, Anne, you did catch me in the middle of something, but..." She glanced at the bathroom door, digging for an excuse to go in there and look at her Dex phone, as she thought of her completely secure cell phone. "Just let me put something away in the bathroom. I was...doing something."

Oh brother. Gabe would call her an amateur. And where the hell *was* he when she needed him, anyway?

"Of course." Anne gave her a nudge, almost too encouraging. "I'll wait here and look at my little almost grandson." She smiled. "You're like a daughter to me, you know."

Right now, she didn't know anything. "I know," Lila said. "And I'm sorry for the grief I caused."

"I'm just happy I found you and that we're together again." *Th*at. Toge*th*er.

She stood, anxious to get to that phone. "Okay, I'll be right back."

"Take your time," Anne said with the smile. A genuine, loving, kind, maternal smile.

Lila stepped into the bathroom, good training making sure she left the door open enough to be able to look in the bathroom mirror and see Anne's reflection in the mirror over the dresser in the bedroom. From that angle, Anne couldn't see her at all, through the door or in the mirror.

As silently as possible, Lila reached into her bag, sliding the hidden zipper to get the phone. Before pulling it out, she looked up to check her unexpected guest.

Who was looking at the bottom of the tissue box.

Why? Her heart rate kicked up as more sirens screamed in her head. *Not good. Not safe. Not right.*

With a slow inhale to stay perfectly calm, she tapped in Gabe's birthday and read the last message.

Twice. Three times.

What the hell was he talking about? This wasn't from Dexter. It was nonsense. This was something that someone would…

And then she saw the timestamp for when it had been read.

Her knees weakened as at least one of the missing puzzle pieces snapped into place. Gabe read this last night. And spent the following seven hours thinking she'd been lying to him from the moment they met.

Only years of CIA schooling kept her from running out of the room screaming for him.

One person could have access to Dexter's phone. One person who showed up out of the blue, knew too much, had a new and bizarre vocal tic, and just checked the bottom of a tissue box...which, if that's where she'd planted a bug, would tell her exactly when she could safely arrive. But how?

Poppy brought that box last night. A tissue box rejected by the new and difficult guest at the resort.

Had Anne Crain, the sweet, beguiling, little senator's wife somehow gotten an implant in Lila's head? And bugged her room?

Questions. Too many questions. It was time to get answers.

Bracing herself for the confrontation, Lila watched Anne put the tissue box down, stand up, and walk out of view of the mirror.

Damn it.

Then she heard the dresser drawer open, and she realized her mistake. Anne Crain was now armed, and Lila wasn't.

Chapter Twenty-Nine

How could he have been so fucking stupid? How could he have trusted *anyone*?

Gabe made a lot of mistakes in his life, and he owned up to them. He had a short fuse and liked things done his way. He was secretive and closed off and didn't trust easily. He fucking swore like a sailor getting his balls cut off.

And, yeah, he preferred to work alone because most people were idiots.

But this time? *He* was the idiot.

He practically spit out the taste of self-loathing that rose like puke in his throat. He told her he loved her. Stuck his dick in a stranger and said things he'd never imagined saying to anyone except Isadora.

But *she wasn't Isadora.* Until that moment that he learned she wasn't the woman he once loved, he hadn't really realized just how bone-deep he wanted her to be telling the truth. He wanted Isadora to be alive. He wanted it like he wanted his next breath. As much as he wanted that kid to be his son.

But he got played, and easily, too. She was right. Half the power in an undercover gig was that people believed what they wanted to believe. Just like Nino told him.

It's very easy to believe a woman is who you want her to be because she happens to be who you need her to be.

Well, right you are, old Italian man. When was Gabe going to listen to that windbag of wisdom?

Only fucking morons made the same mistake twice.

Darya Andropov was first, and she was dead. Now Lila Wickham or whoever the holy fuck she was would be his second. And after he got the answers he wanted, she might be dead, too.

Someone was going to be dead, and it sure as shit wasn't going to be him.

But first, he needed information, and he wasn't getting it from that lying whore. She'd make up some excuse, tell him that Dexter hadn't written that, talk him into sex, and make an inside joke that he'd think only Isa could know.

And he'd go blindly, stupidly, fucktastically forward.

He physically shook off the fury, channeling all his anger into getting his hands around Dexter Crain's throat.

After he left, he dismissed the bodyguards because she didn't need protection and he didn't want them breathing down his neck. Then he circled Artemisia twice, studying the lemony-colored villa with a side patio that looked out at the water, searching for signs of life. It was early enough that Dexter could still be asleep, but the place definitely looked closed up, as if no guest had checked in.

He called the front desk to confirm it had been rented and learned it had, to Anne Porter, who had a reservation and legitimate Canadian ID, which was why he hadn't been notified.

Then was his wife in on it? Or some other woman Dex used as a cover?

He'd find out, and soon.

Making sure no guests were anywhere near the villa,

Gabe made his way closer, peeking in a side window, but all of the plantation shutters inside were closed tight. From the outside, it looked completely empty. He rounded the back to the pool area, also deserted, climbing up to look over the privacy fence, seeing no towels or shoes or empty glasses from the night before.

Looked like Casa Blanca housekeeping had just left the place.

If the villa was empty, then the inside security bar would be open and his passkey would work.

He approached the front door, the Glock he'd hidden outside so Lila wouldn't see him leaving armed was ready in his right hand. With his other hand, he used the card key, turned the knob, and entered.

Either no one was here, or someone was stupid. Dexter Crain was stupid. But then, so was Gabe. There was plenty of stupid to go around these days.

Inside, the rooms were dim from the drawn shutters, since, like all the villas, it was built to either open up to paradise or close off the relentless Florida sun. First, he dead-bolted the security bar so no one could come in while he was here, and then he looked around the living area, again seeing no sign of life whatsoever.

He scanned it all, satisfied the rooms were empty. He headed down the hall to the master suite, finding a closed door. Was Dex asleep in there on the bed? If he was, he was dumber than Gabe and clueless about personal security.

Something told him he wasn't quite that witless.

Still, Gabe lifted his weapon, braced, and used his elbow to flip the fancy knob and pop the door open.

The room was empty and dark except for an oversize tote bag resting on the giant four-poster bed, which, like the one in Rockrose, was low to the ground and draped to the floor in layers of sheer fabric. The bag looked like a woman's tote, bearing the brown and gold insignias of an overpriced Louis Vuitton. Before going to it, he checked the room, the closet, and the en suite. Everything was empty.

The bag had no tags but was unzipped and stuffed with women's clothing. He pulled it closer to where he stood at the foot of the bed and, using his free hand, dug around. Just loose, unfolded tops and slacks, a pair of sneakers, and—

Something cold and square. He pulled out a solid metal cube the shape of a computer hard drive, but that's not what this was. It wasn't even steel or iron. This sucker was titanium. He angled it toward the light, peering at the writing on the side.

Russian writing that even he, a non-Russian speaker, could read. Sevtronics. He'd seen that name on enough electronic devices to recognize the Cyrillic letters.

Turning it over, he frowned at a blue flashing light and tiny digital numbers. Numbers that were…counting down.

This wasn't a hard drive, he realized in horror. This was a—

Two hands circled his ankles and yanked so hard, Gabe flipped right on his back with a stunning thud. Before he could breathe, two men emerged from under the bed, one nearly breaking Gabe's arm to get his gun, the other slamming a fucker of a fist right in his face.

Goddamn son of a bitch! He swung, but that arm was stopped by the brute who got behind him and yanked both arms while the other guy just started going to town. In between fists to his face, Gabe recognized the man pummeling him. The same guy who'd climbed off the boat in the harbor.

Knuckles smashed into his face and head, and a knee to the balls sent white-hot pain screaming through his body.

Silent. Brutal. And a fucking bomb was a foot away on the bed.

He grunted and groaned with every punch, one eye already shut from a hit. And another one to the—*oof.* His rib cracked, and agony ricocheted to his brain.

They still hadn't said a word, but they were professional. Icy. Nasty. Vicious. And thorough. He blacked out for a second, feeling his head fall, and the bastard behind him got in one more frenzy on Gabe's kidney.

Fuckface in front of him kicked his shin with a boot and gave one last thwack to his balls, making Gabe moan like a sick animal.

Then he was down. On the ground. Cracked and beaten and stomped, and finally, there was something on his chest. A boot. A knee. The suitcase with a bomb? He had no idea.

Everything hurt. Went beyond hurt. Kissed death.

And one of them lifted his head and smacked it so hard on the wood floor he heard his teeth crack.

The same question burned in his brain. How could he have been so fucking stupid? How could he have trusted *anyone*?

Betrayed. Betrayed. He'd been *betrayed*. She'd done this to him. She had…

Then he started to fade. Blackness engulfed him. Pain turned to numbness. And finally, nothing.

"I've thought so much about your mother, dear. Are you able to talk about her now?"

Lila took a steadying breath and slowly opened the door fully, finding Anne sitting at the bottom of the bed, letting the messy folds of the comforter casually hide her right hand. Anyone might think she was just sitting there quietly, but Lila knew better. She knew exactly what was hidden under the bedding. She gave a smile and turned her head like she was thinking, stealing the quickest glance at the dresser.

As she suspected, the top drawer was open just a few inches. Enough for a slender hand to reach in and pull out a gun. But she couldn't put Anne on alert; she couldn't give away what she knew. Playing dumb and innocent would be so much better. And give her a minute to gain the advantage she needed.

"Of course I can talk about her now."

First order, find out what was of such interest on that tissue box. Taking a few steps toward the nightstand, she sized up the room, trying to choose a spot for the most strategic advantage to overpower the other woman. She had to be careful. One wrong word and that hidden gun could make an appearance.

"But talking about my mother still does make me a little weepy," she added a believable sniffle, taking a step between the bed and the French doors.

"I imagine it does."

"Especially seeing you," Lila said. "It makes me miss her." She took a noisy swallow as if a sob was welling up. "And since I've mourned someone, I can only imagine how you mourned my death."

Anne angled her head and smiled but didn't get up, which would be the normal reaction. Of course not. Nothing was normal about this encounter.

Lila sniffed again and slowly reached for a tissue to wipe her eyes, knocking the box off the nightstand with what she hoped looked like a natural move. The box fell on its side, and Lila caught Anne's quick look at the floor where it landed.

"Clumsy," Lila whispered, bending at the knees to get it and not give Anne an advantage. "And still teary, even after all these years."

As she touched the side of the box, eyes on Anne, she felt a hard disk on the bottom.

A listening device.

That's how Anne had known exactly when to make the phone vibrate so Gabe would look at it while he was in the bathroom. How she'd controlled them like a puppeteer.

But why?

Anne might know the implant was out. She might know that Gabe and Lila suspected Russian involvement. But she didn't know Lila was on to her yet.

Or did she? The other woman was definitely more guarded since Lila had gone into the bathroom, with her back a little straighter, her smile a little faker.

Lila took a slow step to the bed, pretending to be so overwhelmed by the thought of her mother that she had to sit close to Anne, not far from that hand that stayed under the bedcovers, a finger no doubt on the trigger.

Her heart kicked higher, but every other muscle stayed focused and steady, with one simple thought: She had to live long enough to make sure Gabe knew she hadn't lied to him. That was all the motivation she needed.

"Isa?" Anne asked. "Are you all right?"

"It's just…thinking of my mother. And it's been a long time since anyone called me that." She brought the tissue to her eyes again, inching slightly closer. If she could slam her hand down on top of the gun, she had a chance. But if she missed the spot where the gun was, she'd be dead.

She had to try. Had to succeed. "Anne…"

"Yes?"

She leaned a little closer, her thigh probably inches from that pistol. “Have to ask you a question.” She pictured the word in the Russian alphabet, the pronunciation easily coming back to her.

Почему? Why?

“Of course, dear. Ask me anything.”

“*Patchimoo*?” She pronounced the word in perfect Russian, and in that split second of surprise sparking in Anne’s eyes, Lila slammed her hand down on the lump in the bed, the butt of the gun hitting the heel of her hand.

“Isa!” Anne tried to jerk the gun out, but Lila moved as fast as lightning, crashing her other knee over Anne’s hand so hard she heard bones crunch.

Anne let out a shriek and tried to pull out her hand, but Lila jumped fast, taking advantage of her size and youth, pushing the other woman back on the bed until she was flat and helpless.

“*Patchimoo*?” Lila practically spat the Russian word. *Why*? It was all she wanted to know.

Anne’s brown eyes popped wide, and her mouth dropped. “What are you doing, Isa?”

For one second, one blink of an eye, she doubted, but not enough to move. “*Patchimoo*?” She pressed down so hard she stole the breath from the petite woman.

“Who? What is patchy…”

Lila thrust her fist harder into Anne’s chest. “Who are you, Anne Crain? Why did you plant a listening device in this room? Why is that bogus text on my phone that only Dexter uses? And why, for the love of God, did you bury an implant in my head that gave me headaches to the point of considering suicide?”

She relaxed a little, her eyes closing as if she were shutting down.

Lila didn't back off. "Answer me!"

"You were always an excellent way to keep track of Gabriel Rossi, and when the CIA decided your new role, we decided it was the right time and way to use you."

We? What? "The CIA did this to me?"

"They changed you. The implant? That was the work of the *siloviki*," she said, letting her full Russian accent out now. "My family for thirty years now."

The *siloviki*? The restructured power players of the KGB that she and Gabe just discussed? Anne was one of them? Married to the head of the Senate Intelligence Committee? Or was he…

"And Dexter?"

"An incredible source of information to us." She narrowed her eyes to slits. "It wasn't exactly pleasant being married to him, but it was my job, and I had to stay there until they were ready to use me to my full extent."

Anne Crain was… "A Russian sleeper agent?"

"We don't use that expression anymore," she said. "It's old school and left over from the KGB. We call it an extended assignment, but I am quite ready for this one to be over. Of course, I wouldn't leave until I took the vengeance Viktor wanted the most. I promised I would, before he died. And now I have."

"Viktor?"

"Solov. My cousin."

Viktor Solov…the man Gabe had been spying on when he'd been involved with a double agent and killed her. "Sevtronics."

Anne managed a nod, struggling, but obviously knowing who had the physical control here. "Makers of fine electronic devices, like the one that allowed us to have some measure of control over you."

"Why?" The question pounded. "Why would you need to control me? My jobs have had nothing to do with Russia."

"Viktor didn't want you, my dear. You were merely a means to Gabriel Rossi. The implant tracked your whereabouts and, of course, made sure we knew if you were getting emotionally involved with someone else. The side effects? Headaches that can't be helped."

Fury blasted through her like a cannon shot. "Why did you do that to me?"

"Because I knew that no matter what happened to you and your little undercover job of taking down the terrorists, we knew you'd return to him eventually. At least, once I dug through Dexter's files and discovered you were pregnant, I knew."

"This is about Gabe?"

"This is about Darya Andropov." Sparks flashed in her eyes. "She wasn't some *expendable* double agent. She was Viktor Solov's beloved stepdaughter. And when your lover killed her, he signed his own death warrant. Which is…due. Now. Today."

Her skin pricked with awareness and realization. "Gabe?"

"He's thorough and safe and smart and maddeningly difficult to kill, as you might imagine. We thought we had him at the harbor after I found out from Dex that they were sending Foster here. I knew it could work, but not quite."

"And you killed Foster."

She managed a shrug. "It's Gabe we want. And you weakened him, Isadora, which helped so much." She smiled. Actually smiled, and Lila wanted to slap her. "Once I was able to use our technology to transfer Dexter's phone to mine, it was just a matter of controlling you with texts."

"You will never hurt Gabe Rossi," she ground out, adding more pressure.

But Anne didn't snap. Yet. "It's too late," she said. "You can't save him. It's finished."

Lila had to stop herself from jerking backward enough to give Anne any advantage. Instead, she channeled her fury toward the other woman. "What do you mean?"

Anne just smiled, a sickening, fake smile that said…he was already dead.

White, hot, numbing fear exploded in her, starting in her chest and vibrating out through every nerve ending in her body. It couldn't be true!

"He has eight"—Anne tilted her head to look at the clock next to the bed—"seven minutes."

"What?" Lila recoiled in horror.

"A Sevtronics device is never inaccurate, and this one? Designed to kill anything in a fifteen-foot radius. The titanium will remain intact, so there will be no doubt who set the explosive. The *siloviki* don't want some random terrorist getting credit for killing Gabriel Rossi. They have a message to send, straight to the CIA."

She had to help him. She had to. Lila loosened her grip in shock, just enough for Anne to yank the gun out. Before it was free, Lila kicked it hard, knocking the weapon onto the bed.

It was woman to woman now, and Lila was much stronger than Anne. Anne yanked at Lila's hair, but she shook it off and landed a solid thwack to her jaw, shocking her enough so Lila regained control.

A sleeper agent out of practice and thirty years her senior was no match for Lila.

But should she take the time to fight her—kill her—or save Gabe? "Where is he?" she demanded.

Another bitchy smile.

And another body-shaking spurt of adrenaline crackled

through her as she knew without a doubt where he'd gone. The villa where the bogus text said Dex was. That's where he went…right into a deadly trap.

But she had time to save him.

She whipped around, scooped up the gun, and popped to her feet, not even looking behind her as she started toward the French doors.

"Don't make me shoot you, Isadora."

She froze, hearing the sound of a safety latch at the same time Anne spoke. Without moving, Lila's gaze shifted to the mirror, able to see that Anne indeed had a weapon aimed directly at Lila's back.

Her whole body tightened for a second, bracing for the shot, but then she saw something flicker in Anne's expression. Sadness. Hesitation. Weakness.

"I don't want to kill you," the woman said softly. "It's Gabriel Rossi who needs to die. That was the only reason I agreed to this."

"Really." Could she turn and shoot faster than Anne? Unlikely.

"I really grew fond of you when you lived with us."

"You did?" she asked, purposely letting her voice crack and narrowing her eyes so that her entire being was focused on the reflection in the mirror. She'd have to do this without turning around, without giving herself away, and without missing.

"I know it's hard to believe, but you did become like another child to me."

Lila inched the gun to just the right level without moving a visible muscle in her back. "Oh, Anne." She let it look like her shoulders fell on a sad sigh, using that slight movement to mask the fact that she was slowly turning her hand, getting the gun between her arm and waist.

"I don't want to kill you, Isadora."

Lila slid her finger over the trigger and inched her head just enough to get her aim in the reflection. Right…there.

"But I will if you—"

She fired, and the bullet hit Anne directly between the eyes, making her grunt, stare, then fall back as blood trickled from a perfectly placed hole.

Lila turned then and took one more look at the woman who was already dead. "That's for all the headaches you gave me," she whispered.

Then she ran with only one thought driving her into the hot morning sun.

She had to save Gabe.

Chapter Thirty

Pain. Fucking, agonizing, motherhumping, ballbusting misery that no human should endure.

And that was what Gabe felt in his heart.

He woke with a sharp clarity, barely aware of the throbbing shots of pain from a few broken ribs, a cracked nose, a battered head, and a hammering to his manparts. He still hurt worse in his soul, destroyed by a woman who'd betrayed him, hired thugs to kick the shit out of him, and left him to die.

Because that was surely what this blackness that surrounded him was. Death.

Somehow, he managed to peer through the slit of one of his swollen eyes. The faintest light. But something was on top of him. Almost on top of him.

The bed. He was under the bed—where the bastards had tied him, with a gag stuffed in his mouth—too broken to move. And that damn bomb was probably a foot above his head on the other side of this mattress. So he'd better move, and fast.

He tried to shift, but he was stuffed tight into the space, and that pulled the bindings tighter on his wrists. Legs were free, though. He had to get the fuck out of—

Three loud thumps stopped him. Coming back for more,

guys? No, no, those professional pricks wouldn't knock. Another thump. Then silence.

If someone came in here, they were either there to make sure the job was done right or…they'd get themselves killed.

Or maybe someone came to help him. Maybe…Lila.

Fat fucking chance. She and Dex were probably toasting their success right now. But why would—

A gunshot echoed down the halls, followed by the sound of the front door popping open. He listened to fast, fairly light footsteps in the living area, moving through the house, silent.

A woman. Definitely a woman.

"Gabe, damn it! Where are you?"

His woman. Or so he'd naïvely thought.

It took everything in him to stay silent.

"Gabe?" Her voice was sheer exasperation.

Soundlessly, he angled his head, able to see the floor around the bed as he looked toward the door, waiting.

Then she was in the room, her feet bare, with those same red toes he'd spotted on the beach the very first time she approached him. Why hadn't he trusted his instincts? Isadora Winter would have cut off her feet before she painted her toenails red.

"Why aren't you here?" she murmured.

In other words, why didn't the thugs leave your body where they were supposed to?

"Gabe!" It wasn't much more than a strangled whisper, a little bit of agony, a lot of frustration.

But what if she was looking for him…to help him? Or to make sure he was where he was supposed to be when that bomb—

Fuck. That bomb. A Sevtronics device. That couldn't be a coincidence. If she didn't know about it and—

She knew about it. She *had* to. This was her doing.

Wasn't it?

She stopped at the foot of the bed. Exactly where he had been standing when that monster had grabbed his ankles. Of course, they'd stuck him in the other way, his feet at the foot of the bed.

He heard something move on the bed. The bag. With the bomb.

Didn't she know?

Maybe she was checking it, making sure it was still going to explode at the appointed time. Which could be in the next five seconds, in her face.

His heart fell so hard it was a wonder she didn't hear it. All he had to do was move one muscle. Grunt or lift his knee enough to bump the bed that only looked like it sat low to the ground. And she'd know where he was.

If she wanted him dead, she'd leave him there.

If she loved him…

He closed his slit of an eye. It didn't matter if she loved him or not, really. The fact was, he loved her, and if she didn't know there was a bomb in that bag, she would die.

He had to save her, even if she was a lying little spy who broke his heart into a million pieces. And there was always the chance…

"What is this?" she murmured.

He heard the contents of the suitcase pour out onto the bed. Damn it! He jerked his knee hard, slamming against the bottom of the bed frame with a loud moan, making her feet jump back in shock.

"Gabe! Oh my God, Gabe!"

Before he knew what was happening, her hands were on him. And she started getting under the damn bed with him.

"Mmmhmm!" He tried to us his knee to push her out.

She ignored his protests, pulling the gag out of his mouth. "Get out!" he ordered the second he could.

"I will not. You're hurt. You have to let me help you—"

"There's a bomb," he ground out. She didn't know? Was it possible he was wrong?

"Go. Get out!" He ignored the pain in every movement, using his lower half to try and push her but he was jammed under the bed and she was stubborn.

"You're tied—wait!"

She pushed out from under the bed and ran away, her footsteps disappearing down the hall, and seconds later, she was back with a chef's knife.

She stuck her arms under the bed, flat on the floor, and started hacking at the binding that held his right hand.

"Lila…"

She sawed like her life depended on it. "I'm Isadora, Gabe. That text was a fake. You have to believe me. You have to!"

"You have to leave!" he growled at her. "There's a bomb on the bed."

She managed to shoot him a look just as the knife sliced through the binding. "Not until I free you."

He couldn't turn under the bed to do the work, but she shot out, scampered around, and dove to his left side. "Why didn't they just kill me?" Why leave him to blow up?

"Because they want Sevtronics' fingerprints on your death." She ground out every word as she sliced her way through the tie. "They're making a statement."

"About what?"

"Darya."

"What?" He choked the word.

"This is because of her. They're after you because of her. They used me to get to you."

He fought for his breath, staring at her face, stuck into the small space under the bed. She was telling the truth. He knew it in his gut. "How do you know?"

She sawed harder, so close to freeing him. "Anne Crain is a Russian agent trying to kill you. Was. I just put a bullet in her head."

Holy hell, why for one stupid second did he not trust this woman?

"There." She dropped the knife and started to try to pull him from under the bed.

He yowled at the pain and jerked away. "I'll do it."

"You can't do it alone." She pulled harder. "You can't do everything alone."

He let go. Quit fighting. And let her drag him out to freedom, each movement sending blasts of pain through his ribs and head and shoulders, but he didn't care. He didn't care about anything except her.

"Get out of here," he insisted. "That bomb's going to go off."

"We have two minutes," she said, standing, trying to get him up. "We can get it into the bay in two minutes."

He couldn't get it anywhere in two minutes. He could hardly fucking walk, and his right arm was useless, dangling from a dislocated shoulder. He reached into the bag and grabbed the device with his left hand, nodding to the French doors that led to the patio. "Open them."

"Let me take it, Gabe. I can run it to the bay."

"No way." He held it out and glared at her. "Open the doors and get the hell out of here, Lila."

She scurried ahead of him and threw the doors open, and he followed, pain screaming through every cell in his body.

He didn't have the strength. He tried to lift his arm, but the shoulder was dislocated. "Son of a bitch."

"Gabe, give it to me, and I'll run it to safety."

He couldn't hand her a bomb and watch her take off. What the hell was he made of?

"I'm going to put it in the pool, and we'll get out of here." He walked to the water's edge, but she grabbed his arm. "Lila, stop—"

"Gabe, who is that?"

He squinted through his blood-encrusted eyes to see two men running on the beach, leaving Rockrose to escape.

Instinctively, the both ducked low.

"Those are the bastards who did this to me."

"They have to pass us," she said, reaching for the bomb. "Even if they stay on the beach, they have to pass us. Please, Gabe. I can make it, and you can't." She looked from him to the bomb and lifted her brows. "They'll be here in seconds."

Damn right they would. And at this hour, the beach was absolutely deserted. It was the right thing to do, if *he* were doing it.

"Drop it to me after I climb over and jump down there." She ran the rail. "And cover me with this." She held out a pistol.

He took another ragged breath. "You could die."

"I would, for you."

His heart ripped in half. Just tore right down the middle, and all the distrust he'd locked up in there poured out and left him. "Lila..."

But she was already flinging a leg over the railing. Without a second's hesitation, she let herself drop to the grass about six feet below. Then she held her arms up. "Give me the bomb, Gabe."

He leaned all the way over and prayed this wasn't the stupidest thing he'd ever done. What if it went off while she was holding it?

"Gabe!"

He swallowed.

"You have to trust me," she said. "You can't do everything alone. You have to trust me."

He glanced up and saw the two men tearing across a deserted beach. Without giving himself any more time to think, he opened his hand and let an explosive drop into the hands of the woman he loved. And trusted.

"Cover me!" She vaulted away, tucking the bomb under her arm like she was a damn runningback headed for the end zone.

He cocked the gun and braced himself and his firing hand, ignoring all the pain, all the fear, and all the possibility that this could go wrong. Instead, he watched the two men and saw the very instant one of them caught sight of Lila running toward them.

One reached for a gun, and Gabe took a shot, hitting his arm and knocking him down. As he fell, Lila lifted both hands, swung them back over her head, and pitched that motherfucker with every ounce of strength in her body and some he hadn't even thought she had. It sailed at least thirty feet and landed at their feet.

Within a millisecond, the sand lit up with the small but deadly explosion, sending rocks, shells, sparks, and fire over the empty beach, shaking Barefoot Bay with a jolt.

The same jolt that rocked Gabe when she turned and looked at him from the sand, then started running back to him. She reached the wall of the poolside, and he bent over, offering his two hands.

"Come here, Lila. Come here."

She hoisted herself up with ease and fell into his arms.

Somewhere a siren screamed, people ran, and security guards started shouting. But Lila just put her head on Gabe's shoulder where it belonged.

One unit. One thing. One…*one.*

Chapter Thirty-One

Gabe looked down at the head of an eagle behind a shield, part of the massive seal stamped on the lobby floor of the Central Intelligence Agency, and gave Lila's hand a squeeze. Their footsteps fell into rhythm but slowed as they walked over the very spot in this universe where their paths first crossed.

"You were looking down the day I met you," he said.

"And you walked right into me. On purpose."

He leaned into her. "I just wanted to touch you. To see if you were real."

She smiled up at him. "And?"

"You are so real, blondie. And so ready to kick some CIA butt."

She sighed as they neared the reception desk. "I don't want to kick butts. I'm just going to give them the answers they want and hopefully get a few of my own. I want them to stop this horrible practice if it's happening to other agents. And I want to be free to tell our son the truth of who he is and who his grandparents were."

"Lila! Lila."

They both turned at the sound of a man's voice, seeing

the slow-moving silhouette of Dexter Crain emerging through glass doors toward them.

Gabe stiffened, but Lila's instinct was different. She broke free to reach out her arms to the senator. They'd talked but hadn't seen each other in the weeks that had passed since the events unfolded in Barefoot Bay.

Crain and Lila gave each other a silent embrace while the older man pressed his cheek to hers. Gabe stood back and waited to see how this man treated the woman who killed his wife.

"I suppose I owe you a debt of gratitude," Crain whispered.

She closed her eyes and shook her head. "I so wish it could have been different, Dex. I know you loved her."

His shoulders sank. "I don't know," he admitted. "I loved the woman I thought she was, the mother of my children. But she was never who she said she was, and I am just so..." His eyes finally met Gabe's. "Betrayed," he admitted.

Gabe knew the feeling so well, he couldn't stop himself from reaching his hand out. "You have my sympathies, Senator. Gabriel Rossi."

"Hard to believe we've never met, Mr. Rossi." Dex gave him a solid handshake. "I've heard much about your colorful career as a contract agent."

There might have been a little sarcasm around the world *colorful*, but that only ratcheted up Gabe's opinion of the man. Considering how low that opinion had been, it didn't take much. "And I've heard a lot about your colorful career as a senator."

He got a *touché* half smile in return. "I suppose I won't be a senator much longer, as you might suspect. Handing in my resignation after this meeting." He nodded toward the elevator where they were headed. "Then I'll spend some time licking my wounds and wondering how a man could be so blind."

"Don't," Lila said, taking his arm as they walked.

Gabe flanked the other side. "A wise man once told me that it's very easy to believe a woman is who you want her to be because she happens to be who you need her to be."

"Sounds like Nino," Lila said.

Dex gave a soft laugh. "There's truth in what you're saying, but hard to accept when you're the dummy who lived with a Russian sleeper agent for a lifetime."

"Oh, Dex," Lila said, pulling him closer. "Maybe you can write a book and get it out of your system."

"They'll never let me." He poked the elevator button. "What about you, young lady? What are your plans?"

"I'm going back to Barefoot Bay to let Gabe and Rafe get to know one another."

He looked from one to the other as the elevator door opened. "So everything's out in the open?" He turned to Gabe with an unwavering gaze. "I shouldn't have encouraged her to leave Cuba, son. She was happy."

Fat lot of good that did now.

"Is there any way I can make it up to you?" he asked Gabe as the elevator doors opened to their floor.

"As a matter of fact..." Gabe shot a look to Lila. "Why don't you go in and do the small talk, Lila? That meeting won't start until Hollings shows up, and I guarantee you he's not ten minutes early, like we are. The senator and I will be in shortly."

She gave a hesitant frown to Gabe and then the senator. "Are you sure?"

Dex put his hand on her shoulder. "Give me this time and chance, Lila. I want to talk to him."

"Okay." She patted his hand and reached out to Gabe. "It would be nice if you two could be friends."

"We'll start small," Gabe said, giving a light kiss to her hair. "Save me a seat next to you so you're able to hear me mock those idiots."

When she left, Gabe turned back to Dexter. "I need a favor, Dex."

The senator gave a quizzical look. "If I'm capable of favors anymore."

"I think you can do this." Gabe nudged him down the hall and reached into his pocket. "This way."

Of course, there was small talk and coffee, and nobody said anything that mattered until the director showed up. Lila recognized some faces among the eight or ten attendees, but definitely not all. The moment Director Jeffrey Hollings entered, they all grew silent in the presence of the leader of the CIA.

Gabe sauntered in behind him, came up to Lila with a slow smile, and took her hand. Without a word, he guided them to chairs next to each other along the side of the massive mahogany table in the middle of the room.

Dexter was MIA, but Hollings took a seat at the head of the table. The director was a salt-and-pepper handsome fifty-year-old with clear blue eyes and an air of unquestionable authority.

Except, Lila had a feeling Gabe would have no problem questioning it.

After a moment, Hollings gave a nod to Lila. "For the benefit of this group, Ms. Wickham, can you recount your entire story?"

Next to her, Gabe gave a soft grunt of displeasure. That didn't take long.

"Is that a problem, Mr. Rossi?"

"It's a waste of time," Gabe shot back. "You know her story. You know my story. You know poor dead David Foster's story, although we don't. So why don't we start there?"

Hollings didn't flinch. "Agent Foster was sent by me to warn Ms. Wickham of a credible threat we learned of through classified means."

Gabe angled his head as if *classified means* held no weight with him. Hollings ignored it and continued.

"I told Senator Crain that we were sending Foster. The senator's phone was compromised by Mrs. Crain, who launched the series of events that we're discussing. Foster received texts to go to the harbor, unwittingly walking into a plan to make it look like he'd killed both of you in a shootout, but you foiled that plan. The texts you were receiving weren't from him."

One of the analysts across the table let out a sigh. "Sevtronics has world-class devices."

"Why don't we get some of them?" Gabe asked.

Hollings gave Gabe a harsh look. "As you know, our sole means of infiltrating that company didn't end well."

It ended with Gabe killing the CEO's stepdaughter, Lila thought.

"But we are grateful for the work you both did," Hollings added quickly. "Frankly, we'd known for years that there was a mole somewhere at the congressional level, and we now know that was Anne Crain. We were looking for Russian intelligence agents, not individual associated with the *siloviki*. But they are sly. The two men who were killed on the beach have been identified as Russians associated with that organization, and we now know that they even made Mrs. Crain's legitimate-looking reservation appear through the resort booking service."

"What's the retribution from Moscow?" Lila asked.

"According to our agents on the ground, the Russians are distancing themselves from this. The *siloviki* are not government sanctioned and work entirely independently of Putin or any Russian intelligence agency."

"Who was Anne, really?" Lila inched forward, anxious to have this question answered.

"She was Eva Solov, the cousin of Viktor Solov, head of Sevtronics. Eva was 'killed' years ago, but she managed to get to Canada, where she assumed her new identity as Anne Porter. Her assignment was simply to get to Washington, DC, and, in the most calculating and strategic way, attach herself to the most powerful people she could."

"She certainly did that." Dexter Crain walked into the room carrying a large cardboard storage box that he dropped onto the table. Without explanation, he took the closest chair and pinned his gaze on Director Hollings. "Anne Porter came after me when I was a freshman congressman, and I never knew what hit me. I don't know what secrets she managed to get from me in more than two decades of marriage, but she was clearly a stealthy, skilled sleeper agent."

Grief tinged his voice, though Lila knew Dex well enough to know he was working hard to hide that. Poor man. This had ended so much worse than just a tarnished reputation; he'd lost the woman he loved, and the woman he thought loved him.

Hollings finally nodded. "The whole system failed," he said, his tone gentle for the first time since they started.

In other words, it wasn't the fault of one besotted young congressman.

"Her instructions were quite simple," one of the other deputies added, checking his notes. "She was told to wait until they had something they wanted her to do, until she could be at the right time and the right place for the right reasons." He shifted his gaze to Lila. "That all happened with you because of your relationship with Mr. Rossi, who had become a target of Solov's. Lila, you became the puppet to get to him, and your friendship with Dexter was one of the strings they used to get you where they wanted you."

"Using the implant?"

Hollings shifted ever so slightly in his seat. "That made sure you didn't have the opportunity to get emotionally attached to anyone else."

"I could have done that," Gabe muttered, squeezing her hand under the table.

"And now, Ms. Wickham," the director said. "After a few more questions for research and file purposes, we'd like to close this chapter of CIA history forever."

Gabe leaned forward. "Not so fast."

Hollings answered with the rise of one black brow.

"Lila Wickham is really Isadora Winter."

Hollings didn't react.

"And she deserves the right and privilege to share that information with anyone she chooses, with impunity."

The director took in a breath as if he were about to launch into his argument, but Dexter slammed his hands on the table. "I agree."

Every eye turned to him.

"Senator?" Hollings asked. "Your reputation is on the line as much as the CIA's if the program that she participated in becomes public."

"The program she participated in cost her dearly," Dex replied. "And let's address the elephant in the room, shall we?" He stood slowly and pointed to one of the agents at the table. "That man has headaches, doesn't he?"

The agent swallowed and gave a quick look to Hollings.

"And that agent right there?" He pointed to another woman. "She was working undercover in Crimea after the Russian invasion, took sick, and has had severe headaches since she's returned to her family. That's why they're here, isn't it? Your questions are not for research and file purposes, but because they suffered the same way Lila did."

"No." Lila lifted her hands to her mouth to contain any noise, her gaze falling on the other woman, who met Lila's gaze.

"There is an open investigation," Hollings confirmed.

"To do what?" Lila demanded.

"To prevent it from happening to others."

"And that's where I come in," Gabe said.

"Excuse me?" Hollings asked.

Gabe pointed to the box. "In that container is every form of identification that ever belonged to Isadora Winter, from her birth to her fake death, along with the official documents for a child by the name of Gabriel Rafael Rossi Winter." He threw a look at Lila. "That's a mouthful."

She bit back a smile, not at all sure where he was going but so in for the ride.

"We want it back. We want to own those papers and have the right to share them with our son and our family. We want the right to tell our son, and anyone else we choose to trust, who his grandparents were, what work his mother did to make this country safer, and what she sacrificed to do that work. That's what we want."

Hollings flattened him with a dark look. "That is not going to happen, Mr. Rossi."

"Really." Gabe reached into his pocket and pulled something out, cupping it in his palm.

"You've already turned over the implant, Mr. Rossi," Hollings said.

"And yet, I still have a bargaining chip, so to speak." He opened his palm, revealing a flash drive. "With the help of my sister, who, by the way, you would be damn lucky to get as an agent, I have compiled a mountain of files I was able to withdraw when I left Russia many years ago."

He put the drive on the table. "That *might* contain the names of every single employee at Sevtronics, passwords to their computer files, a database of projects, including the work of the nano implant microchip devices, a list of individuals authorized to surgically implant those devices, and how they function. There's also home addresses and cell phone numbers to every member of the *siloviki*, past and present, a list of favored vodka distributors, and some private numbers for the Moscow escort services that the CEO liked to hire." He put his elbows on the table and leaned forward. "Would you like any of that information, Jeff?"

For a long moment, no one said a word or moved. Except Lila, whose heart was beating and soaring in a way that simply couldn't be natural. Gabe had done this for her. He understood how important it was, and somehow—with the help of Dex, it seemed—had done this for her.

She glanced again at the two agents, closing her eyes when the man rubbed his temples as if the headaches were still occurring.

Finally, Hollings stood. "Give her the box," he said, holding out his hand to Gabe. "And I'll take that."

Gabe stood and dropped the flash drive into the other man's hand, but grabbed his fingers before they could be withdrawn. "Don't let anyone else suffer because of this,"

Gabe ordered. "Including the two other agents in the room."

At the other end of the table, Dexter stood. "I would be happy to personally supervise that project," he said. "In fact, I *will* supervise it."

His jaw clenched, Hollings nodded and, without another word, walked out of the conference room. Everyone sat in a second of silence and then burst into spontaneous applause.

All but Lila, who reached up and hugged Gabe and kissed him on the cheek.

For the next hour, after saying good-bye to Dex, Gabe talked to high-level deputies, and Lila sat huddled with the two agents, sharing stories. One had an implant removed; the other risked brain damage to get his out. Some of the information they now had access to from Gabe's files could help the doctors with surgery and treatment.

When they were finished, she and Gabe left the conference room and stepped into the elevator. He carried the box, and they stayed silent until the doors opened and they walked through the iconic lobby, side by side.

"You know," he finally said, "you can be Isadora again. You can change your name, use these papers, and put the entire Lila Wickham chapter behind you."

She thought about that for a moment, wishing the idea captured her heart, but it didn't. "No."

He dropped the box right on the eagle's head with a thud. "No?"

"That's not what I want," she said softly, turning to him. "I want to own that identity and keep those papers, but I love who I am now. I'm stronger, and I'm a fighter, and I've done some amazing things as Lila, including be a good mother to my son. I'm not ashamed of Lila Wickham, and I don't want her chapter behind me. Do you?"

He huffed out a sigh. "Then I think there's a problem."

"A problem?"

He gestured to the box, then bent over, finally getting on one knee to dig through it. "I sold my soul to get this stuff."

"Is that how Dexter helped you?"

"Kind of." He reached into the box and pulled out her passport. "He knew how to open doors so we could get this."

She took it and flipped it open, seeing her old face and name. "Okay. I like having the documentation, for all the reasons you mentioned, but I just don't want to be her again."

"And this." He handed her a folder, opening it to show her birth certificate. Again, she was happy to have it, free of the pressure to hide it, but… "Gabe, what is your point?"

He stayed down on one knee, digging through the box, pulling up another legal document.

She took the paper, taking in a breath when she read the top. "Rafe's birth certificate."

"With my name on it."

"So he is officially and legally your son."

He looked up, his hand deep into the side of the box now, a devilish half smile torturing her. "Someone's gotta teach that kid how to behave."

"Gabe…I…"

"And this." He whipped out a cracked driver's license. Again, old face, old name, old her.

"Isadora Winter," he mumbled, looking at it. "You're right, I guess. What kind of a name is that? It's so…WASPy. Winter. And cold. And Wickham. So…crispy."

"Gabe, this isn't about my name."

"Yeah, it is." He pulled something out of the corner of the box, a small velvet pouch. "What you need is a new one. A name with more flavor and color. Something Italian."

At that moment, she realized what the pouch held, and

that he was on one knee, and that all the people around them had stopped moving to watch.

And she couldn't breathe. He was doing this here? In the lobby of the CIA headquarters, smack dab over the CIA seal where they'd met?

"Something like Rossi," he said.

Of course he was. This was Gabe. And this was perfect.

"I think Lila Rossi has a nice ring to it." He emptied the pouch into his palm, and a bright blue stone surrounded by diamonds sparkled in the sunlight that poured into the lobby. "This ring, as a matter of fact."

All she could do was stare into the eyes that were the same color as the gorgeous blue diamond he held in two fingers as he reached up and presented it to her.

"Isadora Winter Lila Wickham, woman of my dreams and best friend I've ever had. I love everything about you, old and new, good and bad, weak and strong. Everything."

"Gabe."

He inched the ring back. "I'm going to get through this speech, Lila, and I'm going to do it without swearing once, to prove to you I can be the man you want by your side to raise Rafe. And maybe a few more."

"You are the man I want by my side," she whispered, noticing that a small crowd gathered. Even well-trained CIA personnel couldn't resist a man on one knee making his declaration.

He cleared his throat and raised the ring again. "From the day I walked into you on this very spot, I knew you were the person I wanted to wake up with, to go to sleep with, to grow old with, and have a family with. You make me laugh. You make me think. You make me whole. And..." He closed his eyes and paused, gathering himself. "You make me *trust*. Will you please change your name one more time and marry me?"

"I love you," she whispered.

He smiled, his eyes welling up. "Say yes, Lila. Just say yes."

But she couldn't say anything. All she could do was press her hands to her mouth and try to contain uncontainable happiness. "Yes."

And for the second time that day, they were applauded. Gabe slipped the ring on her finger, pulled her into his arms, and squeezed her tight.

"Oh, hell *yeah*," he whispered, lowering his mouth to kiss her.

Epilogue

"Gabriel, you're good with funny names." Nino put his hands on his hips and stared out at the beach, currently populated with friends and family, and a whole shit-ton of kids.

"It's one of my many gifts," Gabe agreed.

"What should we call this yearly festival?"

"This cooking competition is going to be an annual event?" He popped a brew, sidling closer to his grandfather in the shade of the flowering trees at the edge of Barefoot Bay.

"I think so. Everyone seems to be having fun. So, we need a name for this day when I cook Italian and Poppy makes Jamaican and everybody votes on what's best. Not that there's any real contest."

"The first annual sausage fest jerk-off." Gabe lifted his beer bottle and gave his grandfather a grin. "Poppy will plotz."

Nino chuckled and wiped his hands on a mopina and lifted the lid of a massive egg-shaped ceramic outdoor cooke to send a mouth-watering whiff of steak and onions right at Gabe. "If I win, she will."

"You won't win."

Nino flashed an angry scowl. "Son, wait until I whip out

the pesto pizza. They'll all be on their knees singing *O Sole Mio*."

Gabe gestured toward the tall, lanky imports Poppy had gone to Jamaica to fetch with her own personal babysitter, Chris Sloane, as an unlikely but remarkably useful escort. "Not those three. The deck is stacked, and you know they're all going to vote for their Aunt Poppy."

Nino lifted his bushy brows. "Sorry, but they like their Uncle Nino. A lot."

"I bet they do." Gabe threw an arm around the old man. "I sure as hell did when you came to live with us. I was about the age of that little one. What's his name?"

He shrugged. "Who knows from those holy names? I call them Skinny, Skinnier, and Skinniest."

"That won't last long living in your house." Gabe pictured the sizable kitchen in the rental on the south end of Mimosa Key where Nino, Poppy, and the Jamaican bobsled team had moved. The refrigerator already featured a picture of a "fat" statue of David that said "Eat More Pasta," stuck there by a green and yellow smiley-face magnet that said "Be happy, mon, you're in Jamaica!"

It wouldn't take long for that to be the most unlikely family home in history. And Gabe had his eye on a bigger house right down the street that had just come on the market. It would make the start of a great family compound on this island. Lila had already slid into a natural role of helping Gabe with the undercover business, which was humming along and making good money.

Even Chris had stayed. He liked the island so much, he invited his partner to move down to the island so Chris could take a job with Luke's company. The former secret service agent was fast becoming the top security specialist on staff, which was great because Rafe still loved the guy.

"I'm kind of jealous of your new brood," he admitted to Nino.

"Jealous?"

"Living with you and learning to cook and figure out life. It's the best childhood a human can have."

Nino beamed at him. "I didn't teach you to figure out life."

"Like hell you didn't, old man. Now you're going to do it all again, with another generation."

With a tight smile, he nodded and gave Gabe a misty-eyed look. "Because of you. If it weren't for you, I'd be rambling around that big house in Boston, hoping a grandkid might come to visit so I could have a reason to…"

"To cook?"

"To live." He squeezed the dishrag in his giant gnarled hand. "I can't thank you enough for that, Gabriel."

"Oh, shut it. I love you, you old bastard. And those grandkids are all coming down in a month for a big beach wedding. They get one whiff of Bareass Bay, and we'll be wearing Angelinos and Rossis all year long down here."

"I'd like that." He shooed Gabe. "Now, get out of my—"

"Nope. Gotta talk to you first."

Nino frowned. "About what?"

"Rafe."

Nino looked toward the beach. "Look at him over there, Gabriel. Playing bocce like…well, like a *ragazzaccio*."

"He is a bad boy, isn't he? God, I love him."

"Bad to the bone marrow."

Gabe gave Nino a look, not sure if he was serious or annihilating English. "I guess it's in his bloodline," Gabe said. "Which I'm going to tell him about today."

"Today?"

Gabe nodded. "Lila and I are taking him for a walk. It's time. You have any advice?"

"Tell him the truth, which won't make a lick of sense to him, but he'll know you're his father, for real and for certain."

"That's what I want." Gabe stuck his hand through his hair and sighed. "Think I'll be good enough, Nino? It's a damn…darn big job."

"Ehhh." He made a typical Italian swipe of his hand. "You'll be good enough. Clean up your mouth."

"I have the mouth of a pastor, for crying out loud."

"And teach him what's important in life—family. First, last, and always."

That's why they were having this conversation today. He wasn't going to just be "Mum's husband." He was Rafe's father. "Count on it," he said.

"And you know what else you need to do, Gabriel?" Nino lowered his glasses and peered over the rims, his old dark eyes full of sincerity and a lifetime of experience. "Don't let the little man become the focus of your life."

Gabe frowned. "He's our kid. I expect him to be the center of everything."

But Nino slowly shook his head. "*She's* the center of your everything." He pointed to Lila, who was crossing the sand holding Rafe's hand now, talking to him. "She is your sun and your moon, your yesterday, and your tomorrow, your first and—"

"I get the idea. She's all that and more."

"You know, she reminds me of my Monica."

Gabe inched back, the compliment stunning him. "I've never heard you say that about anyone."

"Yes, there's something about her." He angled his head, thinking. "There's a sweetness in her heart, you know?"

"Oh, I know."

"And she doesn't take any shit from you, which I love."

"So do I, Gramps."

"Then I expect that kid to spend a lot of nights at my house so you two can be alone to make many more babies for me to feed and teach."

Gabe put his hand on Nino's shoulder, but his gaze was on Lila as she laughed at something Rafe had said, and she'd never looked more beautiful or happier. "You have my word."

"And one more thing."

"Uncle *Ninooooooooo*!" Rafe shouted as he broke into a run.

"What's that?" Gabe asked him.

"I don't want him to call me Uncle Nino."

Gabe's jaw loosened. "But that's what we call you."

"Uncle Ninoooooooo!" He was only about thirty feet away now, tear-assing across the sand.

"What do you want him to call you?"

"What do you want him to call you?" Nino shot back.

He didn't have to think about it. "Dad?"

"And I want to be Great-Grandpa."

Rafe ran right to Nino, who picked up the tiny frame in his massive hands, lifting him easily. "You hear that, child? I'm your great-grandpa."

Lila finally caught up, her eyes widening in surprise. "You told him already?" she whispered.

Gabe shook his head and reached for her, pulling her close to his side.

"Great-Grandpa?" Rafe hollered at his usual ear-shattering decibel level. "You are my great-grandpa?"

"He is," Gabe said, easily taking the child from Nino's grip and flipping him over his shoulder. "And I…" He looked at Lila, who gave a slight shrug of permission. "I am…"

"You are Gabe Man!" He bounced on both feet until Gabe snagged one hand and Lila took the other.

"Let's take a walk," Gabe said. "We want to tell you a story."

"I like *storieeeeeeees*."

As they walked, they lifted him and let him swing in the air.

"Does it start with once upon a time?" Rafe asked.

Gabe looked over his shoulder and caught Nino watching, and wiping a tear from his soft, old Italian heart.

"Yes," Gabe said. "Once upon a time, there was…a beautiful princess."

"Ewww. I hate princess stories."

"Yeah, me, too. But this princess was different. She was really a warrior trapped in the body of a…a…"

"Translator," Lila said.

"Yay, warrior!" Rafe jumped on the sand. "Then what happened?"

"Then…" He looked at Lila for help, but she just smiled at him, waiting. "Then…" Gabe finally stopped walking, realizing they were right on the very place where he'd read that letter and met the woman who changed the game.

He crouched down to come face-to-face with his son. "The warrior princess met the most…the most…"

Lila got next to him. "She met the most handsome, funny, smart, lovable, wisecracking, talented super spy."

Gabe threw her a look. "*Super* spy?"

"You're the super guy?" Rafe asked.

"Yes, and your mum is the warrior princess."

His eyes grew as he turned blissfully quiet and looked from one to the other. "Then what am I?"

"You, Gabriel Rafael Wickham Rossi, are our son. My

son," Gabe whispered, putting his hands on Rafe's narrow shoulders. "My son."

"I know that," he said.

"You do?"

"You look like me. But what *am* I? A flying hero dinosaur killer?"

Gabe laughed. "If that's what you want to be. You can be whatever you want."

"I know!" He broke away and started running, his arms wide as he zoomed and careened circles around them. "Dino killerrrrrrr!"

He took off, kicking sand, leaving Gabe and Lila standing with the sun pressing down on their anticlimactic moment.

"So," Gabe said, putting an arm around her. "That went well."

She laughed and rested her head on his shoulder. "You can tell me the story, Gabe. Start with the part where they meet."

He pressed a kiss on her head. "I'm not much for telling stories."

"Make it short and easy."

"Okay." He kissed her again, loving the feel of her head where it belonged. "They meet, they fall in love, take a detour, have a kid, hook up again, knock off some baddies, say their vows, have a bunch more kids, grow their business to international greatness, and live happily ever after."

She sighed contendedly. "The end."

"The end? Not a chance, blondie. It's just the beginning."

Books Set in Barefoot Bay

The Barefoot Bay Billionaires
Secrets on the Sand
Seduction on the Sand
Scandal on the Sand

The Barefoot Bay Brides
Barefoot in White
Barefoot in Lace
Barefoot in Pearls

Barefoot Bay Undercover
Barefoot Bound (prequel)
Barefoot with a Bodyguard
Barefoot with a Stranger
Barefoot with a Bad Boy (Gabe's book!)

The Original Barefoot Bay Quartet
Barefoot in the Sand
Barefoot in the Rain
Barefoot in the Sun
Barefoot by the Sea

About the Author

Roxanne St. Claire is a *New York Times* and *USA Today* bestselling author of well over forty novels of suspense and romance, including many popular series and stand-alone books. Her entire backlist, including excerpts and buy links, can be found at www.roxannestclaire.com.

In addition to being a six-time nominee and one-time winner of the prestigious Romance Writers of America RITA Award, Roxanne's novels have won the National Reader's Choice Award for best romantic suspense three times and the Borders Top Pick in Romance, as well as the Daphne du Maurier Award, the HOLT Medallion, the Maggie, Booksellers Best, Book Buyers Best, the Award of Excellence, and many others. Her books have been translated into dozens of languages and are routinely included as a Doubleday/Rhapsody Book Club Selection of the Month.

Roxanne lives in Florida with her family and can be reached via her website, www.roxannestclaire.com, her Facebook reader page, www.facebook.com/roxannestclaire, and Twitter at www.twitter.com/roxannestclaire.

CPSIA information can be obtained at www.ICGtesting.com
Printed in the USA
LVOW11s0514200516

489059LV00003B/200/P